Kai Lung's Golden Hours

Ernest Bramah

Table of Contents

Kai Lung's Golden Hours

Ernest Bramah

The Kai Lung stories have for many years been in high favour among those who relish sophisticated humour. One of the first to recognize their distinction was Hilaire Belloc, who, in his Introduction, records the impact made upon him when he first made the acquaintance of these masterpieces of narrative. Kai Lung is an itinerant story–teller in ancient China. "I spread my mat," he says, "wherever my uplifted voice can entice together a company to listen," and his powers of enchantment are abundantly revealed in this volume. He incurs the enmity of a sinister figure called Ming–shu, who is the confidential agent of the Mandarin, Shan Tien, and has to defend himself in the Mandarin's court against a series of treasonable charges. Kai Lung's defence takes the original form of inducing the Mandarin to listen to a recital of the traditional tales of China, and so well does he beguile the capricious tyrant that he secures one

1

adjournment after the other and, finally, his freedom—as well as the love of the maiden Hwa–Mei.

PREFACE

Homo faber. Man is born to make. His business is to construct: to plan: to carry out the plan: to fit together, and to produce a finished thing.

That human art in which it is most difficult to achieve this end (and in which it is far easier to neglect it than in any other) is the art of writing. Yet this much is certain, that unconstructed writing is at once worthless and ephemeral: and nearly the whole of our modern English writing is unconstructed.

The matter of survival is perhaps not the most important, though it is a test of a kind, and it is a test which every serious writer feels most intimately. The essential is the matter of excellence: that a piece of work should achieve its end. But in either character, the character of survival or the character of intrinsic excellence, construction deliberate and successful is the fundamental condition.

It may be objected that the mass of writing must in any age neglect construction. We write to establish a record for a few days: or to send a thousand unimportant messages: or to express for others or for ourselves something very vague and perhaps very weak in the way of emotion, which does not demand construction and at any rate cannot command it. No writer can be judged by the entirety of his writings, for these would include every note he ever sent round the corner; every memorandum he ever made upon his shirt cuff. But when a man sets out to write as a serious business, proclaiming that by the nature of his publication and presentment that he is doing something he thinks worthy of the time and place in which he lives and of the people to whom he belongs, then if he does not construct he is negligible.

Yet, I say, the great mass of men to–day do not attempt it in the English tongue, and the proof is that you can discover in their slipshod pages nothing of a seal or stamp. You do not, opening a book at random, say at once: "This is the voice of such and such a one." It is no one's manner or voice. It is part of a common babel.

2

Therefore in such a time as that of our decline, to come across work which is planned, executed and achieved has something of the effect produced by the finding of a wrought human thing in the wild. It is like finding, as I once found, deep hidden in the tangled rank grass of autumn in Burgundy, on the edge of a wood not far from Dijon, a neglected statue of the eighteenth century. It is like coming round the corner of some wholly desolate upper valley in the mountains and seeing before one a well-cultivated close and a strong house in the midst.

It is now many years—I forget how many; it may be twenty or more, or it may be a little less—since The Wallet of Kai Lung was sent me by a friend. The effect produced upon my mind at the first opening of its pages was in the same category as the effect produced by the discovery of that hidden statue in Burgundy, or the coming upon an unexpected house in the turn of a high Pyrenean gorge. Here was something worth doing and done. It was not a plan attempted and only part achieved (though even that would be rare enough to-day, and a memorable exception); it was a thing intended, wrought out, completed and established. Therefore it was destined to endure and, what is more important, it was a success.

The time in which we live affords very few of such moments of relief: here and there a good piece of verse, in The New Age or in the now defunct Westminster: here and there a lapidary phrase such as a score or more of Blatchford's which remain fixed in my memory. Here and there a letter written to the newspapers in a moment of indignation when the writer, not trained to the craft, strikes out the metal justly at white heat. But, I saw, the thing is extremely rare, and in the shape of a complete book rarest of all.

The Wallet of Kai Lung was a thing made deliberately, in hard material and completely successful. It was meant to produce a particular effect of humour by the use of a foreign convention, the Chinese convention, in the English tongue. It was meant to produce a certain effect of philosophy and at the same time it was meant to produce a certain completed interest of fiction, of relation, of a short epic. It did all these things.

It is one of the tests of excellent work that such work is economic, that is, that there is nothing redundant in order or in vocabulary, and at the same time nothing elliptic—in the full sense of that word: that is, no sentence in which so much is omitted that the reader is left puzzled. That is the quality you get in really good statuary—in Houdon, for instance, or in that triumph the archaic Archer in the Louvre. The Wallet of Kai Lung satisfied all these conditions.

I do not know how often I have read it since I first possessed it. I know how many copies there are in my house—just over a dozen. I know with what care I have bound it constantly for presentation to friends. I have been asked for an introduction to this its successor, Kai Lung's Golden Hours. It is worthy of its forerunner. There is the same plan, exactitude, working–out and achievement; and therefore the same complete satisfaction in the reading, or to be more accurate, in the incorporation of the work with oneself.

All this is not extravagant praise, nor even praise at all in the conventional sense of that term. It is merely a judgment: a putting into as carefully exact words as I can find the appreciation I make of this style and its triumph.

The reviewer in his art must quote passages. It is hardly the part of a Preface writer to do that. But to show what I mean I can at least quote the following:

"Your insight is clear and unbiased," said the gracious Sovereign. "But however entrancing it is to wander unchecked through a garden of bright images, are we not enticing your mind from another subject of almost equal importance?"

Or again:

"It has been said," he began at length, withdrawing his eyes reluctantly from an usually large insect upon the ceiling and addressing himself to the maiden, "that there are few situations in life that cannot be honourably settled, and without any loss of time, either by suicide, a bag of gold, or by thrusting a despised antagonist over the edge of a precipice on a dark night."

Or again:

"After secretly observing the unstudied grace of her movements, the most celebrated picture–marker of the province burned the implements of his craft, and began life anew as a trainer of performing elephants."

You cannot read these sentences, I think, without agreeing with what has been said above. If you doubt it, take the old test and try to write that kind of thing yourself.

In connection with such achievements it is customary to-day to deplore the lack of public appreciation. Either to blame the hurried millions of chance readers because they have only bought a few thousands of a masterpiece; or, what is worse still, to pretend that good work is for the few and that the mass will never appreciate it—in reply to which it is sufficient to say that the critic himself is one of the mass and could not be distinguished from others of the mass by his very own self were he a looker-on.

In the best of times (the most stable, the least hurried) the date at which general appreciation comes is a matter of chance, and to-day the presentation of any achieved work is like the reading of Keats to a football crowd. It is of no significance whatsoever to English Letters whether one of its glories be appreciated at the moment it issues from the press or ten years later, or twenty, or fifty. Further, after a very small margin is passed, a margin of a few hundreds at the most, it matters little whether strong permanent work finds a thousand or fifty thousand or a million of readers. Rock stands and mud washes away.

What is indeed to be deplored is the lack of communication between those who desire to find good stuff and those who can produce it: it is in the attempt to build a bridge between the one and the other that men who have the privilege of hearing a good thing betimes write such words as I am writing here.

HILAIRE BELLOC

KAI LUNG'S GOLDEN HOURS

CHAPTER I. The Encountering of Six within a Wood

ONLY at one point along the straight earth-road leading from Loo-chow to Yu-ping was there any shade, a wood of stunted growth, and here Kai Lung cast himself down in refuge from the noontide sun and slept. When he woke it was with the sound of discreet laughter trickling through his dreams. He sat up and looked around. Across the glade two maidens stood in poised expectancy within the shadow of a wild fig-tree, both their gaze and their manner denoting a fixed intention to be prepared for any emergency. Not being desirous that this should tend towards their abrupt departure, Kai Lung rose guardedly to his feet, with many gestures of polite reassurance, and having bowed several times to indicate his pacific nature, he stood in an attitude of deferential admiration. At this display the elder and less attractive of the maidens fled, uttering loud and continuous cries of apprehension in order to conceal the direction of her flight. The other remained, however, and even moved a few steps nearer to Kai Lung, as though encouraged by his appearance, so that he was able to regard her varying details more appreciably. As she advanced she plucked a red blossom from a thorny bush, and from time to time she shortened the broken stalk between her jade teeth.

"Courteous loiterer," she said, in a very pearl–like voice, when they had thus regarded one another for a few beats of time, "what is your honourable name, and who are you who tarry here, journeying neither to the east nor to the west?"

"The answer is necessarily commonplace and unworthy of your polite interest," was the diffident reply. "My unbecoming name is Kai, to which has been added that of Lung. By profession I am an incapable relater of imagined tales, and to this end I spread my mat wherever my uplifted voice can entice together a company to listen. Should my feeble efforts be deemed worthy of reward, those who stand around may perchance contribute to my scanty store, but sometimes this is judged superfluous. For this cause I now turn my expectant feet from Loo–chow towards the untried city of Yu–ping, but the undiminished li stretching relentlessly before me, I sought beneath these trees a refuge from the noontide sun."

"The occupation is a dignified one, being to no great degree removed from that of the Sages who compiled The Books," remarked the maiden, with an encouraging smile. "Are there many stories known to your retentive mind?"

"In one form or another, all that exist are within my mental grasp," admitted Kai Lung modestly. "Thus equipped, there is no arising emergency for which I am unprepared."

"There are other things that I would learn of your craft. What kind of story is the most favourably received, and the one whereby your collecting bowl is the least ignored?"

"That depends on the nature and condition of those who stand around, and therein lies much that is essential to the art," replied Kai Lung, not without an element of pride. "Should the company be chiefly formed of the illiterate and the immature of both sexes, stories depicting the embarrassment of unnaturally round–bodied mandarins, the unpremeditated flight of eccentrically–garbed passers–by into vats of powdered rice, the despair of guardians of the street when assailed by showers of eggs and overripe lo–quats, or any other variety of humiliating pain inflicted upon the innocent and unwary, never fail to win approval. The prosperous and substantial find contentment in hearing of the unassuming virtues and frugal lives of the poor and unsuccessful. Those of humble origin, especially tea–house maidens and the like, are only really at home among stories of the exalted and quick–moving, the profusion of their robes, the magnificence of their palaces, and the general high–minded depravity of their lives. Ordinary persons require stories dealing lavishly with all the emotions, so that they may thereby have a feeling of sufficiency when contributing to the collecting bowl."

"These things being so," remarked the maiden, "what story would you consider most appropriate to a company composed of such as she who is now conversing with you?"

"Such a company could never be obtained," replied Kai Lung, with conviction in his tone. "It is not credible that throughout the Empire could be found even another possessing all the engaging attributes of the one before me. But should it be my miraculous fortune to be given the opportunity, my presumptuous choice for her discriminating ears alone would be the story of the peerless Princess Taik and of the noble minstrel Ch'eng, who to regain her presence chained his wrist to a passing star and was carried into the assembly of the gods."

"Is it," inquired the maiden, with an agreeable glance towards the opportune recumbence of a fallen tree, "is it a narration that would lie within the passage of the sun from one branch of this willow to another?"

"Adequately set forth, the history of the Princess Taik and of the virtuous youth occupies all the energies of an agile story–teller for seven weeks," replied Kai Lung, not entirely gladdened that she should deem him capable of offering so meagre an entertainment as that she indicated. "There is a much–flattened version which may be compressed within the narrow limits of a single day and night, but even that requires for certain of the more moving passages the accompaniment of a powerful drum or a

7

hollow wooden fish."

"Alas!" exclaimed the maiden, "though the time should pass like a flash of lightning beneath the allurement of your art, it is questionable if those who await this one's returning footsteps would experience a like illusion. Even now—" With a magnanimous wave of her well-formed hand she indicated the other maiden, who, finding that the danger of pursuit was not sustained, had returned to claim her part.

"One advances along the westward road," reported the second maiden. "Let us fly elsewhere, O allurer of mankind! It may be—"

"Doubtless in Yu-ping the sound of your uplifted voice—" But at this point a noise upon the earth-road, near at hand, impelled them both to sudden flight into the deeper recesses of the wood.

Thus deprived, Kai Lung moved from the shadow of the trees and sought the track, to see if by chance he from whom they fled might turn to his advantage. On the road he found one who staggered behind a laborious wheel-barrow in the direction of Loo-chow. At that moment he had stopped to take down the sail, as the breeze was bereft of power among the obstruction of the trees, and also because he was weary.

"Greeting," called down Kai Lung, saluting him. "There is here protection from the fierceness of the sun and a stream wherein to wash your feet."

"Haply," replied the other; "and a greatly over-burdened one would gladly leave this ill-nurtured earth-road even for the fields of hell, were it not that all his goods are here contained upon an utterly intractable wheel-barrow."

Nevertheless he drew himself up from the road to the level of the wood and there reclined, yet not permitting the wheel-barrow to pass beyond his sight, though he must thereby lie half in the shade and half in the heat beyond. "Greeting, wayfarer."

"Although you are evidently a man of some wealth, we are for the time brought to a common level by the forces that control us," remarked Kai Lung. "I have here two onions, a gourd and a sufficiency of millet paste. Partake equally with me, therefore, before you resume your way. In the meanwhile I will procure water from the stream near by, and to this end my collecting bowl will serve."

When Kai Lung returned he found that the other had added to their store a double handful of dates, some snuff and a little jar of oil. As they ate together the stranger thus disclosed his mind:

"The times are doubtful and it behoves each to guard himself. In the north the banners of the 'Spreading Lotus' and the 'Avenging Knife' are already raised and pressing nearer every day, while the signs and passwords are so widely flung that every man speaks slowly and with a double tongue. Lately there have been slicings and other forms of vigorous justice no farther distant than Loo–chow, and now the Mandarin Shan Tien comes to Yu–ping to flatten any signs of discontent. The occupation of this person is that of a maker of sandals and coverings for the head, but very soon there will be more wooden feet required than leather sandals in Yu–ping, and artificial ears will be greater in demand than hats. For this reason he has got together all his goods, sold the more burdensome, and now ventures on an untried way."

"Prosperity attend your goings. Yet, as one who has set his face towards Yu–ping, is it not possible for an ordinary person of simple life and unassuming aims to escape persecution under this same Shan Tien?"

"Of the Mandarin himself those who know speak with vague lips. What is done is done by the pressing hand of one Ming–shu, who takes down his spoken word; of whom it is truly said that he has little resemblance to a man and still less to an angel."

"Yet," protested the story–teller hopefully, "it is wisely written: 'He who never opens his mouth in strife can always close his eyes in peace.'"

"Doubtless," assented the other. "He can close his eyes assuredly. Whether he will ever again open them is another matter."

With this timely warning the sandal–maker rose and prepared to resume his journey. Nor did he again take up the burden of his task until he had satisfied himself that the westward road was destitute of traffic.

9

"A tranquil life and a painless death," was his farewell parting. "Jung, of the line of Hai, wishes you well." Then, with many imprecations on the relentless sun above, the inexorable road beneath, and on every detail of the evilly–balanced load before him, he passed out on his way.

It would have been well for Kai Lung had he also forced his reluctant feet to raise the dust, but his body clung to the moist umbrage of his couch, and his mind made reassurance that perchance the maiden would return. Thus it fell that when two others, who looked from side to side as they hastened on the road, turned as at a venture to the wood they found him still there.

"Restrain your greetings," said the leader of the two harshly, in the midst of Kai Lung's courteous obeisance; "and do not presume to disparage yourself as if in equality with the one who stands before you. Have two of the inner chamber, attired thus and thus, passed this way? Speak, and that to a narrow edge."

"The road lies beyond the perception of my incapable vision, chiefest," replied Kai lung submissively. "Furthermore, I have slept."

"Unless you would sleep more deeply, shape your stubborn tongue to a specific point," commanded the other, touching a meaning sword. "Who are you who loiter here, and for what purpose do you lurk? Speak fully, and be assured that your word will be put to a corroding test."

Thus encouraged, Kai Lung freely disclosed his name and ancestry, the means whereby he earned a frugal sustenance and the nature of his journey. In addition, he professed a willingness to relate his most recently–acquired story, that entitled "Wu–yong: or The Politely Inquiring Stranger", but the offer was thrust ungracefully aside.

"Everything you say deepens the suspicion which your criminal–looking face naturally provokes," said the questioner, putting away his tablets on which he had recorded the replies. "At Yu–ping the matter will be probed with a very definite result. You, Li–loe, remain about this spot in case she whom we seek should pass. I return to speak of our unceasing effort."

"I obey," replied the dog-like Li-loe. "What men can do we have done. We are no demons to see through solid matter."

When they were alone, Li-loe drew nearer to Kai Lung and, allowing his face to assume a more pacific bend, he cast himself down by the story-teller's side.

"The account which you gave of yourself was ill contrived," he said. "Being put to the test, its falsity cannot fail to be discovered."

"Yet," protested Kai Lung earnestly, "in no single detail did it deviate from the iron line of truth."

"Then your case is even more desperate than before," exclaimed Li-loe. "Know now that the repulsive-featured despot who has just left us is Ming-shu, he who takes down the Mandarin Shan Tien's spoken word. By admitting that you are from Loo-chow, where disaffection reigns, you have noosed a rope about your neck, and by proclaiming yourself as one whose habit it is to call together a company to listen to your word you have drawn it tight."

"Every rope has two ends," remarked Kai Lung philosophically, "and to-morrow is yet to come. Tell me rather, since that is our present errand, who is she whom you pursue and to what intent?"

"That is not so simple as to be contained within the hollow of an acorn sheath. Let it suffice that she has the left ear of Shan Tien, even as Ming-shu has the right, but on which side his hearing is better it might be hazardous to guess."

"And her meritorious name?"

"She is of the house of K'ang, her name being Hwa-mei, though from the nature of her charm she is ofttime called the Golden Mouse. But touching this affair of your own immediate danger: we being both but common men of the idler sort, it is only fitting that when high ones threaten I should stand by you."

"Speak definitely," assented Kai Lung, "yet with the understanding that the full extent of my store does not exceed four or five strings of cash."

11

"The soil is somewhat shallow for the growth of deep friendship, but what we have we will share equally between us." With these auspicious words Li−loe possessed himself of three of the strings of cash and displayed an empty sleeve. "I, alas, have nothing. The benefits I have in mind are of a subtler and more priceless kind. At Yu−ping my office will be that of the keeper of the doors of the yamen, including that of the prison−house. Thus I shall doubtless be able to render you frequent service of an inconspicuous kind. Do not forget the name of Li−loe."

By this time the approaching sound of heavy traffic, heralded by the beating of drums, the blowing of horns and the discharge of an occasional firework, indicated the passage of some dignified official. This, declared Li−loe, could be none other than the Mandarin Shan Tien, resuming his march towards Yu−ping, and the doorkeeper prepared to join the procession at his appointed place. Kai Lung, however, remained unseen among the trees, not being desirous of obtruding himself upon Ming−shu unnecessarily. When the noise had almost died away in the distance he came forth, believing that all would by this time have passed, and approached the road. As he reached it a single chair was hurried by, its carriers striving by increased exertion to regain their fellows. It was too late for Kai Lung to retreat, whoever might be within. As it passed a curtain moved somewhat, a symmetrical hand came discreetly forth, and that which it held fell at his feet. Without varying his attitude he watched the chair until it was out of sight, then stooped and picked something up—a red blossom on a thorny stalk, the flower already parched but the stem moist and softened to his touch.

CHAPTER II. The Inexorable Justice of the Mandarin Shan Tien

"BY having access to this enclosure you will be able to walk where otherwise you must stand. That in itself is cheap at the price of three reputed strings of inferior cash. Furthermore, it is possible to breathe."

"The outlook, in one direction, is an extensive one," admitted Kai Lung, gazing towards the sky. "Here, moreover, is a shutter through which the vista doubtless lengthens."

"So long as there is no chance of you exploring it any farther than your neck, it does not matter," said Li—loe. "Outside lies a barren region of the yamen garden where no one ever comes. I will now leave you, having to meet one with whom I would traffic for a goat. When I return be prepared to retrace your steps to the prison cell."

"The shadow moves as the sun directs," replied Kai Lung, and with courteous afterthought he added the wonted parting: "Slowly, slowly; walk slowly."

In such a manner the story—teller found himself in a highly—walled enclosure, lying between the prison—house and the yamen garden, a few days after his arrival in Yu—ping. Ming—shu had not eaten his word.

The yard itself possessed no attraction for Kai Lung. Almost before Li—loe had disappeared he was at the shutter in the wall, had forced it open and was looking out. Thus long he waited, motionless, but observing every leaf that stirred among the trees and shrubs and neglected growth beyond. At last a figure passed across a distant glade and at the sight Kai Lung lifted up a restrained voice in song:

"At the foot of a bleak and inhospitable mountain An insignificant stream winds its uncared way; Although inferior to the Yangtze—kiang in every detail Yet fish glide to and fro among its crannies Nor would they change their home for the depths of the widest river.

The palace of the sublime Emperor is made rich with hanging curtains. While here rough stone walls forbid repose. Yet there is one who unhesitatingly prefers the latter; For from an open shutter here he can look forth, And perchance catch a glimpse of one who may pass by.

The occupation of the Imperial viceroy is both lucrative and noble; While that of a relater of imagined tales is by no means esteemed. But he who thus expressed himself would not exchange with the other; For around the identity of each heroine he can entwine the personality of one whom he has encountered. And thus she is ever by his side."

"Your uplifted voice comes from an unexpected quarter, minstrel," said a melodious voice, and the maiden whom he had encountered in the wood stood before him. "What crime have you now committed?"

"An ancient one. I presumed to raise my unworthy eyes—"

"Alas, story–teller," interposed the maiden hastily, "it would seem that the star to which you chained your wrist has not carried you into the assembly of the gods."

"Yet already it has borne me half–way—into a company of malefactors. Doubtless on the morrow the obliging Mandarin Shan Tien will arrange for the journey to be complete."

"Yet have you then no further wish to continue in an ordinary existence?" asked the maiden.

"To this person," replied Kai Lung, with a deep–seated look, "existence can never again be ordinary. Admittedly it may be short."

As they conversed together in this inoffensive manner she whom Li–loe had called the Golden Mouse held in her delicately–formed hands a priceless bowl filled with ripe fruit of the rarer kinds which she had gathered. These from time to time she threw up to the opening, rightly deciding that one in Kai Lung's position would stand in need of sustenance, and he no less dexterously held and retained them. When the bowl was empty she continued for a space to regard it silently, as though exploring the many–sided recesses of her mind.

"You have claimed to be a story–teller and have indeed made a boast that there is no arising emergency for which you are unprepared," she said at length. "It now befalls that you may be put to a speedy test. Is the nature of this imagined scene"—thus she indicated the embellishment of the bowl—"familiar to your eyes?"

"It is that known as 'The Willow,'" replied Kai Lung. "There is a story—"

"There is a story!" exclaimed the maiden, loosening from her brow the overhanging look of care. "Thus and thus. Frequently have I importuned him before whom you will appear to explain to me the meaning of the scene. When you are called upon to plead your cause, see to it well that your knowledge of such a tale is clearly shown. He

14

before whom you kneel, craftily plied meanwhile by my unceasing petulance, will then desire to hear it from your lips . . . At the striking of the fourth gong the day is done. What lies between rests with your discriminating wit."

"You are deep in the subtler kinds of wisdom, such as the weak possess," confessed Kai Lung. "Yet how will this avail to any length?"

"That which is put off from to-day is put off from to-morrow," was the confident reply. "For the rest—at a corresponding gong-stroke of each day it is this person's custom to gather fruit. Farewell, minstrel."

When Li-loe returned a little later Kai Lung threw his two remaining strings of cash about that rapacious person's neck and embraced him as he exclaimed:

"Chieftain among doorkeepers, when I go to the Capital to receive the all-coveted title 'Leaf-crowned' and to chant ceremonial odes before the Court, thou shalt accompany me as forerunner, and an agile tribe of selected goats shall sport about thy path."

"Alas, manlet," replied the other, weeping readily, "greatly do I fear that the next journey thou wilt take will be in an upward or a downward rather than a sideway direction. This much have I learned, and to this end, at some cost admittedly, I enticed into loquacity one who knows another whose brother holds the key of Ming-shu's confidence: that to-morrow the Mandarin will begin to distribute justice here, and out of the depths of Ming-shu's malignity the name of Kai Lung is the first set down."

"With the title," continued Kai Lung cheerfully, "there goes a sufficiency of taels; also a vat of a potent wine of a certain kind."

"If," suggested Li-loe, looking anxiously around, "you have really discovered hidden about this place a secret store of wine, consider well whether it would not be prudent to entrust it to a faithful friend before it is too late."

It was indeed as Li-loe had foretold. On the following day, at the second gong-stroke after noon, the order came and, closely guarded, Kai Lung was led forth. The middle court had been duly arranged, with a formidable display of chains, weights, presses, saws, branding irons and other implements for securing justice. At the head of a table draped with red sat the Mandarin Shan Tien, on his right the secretary of his hand, the contemptible Ming–shu. Round about were positioned others who in one necessity or another might be relied upon to play an ordered part. After a lavish explosion of fire–crackers had been discharged, sonorous bells rung and gongs beaten, a venerable geomancer disclosed by means of certain tests that all doubtful influences had been driven off and that truth and impartiality alone remained.

"Except on the part of the prisoners, doubtless," remarked the Mandarin, thereby imperilling the gravity of all who stood around.

"The first of those to prostrate themselves before your enlightened clemency, Excellence, is a notorious assassin who, under another name, has committed many crimes," began the execrable Ming–shu. "He confesses that, now calling himself Kai Lung, he has recently journeyed from Loo–chow, where treason ever wears a smiling face."

"Perchance he is saddened by our city's loyalty," interposed the benign Shan Tien, "for if he is smiling now it is on the side of his face removed from this one's gaze."

"The other side of his face is assuredly where he will be made to smile ere long," acquiesced Ming–shu, not altogether to his chief's approval, as the analogy was already his. "Furthermore, he has been detected lurking in secret meeting–places by the wayside, and on reaching Yu–ping he raised his rebellious voice inviting all to gather round and join his unlawful band. The usual remedy in such cases during periods of stress, Excellence, is strangulation."

"The times are indeed pressing," remarked the agile–minded Mandarin, "and the penalty would appear to be adequate." As no one suffered inconvenience at his attitude, however, Shan Tien's expression assumed a more unbending cast.

"Let the witnesses appear," he commanded sharply.

"In so clear a case it has not been thought necessary to incur the expense of hiring the usual witnesses," urged Ming–shu; "but they are doubtless clustered about the opium floor and will, if necessary, testify to whatever is required."

16

"The argument is a timely one," admitted the Mandarin. "As the result cannot fail to be the same in either case, perhaps the accommodating prisoner will assist the ends of justice by making a full confession of his crimes?"

"High Excellence," replied the story–teller, speaking for the first time, "it is truly said that that which would appear as a mountain in the evening may stand revealed as a mud–hut by the light of day. Hear my unpainted word. I am of the abject House of Kai and my inoffensive rice is earned as a narrator of imagined tales. Unrolling my threadbare mat at the middle hour of yesterday, I had raised my distressing voice and announced an intention to relate the Story of Wong Ts'in, that which is known as 'The Legend of the Willow Plate Embellishment,' when a company of armed warriors, converging upon me—"

"Restrain the melodious flow of your admitted eloquence," interrupted the Mandarin, veiling his arising interest. "Is the story, to which you have made reference, that of the scene widely depicted on plates and earthenware?"

"Undoubtedly. It is the true and authentic legend as related by the eminent Tso–yi."

"In that case," declared Shan Tien dispassionately, "it will be necessary for you to relate it now, in order to uphold your claim. Proceed."

"Alas, Excellence," protested Ming–shu from a bitter throat, "this matter will attenuate down to the stroke of evening rice. Kowtowing beneath your authoritative hand, that which the prisoner only had the intention to relate does not come within the confines of his evidence."

"The objection is superficial and cannot be sustained," replied Shan Tien. "If an evilly–disposed one raised a sword to strike this person, but was withheld before the blow could fall, none but a leper would contend that because he did not progress beyond the intention thereby he should go free. Justice must be impartially upheld and greatly do I fear that we must all submit."

With these opportune words the discriminating personage signified to Kai Lung that he should begin.

The Story of Wong T'sin and the Willow Plate Embellishment

Wong Ts'in, the rich porcelain maker, was ill at ease within himself. He had partaken of his customary midday meal, flavoured the repast by unsealing a jar of matured wine, consumed a little fruit, a few sweetmeats and half a dozen cups of unapproachable tea, and then retired to an inner chamber to contemplate philosophically from the reposeful attitude of a reclining couch.

But upon this occasion the merchant did not contemplate restfully. He paced the floor in deep dejection and when he did use the couch at all it was to roll upon it in a sudden access of internal pain. The cause of his distress was well known to the unhappy person thus concerned, nor did it lessen the pangs of his emotion that it arose entirely from his own ill-considered action.

When Wong Ts'in had discovered, by the side of a remote and obscure river, the inexhaustible bed of porcelain clay that ensured his prosperity, his first care was to erect adequate sheds and labouring-places; his next to build a house sufficient for himself and those in attendance round about him.

So far prudence had ruled his actions, for there is a keen edge to the saying: "He who sleeps over his workshop brings four eyes into the business," but in one detail Wong T'sin's head and feet went on different journeys, for with incredible oversight he omitted to secure the experience of competent astrologers and omen-casters in fixing the exact site of his mansion.

The result was what might have been expected. In excavating for the foundations, Wong T'sin's slaves disturbed the repose of a small but rapacious earth-demon that had already been sleeping there for nine hundred and ninety-nine years. With the insatiable cunning of its kind, this vindictive creature waited until the house was completed and then proceeded to transfer its unseen but formidable presence to the quarters that were designed for Wong Ts'in himself. Thenceforth, from time to time, it continued to revenge itself for the trouble to which it had been put by an insidious persecution. This frequently took the form of fastening its claws upon the merchant's digestive organs, especially after he had partaken of an unusually rich repast (for in some way the display of certain viands excited its unreasoning animosity), pressing heavily upon his chest, invading his repose with dragon-dreams while he slept, and the like. Only by the exercise of an ingenuity greater than its own could Wong Ts'in succeed in baffling its ill–conditioned spite.

On this occasion, recognizing from the nature of his pangs what was taking place, Wong Ts'in resorted to a stratagem that rarely failed him. Announcing in a loud voice that it was his intention to refresh the surface of his body by the purifying action of heated vapour, and then to proceed to his mixing–floor, the merchant withdrew. The demon, being an earth–dweller with the ineradicable objection of this class of creatures towards all the elements of moisture, at once relinquished its hold, and going direct to the part of the works indicated, it there awaited its victim with the design of resuming its discreditable persecution.

Wong Ts'in had spoken with a double tongue. On leaving the inner chamber he quickly traversed certain obscure passages of his house until he reached an inferior portal. Even if the demon had suspected his purpose it would not have occurred to a creature of its narrow outlook that anyone of Wong Ts'in's importance would make use of so menial an outway. The merchant therefore reached his garden unperceived and thenceforward maintained an undeviating face in the direction of the Outer Expanses. Before he had covered many li he was assured that he had indeed succeeded for the time in shaking off his unscrupulous tormentor. His internal organs again resumed their habitual calm and his mind was lightened as from an overhanging cloud.

There was another reason why Wong Ts'in sought the solitude of the thinly–peopled outer places, away from the influence and distraction of his own estate. For some time past a problem that had once been remote was assuming dimensions of increasing urgency. This detail concerns Fa Fai, who had already been referred to by a person of literary distinction, in a poetical analogy occupying three written volumes, as a pearl–tinted peach–blossom shielded and restrained by the silken net–work of wise parental affection (and recognizing the justice of the comparison, Wong Ts'in had been induced to purchase the work in question). Now that Fa Fai had attained an age when she could fittingly be sought in marriage the contingency might occur at any time, and the problem confronting her father's decision was this: owing to her incomparable perfection Fa Fai must be accounted one of Wong Ts'in's chief possessions, the other undoubtedly being his secret process of simulating the lustrous effect of pure gold embellishment on china by the application of a much less expensive substitute. Would it be more prudent to concentrate the power of both influences and let it become known that with Fa Fai would go the essential part of his very remunerative clay enterprise, or would it be more prudent to divide these attractions and secure two distinct influences, both concerned about his welfare? In the first case there need be no reasonable limit to the extending vista of his ambition, and he might even aspire to greet as a son the highest functionary of the province—an official of such heavily–sustained importance that when he went about it required six chosen slaves to carry him, and of late it had been considered more prudent to employ eight.

If, on the other hand, Fa Fai went without any added inducement, a mandarin of moderate rank would probably be as high as Wong Ts'in could look, but he would certainly be able to adopt another of at least equal position, at the price of making over to him the ultimate benefit of his discovery. He could thus acquire either two sons of reasonable influence, or one who exercised almost unlimited authority. In view of his own childlessness, and of his final dependence on the services of others, which arrangement promised the most regular and liberal transmission of supplies to his expectant spirit when he had passed into the Upper Air, and would his connection with one very important official or with two subordinate ones secure him the greater amount of honour and serviceable recognition among the more useful deities?

To Wong Ts'in's logical mind it seemed as though there must be a definite answer to this problem. If one manner of behaving was right the other must prove wrong, for as the wise philosopher Ning–hy was wont to say: "Where the road divides, there stand two Ning–hys." The decision on a matter so essential to his future comfort ought not to be left to chance. Thus it had become a habit of Wong Ts'in's to penetrate the Outer Spaces in the hope of there encountering a specific omen.

Alas, it has been well written: "He who thinks that he is raising a mound may only in reality be digging a pit." In his continual search for a celestial portent among the solitudes Wong Ts'in had of late necessarily somewhat neglected his earthly (as it may thus be expressed) interests. In these emergencies certain of the more turbulent among his workers had banded themselves together into a confederacy under the leadership of a craftsman named Fang. It was the custom of these men, who wore a badge and recognized a mutual oath and imprecation, to present themselves suddenly before Wong Ts'in and demand a greater reward for their exertions than they had previously agreed to, threatening that unless this was accorded they would cast down the implements of their labour in unison and involve in idleness those who otherwise would have continued at their task. This menace Wong Ts'in bought off from time to time by agreeing to their exactions, but it began presently to appear that this way of appeasing them resembled Chou Hong's method of extinguishing a fire by directing jets of wind against it. On the day with which this related story has so far concerned itself, a band of the most highly remunerated and privileged of the craftsmen had appeared before Wong Ts'in with the intolerable Fang at their head. These men were they whose skill enabled them laboriously to copy upon the surfaces of porcelain a given scene without appreciable deviation from one to the other, for in those remote cycles of history no other method was yet known or even dreamed of.

"Suitable greetings, employer of our worthless services," remarked their leader, seating himself upon the floor unbidden. "These who speak through the mouth of the cringing mendicant before you are the Bound–together Brotherhood of Colour–mixers and Putters–on of Thought–out Designs, bent upon a just cause."

"May their Ancestral Tablets never fall into disrepair," replied Wong Ts'in courteously. "For the rest—let the mouth referred to shape itself into the likeness of a narrow funnel, for the lengthening gong–strokes press round about my unfinished labours."

"That which in justice requires the amplitude of a full–sized cask shall be pressed down into the confines of an inadequate vessel," assented Fang. "Know then, O battener upon our ill–requited skill, how it has come to our knowledge that one who is not of our Brotherhood moves among us and performs an equal task for a less reward. This is our spoken word in consequence: in place of one tael every man among us shall now take two, and he who before has laboured eight gongs to receive it shall henceforth labour four. Furthermore, he who is speaking shall, as their recognized head and authority, always be addressed by the honourable title of 'Polished,' and the dog who is not one of us shall be cast forth."

"My hand itches to reward you in accordance with the inner prompting of a full heart," replied the merchant, after a well–sustained pause. "But in this matter my very deficient ears must be leading my threadbare mind astray. The moon has not been eaten up since the day when you stood before me in a like attitude and bargained that every man should henceforth receive a full tael where hitherto a half had been his portion, and that in place of the toil of sixteen gong–strokes eight should suffice. Upon this being granted all bound themselves by spoken word that the matter should stand thus and thus between us until the gathering–in of the next rice harvest."

"That may have been so at the time," admitted Fang, with dog–like obstinacy, "but it was not then known that you had pledged yourself to Hien Nan for tenscore embellished plates of porcelain within a stated time, and that our services would therefore be essential to your reputation. There has thus arisen what may be regarded as a new vista of eventualities, and this frees us from the bondage of our spoken word. Having thus moderately stated our unbending demand, we will depart until the like gong–stroke of to–morrow, when, if our claim be not agreed to, all will cast down their implements of labour with the swiftness of a lightning–flash and thereby involve the whole of your too–profitable undertaking in well–merited stagnation. We go, venerable head; auspicious omens attend your movements!"

"May the All–Seeing guide your footsteps," responded Wong Ts'in, and with courteous forbearance he waited until they were out of hearing before he added—"into a vat of boiling sulphur!"

Thus may the position be outlined when Wei Chang, the unassuming youth whom the black–hearted Fang had branded with so degrading a comparison, sat at his appointed place rather than join in the discreditable conspiracy, and strove by his unaided dexterity to enable Wong Ts'in to complete the tenscore embellished plates by the appointed time. Yet already he knew that in this commendable ambition his head grew larger than his hands, for he was the slowest–working among all Wong Ts'in's craftsmen, and even then his copy could frequently be detected from the original. Not to overwhelm his memory with unmerited contempt it is fitting now to reveal somewhat more of the unfolding curtain of events.

Wei Chang was not in reality a worker in the art of applying coloured designs to porcelain at all. He was a student of the literary excellences and had decided to devote his entire life to the engaging task of reducing the most perfectly matched analogy to the least possible number of words when the unexpected appearance of Fa Fai unsettled his ambitions. She was restraining the impatience of a powerful horse and controlling its movements by means of a leather thong, while at the same time she surveyed the landscape with a disinterested glance in which Wei Chang found himself becoming involved. Without stopping even to consult the spirits of his revered ancestors on so important a decision, he at once burned the greater part of his collection of classical analogies and engaged himself, as one who is willing to become more proficient, about Wong Ts'in's earth—yards. Here, without any reasonable intention of ever becoming in any way personally congenial to her, he was in a position occasionally to see the distant outline of Fa Fai's movements, and when a day passed and even this was withheld he was content that the shadow of the many—towered building that contained her should obscure the sunlight from the window before which he worked.

While Wei Chang was thus engaged the door of the enclosure in which he laboured was thrust cautiously inwards, and presently he became aware that the being whose individuality was never completely absent from his thoughts was standing in an expectant attitude at no great distance from him. As no other person was present, the craftsmen having departed in order to consult an oracle that dwelt beneath an appropriate sign, and Wong Ts'in being by this time among the Outer Ways seeking an omen as to Fa Fai's disposal, Wei Chang did not think it respectful to become aware of the maiden's presence until a persistent distress of her throat compelled him to recognize the incident.

"Unapproachable perfection," he said, with becoming deference, "is it permissible that in the absence of your enlightened sire you should descend from your golden eminence and stand, entirely unattended, at no great distance from so ordinary a person as myself?"

"Whether it be strictly permissible or not, it is only on like occasions that she ever has the opportunity of descending from the solitary pinnacle referred to," replied Fa Fai, not only with no outward appearance of alarm at being directly addressed by one of a different sex, but even moving nearer to Wei Chang as she spoke. "A more essential detail in the circumstances concerns the length of time that he may be prudently relied upon to be away?"

"Doubtless several gong—strokes will intervene before his returning footsteps gladden our expectant vision," replied Wei Chang. "He is spoken of as having set his face towards the Outer Ways, there perchance to come within the influence of a portent."

"Its probable object is not altogether unknown to the one who stands before you," admitted Fa Fai, "and as a dutiful and affectionate daughter it has become a consideration with her whether she ought not to press forward, as it were, to a solution on her own account. . . . If the one whom I am addressing could divert his attention from the embellishment of the very inadequate claw of a wholly superfluous winged dragon, possibly he might add his sage counsel on that point."

"It is said that a bull–frog once rent his throat in a well–meant endeavour to advise an eagle in the art of flying," replied Wei Chang, concealing the bitterness of his heart beneath an easy tongue. "For this reason it is inexpedient for earthlings to fix their eyes on those who dwell in very high places."

"To the intrepid, very high places exist solely to be scaled; with others, however, the only scaling they attempt is lavished on the armour of preposterous flying monsters, O youth of the House of Wei!"

"Is it possible," exclaimed Wei Chang, moving forward with so sudden an ardour that the maiden hastily withdrew herself several paces from beyond his enthusiasm, "is it possible that this person's hitherto obscure and execrated name is indeed known to your incomparable lips?"

"As the one who periodically casts up the computations of the sums of money due to those who labour about the earth–yards, it would be strange if the name had so far escaped my notice," replied Fa Fai, with a distance in her voice that the few paces between them very inadequately represented. "Certain details engrave themselves upon the tablets of recollection by their persistence. For instance, the name of Fang is generally at the head of each list; that of Wei Chang is invariably at the foot."

"It is undeniable," admitted Wei Chang, in a tone of well–merited humiliation; "and the attainment of never having yet applied a design in such a manner that the copy might be mistaken for the original has entirely flattened–out this person's self–esteem."

"Doubtless," suggested Fa Fai, with delicate encouragement, "there are other pursuits in which you would disclose a more highly developed proficiency—as that of watching the gyrations of untamed horses, for example. Our more immediate need, however, is to discover a means of defeating the malignity of the detestable Fang. With this object I have for some time past secretly applied myself to the task of contriving a design which, by blending simplicity with picturesque effect, will enable one person in a given length of time to achieve the amount of work hitherto done by two."

With these auspicious words the accomplished maiden disclosed a plate of translucent porcelain, embellished in the manner which she had described. At the sight of the ingenious way in which trees and persons, stream and buildings, and objects of a widely differing nature had been so arranged as to give the impression that they all existed at the same time, and were equally visible without undue exertion on the part of the spectator who regarded them, Wei Chang could not restrain an exclamation of delight.

"How cunningly imagined is the device by which objects so varied in size as an orange and an island can be depicted within the narrow compass of a porcelain plate without the larger one completely obliterating the smaller or the smaller becoming actually invisible by comparison with the other! Hitherto this unimaginative person had not considered the possibility of showing other than dragons, demons, spirits, and the forces which from their celestial nature may be regarded as possessing no real thickness of substance and therefore being particularly suitable for treatment on a flat surface. But this engaging display might indeed be a scene having an actual existence at no great space away."

"Such is assuredly the case," admitted Fa Fai. "Within certain limitations, imposed by this new art of depicting realities as they are, we may be regarded as standing before an open window. The important-looking building on the right is that erected by this person's venerated father. Its prosperity is indicated by the luxurious profusion of the fruit-tree overhanging it. Pressed somewhat to the back, but of dignified proportion, are the outer buildings of those who labour among the clay."

"In a state of actuality, they are of measurably less dignified dimensions," suggested Wei Chang.

"The objection is inept," replied Fa Fai. "The buildings in question undoubtedly exist at the indicated position. If, therefore, the actuality is to be maintained, it is necessary either to raise their stature or to cut down the trees obscuring them. To this gentle-minded person the former alternative seemed the less drastic. As, however, it is regarded in a spirit of no-satisfaction—"

25

"Proceed, incomparable one, proceed," implored Wei Chang. "It was but a breath of thought, arising from a recollection of the many times that this incapable person has struck his unworthy head against the roof—beams of those nobly—proportioned buildings."

"The three stunted individuals crossing the bridge in undignified attitudes are the debased Fang and two of his mercenary accomplices. They are, as usual, bending their footsteps in the direction of the hospitality of a house that announces its purpose beneath the sign of a spreading bush. They are positioned as crossing the river to a set purpose, and the bridge is devoid of a rail in the hope that on their return they may all fall into the torrent in a helpless condition and be drowned, to the satisfaction of the beholders."

"It would be a fitting conclusion to their ill—spent lives," agreed Wei Chang. "Would it not add to their indignity to depict them as struggling beneath the waves?"

"It might do so," admitted Fa Fai graciously, "but in order to express the arisement adequately it would be necessary to display them twice—first on the bridge with their faces turned towards the west, and then in the flood with their faces towards the east; and the superficial might hastily assume that the three on the bridge would rescue the three in the river."

"You are all—wise," said Wei Chang, with well—marked admiration in his voice. "This person's suggestion was opaque."

"In any case," continued Fa Fai, with a reassuring glance, "it is a detail that is not essential to the frustration of Fang's malignant scheme, for already well on its way towards Hien Nan may be seen a trustworthy junk, laden with two formidable crates, each one containing fivescore plates of the justly esteemed Wong Ts'in porcelain."

"Nevertheless," maintained Wei Chang mildly, "the out—passing of Fang would have been a satisfactory detail of the occurrence."

"Do not despair," replied Fa Fai. "Not idly is it written: 'Destiny has four feet, eight hands and sixteen eyes: how then shall the ill—doer with only two of each hope to escape?' An even more ignominious end may await Fang, should he escape drowning, for, conveniently placed by the side of the stream, this person has introduced a spreading willow–tree. Any of its lower branches is capable of sustaining Fang's weight, should a reliable rope connect the two."

"There is something about that which this person now learns is a willow that distinguishes it above all the other trees of the design," remarked Wei Chang admiringly. "It has a wild and yet a romantic aspect."

"This person had not yet chanced upon a suitable title for the device," said Fa Fai, "and a distinguishing name is necessary, for possibly scores of copies may be made before its utility is exhausted. Your discriminating praise shall be accepted as a fortunate omen, and henceforth this shall be known as the Willow Pattern Embellishment."

"The honour of suggesting the title is more than this commonplace person can reasonably carry," protested Wei Chang, feeling that very little worth considering existed outside the earth–shed. "Not only scores, but even hundreds of copies may be required in the process of time, for a crust of rice–bread and handful of dried figs eaten from such a plate would be more satisfying than a repast of many–coursed richness elsewhere."

In this well–sustained and painless manner Fa Fai and Wei Chang continued to express themselves agreeably to each other, until the lengthening gong–strokes warned the former person that her absence might inconvenience Wong Ts'in's sense of tranquillity on his return, nor did Wei Chang contest the desirability of a great space intervening between them should the merchant chance to pass that way. In the meanwhile Chang had explained many of the inner details of his craft so that Fa Fai should the better understand the requirements of her new art.

"Yet where is the Willow plate itself?" said the maiden, as she began to arrange her mind towards departure. "As the colours were still in a receptive state this person placed it safely aside for the time. It was somewhat near the spot where you—"

During the amiable exchange of shafts of polished conversation Wei Chang had followed Fa Fai's indication and had seated himself upon a low bench without any very definite perception of his movements. He now arose with the unstudied haste of one who has inconvenienced a scorpion.

27

"Alas!" he exclaimed, in a tone of the acutest mental distress; "can it be possible that this utterly profane outcast has so desecrated—"

"Certainly comment of an admittedly crushing nature has been imposed on this one's well-meant handiwork," said Fa Fai. With these lightly-barbed words, which were plainly devised to restore the other person's face towards himself, the magnanimous maiden examined the plate which Wei Chang's uprising had revealed.

"Not only has the embellishment suffered no real detriment," she continued, after an adequate glance, "but there has been imparted to the higher lights—doubtless owing to the nature of the fabric in which your lower half is encased—a certain nebulous quality that adds greatly to the successful effect of the various tones."

At the first perception of the indignity to which he had subjected the entrancing Fa Fai's work, and the swift feeling that much more than the coloured adornment of a plate would thereby be destroyed, all power of retention had forsaken Wei Chang's incapable knees and he sank down heavily upon another bench. From this dejection the maiden's well-chosen encouragement recalled him to a position of ordinary uprightness.

"A tombstone is lifted from this person's mind by your gracefully-placed words," he declared, and he was continuing to indicate the nature of his self-reproach by means of a suitable analogy when the expression of Fa Fai's eyes turned him to a point behind himself. There, lying on the spot from which he had just risen, was a second Willow plate, differing in no detail of resemblance from the first.

"Shadow of the Great Image!" exclaimed Chang, in an awe-filled voice. "It is no marvel that miracles should attend your footsteps, celestial one, but it is incredible that this clay-souled person should be involved in the display."

"Yet," declared Fa Fai, not hesitating to allude to things as they existed, in the highly-raised stress of the discovery, "it would appear that the miracle is not specifically connected with this person's feet. Would you not, in furtherance of this line of suggestion, place yourself in a similar attitude on yet another plate, Wei Chang?"

28

Not without many protests that it was scarcely becoming thus to sit repeatedly in her presence, Chang complied with the request, and upon Fa Fai's further insistence he continued to impress himself, as it were, upon a succession of porcelain plates, with a like result. Not until the eleventh process was reached did the Willow design begin to lose its potency.

"Ten perfect copies produced within as many moments, and not one distinguishable from the first!" exclaimed Wei Chang, regarding the array of plates with pleasurable emotion. "Here is a means of baffling Fang's crafty confederacy that will fill Wong Ts'in's ears with waves of gladness on his return."

"Doubtless," agreed Fa Fai, with a dark intent. She was standing by the door of the enclosure in the process of making her departure, and she regarded Wei Chang with a set deliberation. "Yet," she continued definitely, "if this person possessed that which was essential to Wong Ts'in's prosperity, and Wong Ts'in held that which was necessary for this one's tranquillity, a locked bolt would be upon the one until the other was pledged in return."

With these opportune words the maiden vanished, leaving Wei Chang prostrating himself in spirit before the many-sidedness of her wisdom.

Wong T'sin was not altogether benevolently inclined towards the universe on his return a little later. The persistent image of Fang's overthreatening act still corroded the merchant's throat with bitterness, for on his right he saw the extinction of his business as unremunerative if he agreed, and on his left he saw the extinction of his business as undependable if he refused to agree.

Furthermore, the omens were ill-arranged.

On his way outwards he had encountered an aged man who possessed two fruit-trees, on which he relied for sustenance. As Wong Ts'in drew near, this venerable person carried from his dwelling two beaten cakes of dog-dung and began to bury them about the root of the larger tree. This action, on the part of one who might easily be a disguised wizard, aroused Wong Ts'in's interest.

29

"Why," he demanded, "having two cakes of dung and two fruit–trees, do you not allot one to each tree, so that both may benefit and return to you their produce in the time of your necessity?"

"The season promises to be one of rigour and great need," replied the other. "A single cake of dung might not provide sufficient nourishment for either tree, so that both should wither away. By reducing life to a bare necessity I could pass from one harvest to another on the fruit of this tree alone, but if both should fail I am undone. To this end I safeguard my existence by ensuring that at least the better of the two shall thrive."

"Peace attend your efforts!" said Wong Ts'in, and he began to retrace his footsteps, well content.

Yet he had not covered half the distance back when his progress was impeded by an elderly hag who fed two goats, whose milk alone preserved her from starvation. One small measure of dry grass was all that she was able to provide them with, but she divided it equally between them, to the discontent of both.

"The season promises to be one of rigour and great need," remarked Wong Ts'in affably, for the being before him might well be a creature of another part who had assumed that form for his guidance. "Why do you not therefore ensure sustenance to the better of the two goats by devoting to it the whole of the measure of dry grass? In this way you would receive at least some nourishment in return and thereby safeguard your own existence until the rice is grown again."

"In the matter of the two goats," replied the aged hag, "there is no better, both being equally stubborn and perverse, though one may be finer–looking and more vainglorious than the other. Yet should I foster this one to the detriment of her fellow, what would be this person's plight if haply the weaker died and the stronger broke away and fled! By treating both alike I retain a double thread on life, even if neither is capable of much."

"May the Unseen weigh your labours!" exclaimed Wong Ts'in in a two–edged voice, and he departed.

When he reached his own house he would have closed himself in his own chamber with himself had not Wei Chang persisted that he sought his master's inner ear with a heavy project. This interruption did not please Wong Ts'in, for he had begun to recognize the day as being unlucky, yet Chang succeeded by a device in reaching his side, bearing in his hands a guarded burden.

Though no written record of this memorable interview exists, it is now generally admitted that Wei Chang either involved himself in an unbearably attenuated caution before he would reveal his errand, or else that he made a definite allusion to Fa Fai with a too sudden conciseness, for the slaves who stood without heard Wong Ts'in clear his voice of all restraint and express himself freely on a variety of subjects. But this gave place to a subdued murmur, ending with the ceremonial breaking of a plate, and later Wong Ts'in beat on a silver bell and called for wine and fruit.

The next day Fang presented himself a few gong–strokes later than the appointed time, and being met by an unbending word he withdrew the labour of those whom he controlled. Thenceforth these men, providing themselves with knives and axes, surrounded the gate of the earth–yards and by the pacific argument of their attitudes succeeded in persuading others who would willingly have continued at their task that the air of Wong Ts'in's sheds was not congenial to their health. Towards Wei Chang, whose efforts they despised, they raised a cloud of derision, and presently noticing that henceforth he invariable clad himself in lower garments of a dark blue material (to a set purpose that will be as crystal to the sagacious), they greeted his appearance with cries of: "Behold the sombre one! Thou dark leg!" so that this reproach continues to be hurled even to this day at those in a like case, though few could answer why.

Long before the stipulated time the tenscore plates were delivered to Hien Nan. So greatly were they esteemed, both on account of their accuracy of unvarying detail and the ingenuity of their novel embellishment, that orders for scores, hundreds and even thousands began to arrive from all quarters of the Empire. The clay enterprise of Wong Ts'in took upon itself an added lustre, and in order to deal adequately with so vast an undertaking the grateful merchant adopted Wei Chang and placed him upon an equal footing with himself. On the same day Wong Ts'in honourably fulfilled his spoken word and the marriage of Wei Chang and Fa Fai took place, accompanied by the most lavish display of fireworks and coloured lights that the province had ever seen. The controlling deities approved, and they had seven sons, one of whom had seven fingers upon each hand. All these sons became expert in Wei Chang's process of transferring porcelain embellishment, for some centuries elapsed before it was discovered that it was not absolutely necessary to sit upon each plate to produce the desired effect.

This chronicle of an event that is now regarded as almost classical would not be complete without an added reference to the ultimate end of the sordid Fang.

Fallen into disrepute among his fellows owing to the evil plight towards which he had enticed them, it became his increasing purpose to frequent the house beyond the river. On his return at nightfall he invariably drew aside on reaching the bridge, well knowing that he could not prudently rely upon his feet among so insecure a crossing, and composed himself to sleep amid the rushes. While in this position one night he was discovered and pushed into the river by a devout ox (an instrument of high destinies), where he perished incapably.

Those who found his body, not being able to withdraw so formidable a weight direct, cast a rope across the lower branch of a convenient willow–tree and thus raised it to the shore. In this striking manner Fa Fai's definite opinion achieved a destined end.

CHAPTER III. The Degraded Persistence of the Effete Ming–shu

AT about the same gong–stroke as before, Kai Lung again stood at the open shutter, and to him presently came the maiden Hwa–mei, bearing in her hands a gift of fruit.

"The story of the much–harassed merchant Wong Ts'in and of the assiduous youth Wei Chang has reached this person's ears by a devious road, and though it doubtless lost some of the subtler qualities in the telling, the ultimate tragedy had a convincing tone," she remarked pleasantly.

"It is scarcely to be expected that one who has spent his life beneath an official umbrella should have at his command the finer analogies of light and shade," tolerantly replied Kai Lung. "Though by no means comparable with the unapproachable history of the Princess Taik and the minstrel Ch'eng as a means for conveying the unexpressed aspirations of the one who relates towards the one who is receptive, there are many passages even in the behaviour of Wei Chang into which this person could infuse an unmistakable stress of significance were he but given the opportunity."

"The day of that opportunity has not yet dawned," replied the Golden Mouse; "nor has the night preceding it yet run its gloomy course. Foiled in his first attempt, the vindictive Ming–shu now creeps towards his end by a more tortuous path. Whether or not dimly suspecting something of the strategy by which your imperishable life was preserved to–day, it is no part of his depraved scheme that you should be given a like opportunity again. To–morrow another will be led to judgment, one Cho–kow, a tribesman of the barbarian land of Khim."

"With him I have already conversed and shared rice," interposed Kai Lung. "Proceed, elegance."

"Accused of plundering mountain tombs and of other crimes now held in disrepute, he will be offered a comparatively painless death if he will implicate his fellows, of whom you will be held to be the chief. By this ignoble artifice you will be condemned on his testimony in your absence, nor will you have any warning of your fate until you are led forth to suffer."

Then replied Kai Lung, after a space of thought: "Not ineptly is it written: 'When the leading carriage is upset the next one is more careful,' and Ming–shu has taken the proverb to his heart. To counteract his detestable plot will not be easy, but it should not be beyond our united power, backed by a reasonable activity on the part of our protecting ancestors."

"The devotional side of the emergency has had this one's early care," remarked Hwa–mei. "From daybreak to–morrow six zealous and deep–throated monks will curse Ming–shu and all his ways unceasingly, while a like number will invoke blessings and success upon your enlightened head. In the matter of noise and illumination everything that can contribute has been suitably prepared."

"It is difficult to conjecture what more could be done in that direction," confessed Kai Lung gratefully.

"Yet as regards a more material effort—?" suggested the maiden, amid a cloud of involving doubt.

"If there is a subject in which the imagination of the Mandarin Shan Tien can be again enmeshed it might be yet accomplished," replied Kai Lung. "Have you a knowledge of any such deep concern?"

"Truly there is a matter that disturbs his peace of late. He has dreamed a dream three times, and its meaning is beyond the skill of any man to solve. Yet how shall this avail you who are no geomancer?"

"What is the nature of the dream?" inquired Kai Lung. "For remember, 'Though Shen–fi has but one gate, many roads lead to it.'"

"The substance of the dream is this: that herein he who sleeps walks freely in the ways of men wearing no robe or covering of any kind, yet suffering no concern or indignity therefrom; that the secret and hidden things of the earth are revealed to his seeing eyes; and that he can float in space and project himself upon the air at will. These three things are alien to his nature, and being three times repeated, the uncertainty assails his ease."

"Let it, under your persistent care, assail him more and that unceasingly," exclaimed Kai Lung, with renewed lightness in his voice. "Breathe on the surface of his self–repose as a summer breeze moves the smooth water of a mountain lake—not deeply, but never quite at rest. Be assured: it is no longer possible to doubt that powerful Beings are interested in our cause."

"I go, oppressed one," replied Hwa–mei. "May this period of your ignoble trial be brought to a distinguished close."

On the following day at the appointed hour Cho-kow was led before the Mandarin Shan Tien, and the nature of his crimes having been explained to him by the contemptible Ming-shu, he was bidden to implicate Kai Lung and thus come to an earlier and less painful end.

"All-powerful," he replied, addressing himself to the Mandarin, "the words that have been spoken are bent to a deceptive end. They of our community are a simple race and doubtless in the past their ways were thus and thus. But, as it is truly said, 'Tian went bare, his eyes could pierce the earth and his body float in space, but they of his seed do but dream the dream.' We, being but the puny descendants—"

"You have spoken of one Tian whose attributes were such, and of those who dream thereof," interrupted the Mandarin, as one who performs a reluctant duty. "That which you adduce to uphold your cause must bear the full light of day."

"Alas, omnipotence," replied Cho-kow, "this concerns the doing of the gods and those who share their line. Now I am but an ill-conditioned outcast from the obscure land of Khim, and possess no lore beyond what happens there. Haply the gods that rule in Khim have a different manner of behaving from those in the Upper Air above Yu-ping, and this person's narration would avoid the semblance of the things that are and he himself would thereby be brought to disrepute."

"Suffer not that apprehension to retard your impending eloquence," replied Shan Tien affably. "Be assured that the gods have exactly the same manner of behaving in every land."

"Furthermore," continued Cho-kow, with patient craft, "I am a man of barbarian tongue, the full half of my speech being foreign to your ear. The history of the much-accomplished Tian and the meaning of the dreams that mark those of his race require for a full understanding the subtle analogies of an acquired style. Now that same Kai Lung whom you have implicated to my band—"

"Excellence!" protested Ming-shu, with a sudden apprehension in his throat, "yesterday our labours dissolved in air through the very doubtful precedent of allowing one to testify what he had had the intention to relate. Now we are asked to allow a tomb-haunter to call a parricide to disclose that which he himself is ignorant of. Press down your autocratic thumb—"

"Alas, instructor," interposed Shan Tien compassionately, "the sympathetic concern of my mind overflows upon the spectacle of your ill-used forbearance, yet you having banded together the two in a common infamy, it is the ancient privilege of this one to call the other to his cause. We are but the feeble mouthpieces of a benevolent scheme of all—embracing justice and greatly do I fear that we must again submit."

With these well—timed words the broad—minded personage settled himself more reposefully among his cushions and signified that Kai Lung should be led forward and begin.

The Story of Ning, the Captive God, and the Dreams tha mark his Race

i. THE MALICE OF THE DEMON, LEOU

When Sun Wei definitely understood that the deities were against him (for on every occasion his enemies prospered and the voice of his own authority grew less), he looked this way and that with a well—considering mind.

He did nothing hastily, but when once a decision was reached it was as unbending as iron and as smoothly finished as polished jade. At about the evening hour when others were preparing to offer sacrifice he took the images and the altars of his Rites down from their honourable positions and cast them into a heap on a waste expanse beyond his courtyard. Then with an axe he unceremoniously detached their incomparable limbs from their sublime bodies and flung the parts into a fire that he had prepared.

"It is better," declared Sun Wei, standing beside the pile, his hands buried within his sleeves—"it is better to be struck down at once, rather than to wither away slowly like a half—uprooted cassia—tree."

When this act of defiance was reported in the Upper World the air grew thick with the cries of indignation of the lesser deities, and the sound of their passage as they projected themselves across vast regions of space and into the presence of the supreme N'guk was like the continuous rending of innumerable pieces of the finest silk.

In his musk—scented heaven, however, N'guk slept, as his habit was at the close of each celestial day. It was with some difficulty that he could be aroused and made to understand the nature of Sun Wei's profanity, for his mind was dull with the smoke of never—ending incense.

"To—morrow," he promised, with a benignant gesture, turning over again on his crystal throne, "some time to—morrow impartial justice shall be done. In the meanwhile—courteous dismissal attend your opportune footsteps."

"He is becoming old and obese," murmured the less respectful of the demons. "He is not the god he was, even ten thousand cycles ago. It were well—"

"But, omnipotence," protested certain conciliatory spirits, pressing to the front, "consider, if but for a short breath of time. A day here is as threescore of their years as these mortals live. By to—morrow night not only Sun Wei, but most of those now dwelling down below, will have Passed Beyond. But the story of his unpunished infamy will live. We shall become discredited and our altar fires extinct. Sacrifice of either food or raiment will cease to reach us. The Season of White Rain is approaching and will find us ill provided. We who speak are but Beings of small part—"

"Peace!" commanded N'guk, now thoroughly disturbed, for the voices of the few had grown into a tumult; "how is it possible to consider with a torrent like the Hoang—Ho in flood pouring through my very ordinary ears? Your omniscient but quite inadequate Chief would think."

At this rebuke the uproar ceased. So deep became the nature of N'guk's profound thoughts that they could be heard rolling like thunder among the caverns of his gigantic brain. To aid the process, female slaves on either side fanned his fiery head with celestial lotus leaves. On the earth, far beneath, cyclones, sand—storms and sweeping water—spouts were forced into being.

"Hear the contemptible wisdom of my ill—formed mouth," said N'guk at length. "If we at once put forth our strength, the degraded Wun Sei is ground—"

"Sun Wei, All—knowing One," murmured an attending spirit beneath his breath.

"—the unmentionable outcast whom we are discussing is immediately ground into powder," continued the Highest, looking fixedly at a distant spot situated directly beyond his painstaking attendant. "But what follows? Henceforth no man can be allowed to whisper ill of us but we must at once seek him out and destroy him, or the obtuse and superficial will exclaim: 'It was not so in the days of—of So—and—So.

Behold'"—here the Great One bent a look of sudden resentment on the band of those who would have reproached him—"'behold the gods become old and obese. They are not the Powers they were. It would be better to address ourselves to other altars.'"

At this prospect many of the more venerable spirits began to lose their enthusiasm. If every mortal who spoke ill of them was to be pursued what leisure for dignified seclusion would remain?

"If, however," continued the dispassionate Being, "the profaner is left to himself he will, sooner or later, in the ordinary course of human intelligence, become involved in some disaster of his own contriving. Then they who dwell around will say: 'He destroyed the alters! Truly the hands of the Unseen are slow to close, but their arms are very long. Lo, we have this day ourselves beheld it. Come, let us burn incense lest some forgotten misdeed from the past lurk in our path.'"

When he had finished speaking all the more reputable of those present extolled his judgment. Some still whispered together, however, whereupon the sagacious N'guk opened his mouth more fully and shot forth tongues of consuming fire among the murmurers so that they fled howling from his presence.

Now among the spirits who had stood before the Pearly Ruler without taking any share in the decision were two who at this point are drawn into the narration, Leou and Ning. Leou was a revengeful demon, ever at enmity with one or another of the gods and striving how he might enmesh his feet in destruction. Ning was a better-class deity, voluptuous but well-meaning, and little able to cope with Leou's subtlety. Thus it came about that the latter one, seeing in the outcome a chance to achieve his end, at once dropped headlong down to earth and sought out Sun Wei.

Sun Wei was reclining at his evening rice when Leou found him. Becoming invisible, the demon entered a date that Sun Wei held in his hand and took the form of a stone. Sun Wei recognized the doubtful nature of the stone as it passed between his teeth, and he would have spat it forth again, but Leou had the questionable agility of the serpent and slipped down the other's throat. He was thus able to converse familiarly with Sun Wei without fear of interruption.

"Sun Wei," said the voice of Leou inwardly, "the position you have chosen is a desperate one, and we of the Upper Air who are well disposed towards you find the path of assistance fringed with two–edged swords."

"It is well said: 'He who lacks a single tael sees many bargains,'" replied Sun Wei, a refined bitterness weighing the import of his words. "Truly this person's friends in the Upper Air are a never–failing lantern behind his back."

At this justly–barbed reproach Leou began to shake with disturbed gravity until he remembered that the motion might not be pleasing to Sun Wei's inner feelings.

"It is not that the well–disposed are slow to urge your claims, but that your enemies number some of the most influential demons in all the Nine Spaces," he declared, speaking with a false smoothness that marked all his detestable plans. "Assuredly in the past you must have led a very abandoned life, Sun Wei, to come within the circle of their malignity."

"By no means," replied Sun Wei. "Until driven to despair this person not only duly observed the Rites and Ceremonies, but he even avoided the Six Offences. He remained by the side of his parents while they lived, provided an adequate posterity, forbore to tread on any of the benevolent insects, safeguarded all printed paper, did not consume the meat of the industrious ox, and was charitable towards the needs of hungry and homeless ghosts."

"These observances are well enough," admitted Leou, restraining his narrow–minded impatience; "and with an ordinary number of written charms worn about the head and body they would doubtless carry you through the lesser contingencies of existence. But by, as it were, extending contempt, you have invited the retaliatory propulsion of the sandal of authority."

"To one who has been pushed over the edge of a precipice, a rut across the path is devoid of menace; nor do the destitute tremble at the departing watchman's cry: 'Sleep warily; robbers are about.'"

"As regards bodily suffering and material extortion, it is possible to attain such a limit as no longer to excite the cupidity of even the most rapacious deity," admitted Leou.

"Other forms of flattening—out a transgressor's self—content remain however. For instance, it has come within the knowledge of the controlling Powers that seven generations of your distinguished ancestors occupy positions of dignified seclusion in the Upper Air."

For the first time Sun Wei's attitude was not entirely devoid of an emotion of concern.

"They would not—?"

"To mark their sense of your really unsupportable behaviour it has been decided that all seven shall return to the humiliating scenes of their former existences in admittedly objectionable forms," replied the outrageous Leou. "Sun Chen, your venerated sire, will become an agile grasshopper; your incomparable grandfather, Yuen, will have the similitude of a yellow goat; as a tortoise your leisurely—minded ancestor Huang, the high public official—"

"Forbear!" exclaimed the conscience—stricken Sun Wei; "rather would this person suffer every imaginable form of torture than that the spirit of one of his revered ancestors should be submitted to so intolerable a bondage. Is there no amiable form of compromise whereby the ancestors of some less devoted and liberally—inspired son might be imperceptibly, as it were, substituted?"

"In ordinary cases some such arrangement is generally possible," conceded Leou; "but not idly is it written: 'There is a time to silence an adversary with the honey of logical persuasion, and there is a time to silence him with the argument of a heavily—directed club.' In your extremity a hostage is the only efficient safeguard. Seize the person of one of the gods themselves and raise a strong wall around your destiny by holding him to ransom."

"'Ho Tai, requiring a light for his pipe, stretched out his hand towards the great sky—lantern,'" quoted Sun Wei.

"'Do not despise Ching To because his armour is invisible,'" retorted Leou, with equal point. "Your friends in the Above are neither feeble nor inept. Do as I shall instruct you and no less a Being than Ning will be delivered into your hand."

Then replied Sun Wei dubiously: "A spreading mango-tree affords a pleasant shade within one's courtyard, and a captive god might for a season undoubtedly confer an enviable distinction. But presently the tree's encroaching roots may disturb the foundation of the house so that the walls fall and crush those who are within, and the head of a restrained god would in the end certainly displace my very inadequate roof-tree."

"A too-prolific root can be pruned back," replied Leou, "and the activities of a bondaged god may be efficiently curtailed. How this shall be accomplished will be revealed to you in a dream: take heed that you do not fail by the deviation of a single hair."

Having thus prepared his discreditable plot, Leou twice struck the walls enclosing him, so that Sun Wei coughed violently. The demon was thereby enabled to escape, and he never actually appeared in a tangible form again, although he frequently communicated, by means of signs and omens, with those whom he wished to involve in his sinister designs.

ii. THE PART PLAYED BY THE SLAVE-GIRL, HIA

Among the remaining possessions that the hostility of the deities still left to Sun Wei at the time of these happenings was a young slave of many-sided attraction. The name of Hia had been given to her, but she was generally known as Tsing-ai on account of the extremely affectionate gladness of her nature.

On the day following that in which Sun Wei and the demon Leou had conversed together, Hia was disporting herself in the dark shades of a secluded pool, as her custom was after the heat of her labours, when a phoenix, flying across the glade, dropped a pearl of unusual size and lustre into the stream. Possessing herself of the jewel and placing it in her mouth, so that it should not impede the action of her hands, Hia sought the bank and would have drawn herself up when she became aware of the presence of one having the guise of a noble commander. He was regarding her with a look in which well-expressed admiration was blended with a delicate intimation that owing to the unparalleled brilliance of her eyes he was unable to perceive any other detail of her appearance, and was, indeed, under the impression that she was devoid of ordinary outline. At the same time, without permitting her glance to be in any but an entirely opposite direction, Hia was able to satisfy herself that the stranger was a person on whom she might prudently lavish the full depths of her regard if the necessity arose. His apparel was rich, voluminous and of colours then unknown within the Empire; his hair long and abundant; his face placid but sincere. He carried no weapons, but wherever he trod there came a yellow flame from below his right foot and a white vapour from beneath his left. His insignia were those of a royal prince, and when he spoke his voice resembled the noise of arrows passing through the upper branches of a prickly forest. His long and pointed nails indicated the high and dignified nature of all his occupations; each nail was protected by a solid sheath, there being amethyst, ruby, topaz, ivory, emerald, white jade, iron, chalcedony, gold and malachite.

When the distinguished–looking personage had thus regarded Hia for some moments he drew an instrument of hollow tubes from a fold of his garment and began to sing of two who, as the outcome of a romantic encounter similar to that then existing, had professed an agreeable attachment for one another and had, without unnecessary delay, entered upon a period of incomparable felicity. Doubtless Hia would have uttered words of high–minded rebuke at some of the more detailed analogies of the recital had not the pearl deprived her of the power of expressing herself clearly on any subject whatever, nor did it seem practicable to her to remove it without withdrawing her hands from the modest attitudes into which she had at once distributed them. Thus positioned, she was compelled to listen to the stranger's well–considered flattery, and this (together with the increasing coldness of the stream as the evening deepened) convincingly explains her ultimate acquiescence to his questionable offers.

Yet it cannot be denied that Ning (as he may now fittingly be revealed) conducted the enterprise with a seemly liberality; for upon receiving from Hia a glance not expressive of discouragement he at once caused the appearance of a suitably–furnished tent, a train of Nubian slaves offering rich viands, rare wine and costly perfumes, companies of expert dancers and musicians, a retinue of discreet elderly women to robe her and to attend her movements, a carpet of golden silk stretching from the water's edge to the tent, and all the accessories of a high–class profligacy.

When the night was advanced and Hia and Ning, after partaking of a many–coursed feast, were reclining on an ebony couch, the Being freely expressed the delight that he discovered in her amiable society, incautiously adding: "Demand any recompense that is within the power of this one to grant, O most delectable of water–nymphs, and its accomplishment will be written by a flash of lightning." In this, however, he merely spoke as the treacherous Leou (who had enticed him into the adventure) had assured him was usual in similar circumstances, he himself being privately of the opinion that the expenditure already incurred was more than adequate to the occasion.

Then replied Hia, as she had been fully instructed against the emergency: "The word has been spoken. But what is precious metal after listening to the pure gold of thy lips, or who shall again esteem gems while gazing upon the full round radiance of thy moon–like face? One thing only remains: remove the various sheaths from off thy hands, for they not only conceal the undoubted perfection of the nails within, but their massive angularity renders the affectionate ardour of your embrace almost intolerable."

At this very ordinary request a sudden flatness overspread Ning's manner and he began to describe the many much more profitable rewards that Hia might fittingly demand. As none of these appeared to entice her imagination, he went on to rebuke her want of foresight, and, still later, having unsuccessfully pointed out to her the inevitable penury and degradation in which her thriftless perversity would involve her later years, to kick the less substantial appointments across the tent.

"The night thickens, with every indication of a storm," remarked Hia pleasantly. "Yet that same impending flash of promised lightning tarries somewhat."

"Truly is it written: 'A gracious woman will cause more strife than twelve armed men can quell,'" retorted Ning bitterly.

"Not, perchance, if one of them bares his nails?" Thus she lightly mocked him, but always with a set intent, as a poised dragon–fly sips water yet does not wet his wings. Whereupon, finally, Ning tore the sheaths from off his fingers and cast them passionately about her feet, immediately afterwards sinking into a profound sleep, for both the measure and the potency of the wine he had consumed exceeded his usual custom. Otherwise he would scarcely have acted in this incapable manner, for each sheath was inscribed with one symbol of a magic charm and in the possession of the complete sentence resided the whole of the Being's authority and power.

Then Hia, seeing that he could no longer control her movements, and that the end to which she had been bending was attained, gathered together the fruits of her conscientious strategy and fled.

When Ning returned to the condition of ordinary perceptions he was lying alone in the field by the river-side. The great sky-fire made no pretence of averting its rays from his uncovered head, and the lesser creatures of the ground did not hesitate to walk over his once sacred form. The tent and all the other circumstances of the quest of Hia had passed into a state of no-existence, for with a somewhat narrow-minded economy the deity had called them into being with the express provision that they need only be of such a quality as would last for a single night.

With this recollection, other details began to assail his mind. His irreplaceable nail-sheaths—there was no trace of one of them. He looked again. Alas! his incomparable nails were also gone, shorn off to the level of his finger-ends. For all their evidence he might be one who had passed his days in discreditable industry. Each moment a fresh point of degradation met his benumbed vision. His profuse and ornamental locks were reduced to a single roughly-plaited coil; his sandals were inelegant and harsh; in place of his many-coloured flowing robes a scanty blue gown clothed his form. He who had been a god was undistinguishable from the labourers of the fields. Only in one thing did the resemblance fail: about his neck he found a weighty block of wood controlled by an iron ring: while they at least were free he was a captive slave.

A shadow on the grass caused him to turn. Sun Wei approached, a knotted thong in one hand, in the other a hoe. He pointed to an unweeded rice-field and with many ceremonious bows pressed the hoe upon Ning as one who confers high honours. As Ning hesitated, Sun Wei pressed the knotted thong upon him until it would have been obtuse to disregard his meaning. Then Ning definitely understood that he had become involved in the workings of very powerful forces, hostile to himself, and picking up the hoe he bent his submissive footsteps in the direction of the laborious rice-field.

iii. THE IN-COMING OF THE YOUTH, TIAN

It was dawn in the High Heaven and the illimitable N'guk, waking to his labours for the day, looked graciously around on the assembled myriads who were there to carry

44

his word through boundless space. Not wanting are they who speak two—sided words of the Venerable One from behind fan—like hands, but when his voice takes upon it the authority of a brazen drum knees become flaccid.

"There is a void in the unanimity of our council," remarked the Supreme, his eye resting like a flash of lightning on a vacant place. "Wherefore tarries Ning, the son of Shin, the Seed—sower?"

For a moment there was an edging of N'guk's inquiring glance from each Being to his neighbour. Then Leou stood audaciously forth.

"He is reported to be engaged on a private family matter," he replied gravely. "Haply his feet have become entangled in a mesh of hair."

N'guk turned his benevolent gaze upon another—one higher in authority.

"Perchance," admitted the superior Being tolerantly. "Such things are. How comes it else that among the earth—creatures we find the faces of the deities—both the good and the bad?"

"How long has he been absent from our paths?"

They pressed another forward—keeper of the Outer Path of the West Expanses, he.

"He went, High Excellence, in the fifteenth of the earth—ruler Chun, whom your enlightened tolerance has allowed to occupy the lower dragon throne for twoscore years, as these earthlings count. Thus and thus—"

"Enough!" exclaimed the Supreme. "Hear my iron word. When the buffoon—witted Ning rises from his congenial slough this shall be his lot: for sixty thousand ages he shall fail to find the path of his return, but shall, instead, thread an aimless flight among the frozen ambits of the outer stars, carrying a tormenting rain of fire at his tail. And Leou, the Whisperer," added the Divining One, with the inscrutable wisdom that marked even his most opaque moments, "Leou shall meanwhile perform Ning's neglected task."

*

For five and twenty years Ning had laboured in the fields of Sun Wei with a wooden collar girt about his neck, and Sun Wei had prospered. Yet it is to be doubted whether this last detail deliberately hinged on the policy of Leou or whether Sun Wei had not rather been drawn into some wider sphere of destiny and among converging lines of purpose. The ways of the gods are deep and sombre, and water once poured out will flow as freely to the north as to the south. The wise kowtows acquiescently whatever happens and thus his face is to the ground. "Respect the deities," says the imperishable Sage, "but do not become familiar with them." Sun Wei was clearly wrong.

To Ning, however, standing on a grassy space on the edge of a flowing river, such thoughts do not extend. He is now a little hairy man of gnarled appearance, and his skin of a colour and texture like a ripe lo-quat. As he stands there, something in the outline of the vista stirs the retentive tablets of his mind: it was on this spot that he first encountered Hia, and from that involvement began the cycle of his unending ill.

As he stood thus, implicated with his own inner emotions, a figure emerged from the river at its nearest point and, crossing the intervening sward, approached. He had the aspect of being a young man of high and dignified manner, and walked with the air of one accustomed to a silk umbrella, but when Ning looked more closely, to see by his insignia what amount of reverence he should pay, he discovered that the youth was destitute of the meagrest garment.

"Rise, venerable," said the stranger affably, for Ning had prostrated himself as being more prudent in the circumstances. "The one before you is only Tian, of obscure birth, and himself of no particular merit or attainment. You, doubtless, are of considerably more honourable lineage?"

"Far from that being the case," replied Ning, "the one who speaks bears now the commonplace name of Lieu, and is branded with the brand of Sun Wei. Formerly, indeed, he was a god, moving in the Upper Space and known to the devout as Ning, but now deposed by treachery."

"Unless the subject is one that has painful associations," remarked Tian considerately, "it is one on which this person would willingly learn somewhat deeper. What, in short,

46

are the various differences existing between gods and men?"

"The gods are gods; men are men," replied Ning. "There is no other difference."

"Yet why do not the gods now exert their strength and raise from your present admittedly inferior position one who is of their band?"

"Behind their barrier the gods laugh at all men. How much more, then, is their gravity removed at the sight of one of themselves who has fallen lower than mankind?"

"Your plight would certainly seem to be an ill-destined one," admitted Tian, "for, as the Verses say: 'Gold sinks deeper than dross.' Is there anything that an ordinary person can do to alleviate your subjection?"

"The offer is a gracious one," replied Ning, "and such an occasion undoubtedly exists. Some time ago a pearl of unusual size and lustre slipped from its setting about this spot. I have looked for it in vain, but your acuter eyes, perchance—"

Thus urged, the youth Tian searched the ground, but to no avail. Then chancing to look upwards, he exclaimed:

"Among the higher branches of the tallest bamboo there is an ancient phoenix nest, and concealed within its wall is a pearl such as you describe."

"That manifestly is what I seek," said Ning. "But it might as well be at the bottom of its native sea, for no ladder could reach to such a height nor would the slender branch support a living form."

"Yet the emergency is one easily disposed of." With these opportune words the amiable person rose from the ground without any appearance of effort or conscious movement, and floating upward through the air he procured the jewel and restored it to Ning.

When Ning had thus learned that Tian possessed these three attainments which are united in the gods alone—that he could stand naked before others without consciousness of shame, that his eyes were able to penetrate matter impervious to those of ordinary persons, and that he controlled the power of rising through the air unaided—he understood that the one before him was a deity of some degree. He therefore questioned him closely about his history, the various omens connected with his life and the position of the planets at his birth. Finding that these presented no element of conflict, and that, furthermore, the youth's mother was a slave, formerly known as Hia, Ning declared himself more fully and greeted Tian as his undoubted son.

"The absence of such a relation is the one thing that has pressed heavily against this person's satisfaction in the past, and the deficiency is now happily removed," exclaimed Tian. "The distinction of having a deity for a father outweighs even the present admittedly distressing condition in which he reveals himself. His word shall henceforth be my law."

"The sentiment is a dutiful one," admitted Ning, "and it is possible that you are now thus discovered in pursuance of some scheme among my more influential accomplices in the Upper Air for restoring to me my former eminence."

"In so meritorious a cause this person is prepared to immerse himself to any depth," declared Tian readily. "Nothing but the absence of precise details restrains his hurrying feet."

"Those will doubtless be communicated to us by means of omens and portents as the requirement becomes more definite. In the meanwhile the first necessity is to enable this person's nails to grow again; for to present himself thus in the Upper Air would be to cover him with ridicule. When the Emperor Chow-sin endeavoured to pass himself off as a menial by throwing aside his jewelled crown, the rebels who had taken him replied: 'Omnipotence, you cannot throw away your knees.' To claim kinship with those Above and at the same time to extend towards them a hand obviously inured to probing among the stony earth would be to invite the averted face of recognition."

"Let recognition be extended in other directions and the task of returning to a forfeited inheritance will be lightened materially," remarked a significant voice.

"Estimable mother," exclaimed Tian, "this opportune stranger is my venerated father, whose continuous absence has been an overhanging cloud above my gladness, but now

48

happily revealed and restored to our domestic altar."

"Alas!" interposed Ning, "the opening of this enterprise forecasts a questionable omen. Before this person stands the one who enticed him into the beginning of all his evil; how then—"

"Let the word remain unspoken," interrupted Hia. "Women do not entice men—though they admittedly accompany them, with an extreme absence of reluctance, in any direction. In her youth this person's feet undoubtedly bore her occasionally along a light and fantastic path, for in the nature of spring a leaf is green and pliable, and in the nature of autumn it is brown and austere, and through changeless ages thus and thus. But, as it is truly said: 'Milk by repeated agitation turns to butter,' and for many years it has been this one's ceaseless study of the Arts whereby she might avert that which she helped to bring about in her unstable youth."

"The intention is a commendable one, though expressed with unnecessary verbiage," replied Ning. "To what solution did your incantations trend?"

"Concealed somewhere within the walled city of Ti–foo are the sacred nail–sheaths on which your power so essentially depends, sent thither by Sun Wei at the crafty instance of the demon Leou, who hopes at a convenient time to secure them for himself. To discover these and bear them forth will be the part allotted to Tian, and to this end has the training of his youth been bent. By what means he shall strive to the accomplishment of the project the unrolling curtain of the future shall disclose."

"It is as the destinies shall decide and as the omens may direct," said Tian. "In the meanwhile this person's face is inexorably fixed in the direction of Ti–foo."

"Proceed with all possible discretion," advised Ning. "In so critical an undertaking you cannot be too cautious, but at the same time do not suffer the rice to grow around your advancing feet."

"A moment," conselled Hia. "Tarry yet a moment. Here is one whose rapidly–moving attitude may convey a message."

"It is Lin Fa!" exclaimed Ning, as the one alluded to drew near—"Lin Fa who guards the coffers of Sun Wei. Some calamity pursues him."

"Hence!" cried Lin Far, as he caught sight of them, yet scarcely pausing in his flight: "flee to the woods and caves until the time of this catastrophe be past. Has not the tiding reached you?"

"We be but dwellers on the farther bounds and no word has reached our ear, O great Lin Fa. Fill in, we pray you, the warning that has been so suddenly outlined."

"The usurper Ah–tang has lit the torch of swift rebellion and is flattening–down the land that bars his way. Already the villages of Yeng, Leu, Liang–li and the Dwellings by the Three Pure Wells are as dust beneath his trampling feet, and they who stayed there have passed up in smoke. Sun Wei swings from the roof–tree of his own ruined yamen. Ah–tang now lays siege to walled Ti–foo so that he may possess the Northern Way. Guard this bag of silver meanwhile, for what I have is more than I can reasonably bear, and when the land is once again at peace, assemble to meet me by the Five–Horned Pagoda, ready with a strict account."

"All this is plainly part of an orderly scheme for my advancement, brought about by my friends in the Upper World," remarked Ning, with some complacency. "Lin Fa has been influenced to the extent of providing us with the means for our immediate need; Sun Wei has been opportunely removed to the end that this person may now retire to a hidden spot and there suffer his dishonoured nails to grow again: Ah–tang has been impelled the raise the banner of insurrection outside Ti–foo so that Tian may make use of the necessities of either side in pursuit of his design. Assuredly the long line of our misfortunes is now practically at an end."

iv. EVENTS ROUND WALLED TI–FOO

Nevertheless, the alternative forced on Tian was not an alluring one. If he joined the band of Ah–tang and the usurper failed, Tian himself might never get inside Ti–foo; if, however, he allied himself with the defenders of Ti–foo and Ah–tang did not fail, he might never get out of Ti–foo. Doubtless he would have reverently submitted his cause to the inspired decision of the Sticks, or some other reliable augur, had he not, while immersed in the consideration, walked into the camp of Ah–tang. The omen of this

50

occurrence was of too specific a nature not to be regarded as conclusive.

Ah-tang was one who had neglected the Classics from his youth upwards. For this reason his detestable name is never mentioned in the Histories, and the various catastrophes he wrought are charitably ascribed to the action of earthquakes, thunderbolts and other admitted forces. He himself, with his lamentable absence of literary style, was wont to declare that while confessedly weak in analogies he was strong in holocausts. In the end he drove the sublime emperor from his capital and into the Outer Lands; with true refinement the annalists of the period explain that the condescending monarch made a journey of inspection among the barbarian tribes on the confines of his Empire.

When Tian, charged with being a hostile spy, was led into the presence of Ah-tang, it was the youth's intention to relate somewhat of his history, but the usurper, excusing himself on the ground of literary deficiency, merely commanded five of his immediate guard to bear the prisoner away and to return with his head after a fitting interval. Misunderstanding the exact requirement, Tian returned at the appointed time with the heads of the five who had charge of him and the excuse that in those times of scarcity it was easier to keep one head than five. This aptitude so pleased Ah-tang (who had expected at the most a farewell apophthegm) that he at once made Tian captain of a chosen band.

Thus was Tian positioned outside the city of Ti-foo, materially contributing to its ultimate surrender by the resourceful courage of his arms. For the first time in the history of opposing forces he tamed the strength and swiftness of wild horses to the use of man, and placing copper loops upon their feet and iron bars between their teeth, he and his band encircled Ti-foo with an ever-moving shield through which no outside word could reach the town. Cut off in this manner from all hope of succour, the stomachs of those within the walls grew very small, and their eyes became weary of watching for that which never came. On the third day of the third moon of their encirclement they sent a submissive banner, and one bearing a written message, into the camp of Ah-tang.

"We are convinced" (it ran) "of the justice of your cause. Let six of your lordly nobles appear unarmed before our ill-kept Lantern Gate at the middle gong-stroke of to-morrow and they will be freely admitted within our midst. Upon receiving a bound assurance safeguarding the limits of our temples, the persons and possessions of our chiefs, and the undepreciated condition of the first wives and virgin daughters of such as be of mandarin rank or literary degree, the inadequate keys of our broken—down defences will be laid at their sumptuous feet.

"With a fervent hand—clasp as of one brother to another, and a passionate assurance of mutual good—will,

KO'EN CHENG, Important Official."

"It is received," replied Ah—tang, when the message had been made known to him. "Six captains will attend."

Alas! it is well written: "There is often a space between the fish and the fish—plate." Mentally inflated at the success of their efforts and the impending surrender of Ti—foo, Tian's band suffered their energies to relax. In the dusk of that same evening one disguised in the skin of a goat browsed from bush to bush until he reached the town. There, throwing off all restraint, he declared his errand to Ko'en Cheng.

"Behold!" he exclaimed, "the period of your illustrious suffering is almost at an end. With an army capable in size and invincible in determination, the ever—victorious Wu Sien is marching to your aid. Defy the puny Ah—tang for yet three days more and great glory will be yours."

"Doubtless," replied Ko'en Cheng, with velvet bitterness: "but the sun has long since set and the moon is not yet risen. The appearance of a solitary star yesterday would have been more foot—guiding than the forecast of a meteor next week. This person's thumb—signed word is passed and to—morrow Ah—tang will hold him to it."

Now there was present among the council one wrapped in a mantle made of rustling leaves, who spoke in a smooth, low voice, very cunning and persuasive, with a plan already shaped that seemed to offer well and to safeguard Ko'en Cheng's word. None remembered to have seen him there before, and for this reason it is now held by some that this was Leou, the Whisperer, perturbed lest the sacred nail—sheaths of Ning should pass beyond his grasp. As to this, says not the Wise One: "When two men cannot agree over the price of an onion who shall decide what happened in the time of

Yu?" But the voice of the unknown prevailed, all saying: "At the worst it is but as it will be; perchance it may be better."

That night there was much gladness in the camp of Ah-tang, and men sang songs of victory and cups of wine were freely passed, though in the outer walks a strict watch was kept. When it was dark the word was passed that an engaging company was approaching from the town, openly and with lights. These being admitted revealed themselves as a band of maidens, bearing gifts of fruit and wine and assurances of their agreeable behaviour. Distributing themselves impartially about the tents of the chiefs and upper ones, they melted the hours of the night in graceful accomplishments and by their seemly compliance dispelled all thought of treachery. Having thus gained the esteem of their companions, and by the lavish persuasion of bemusing wine dimmed their alertness, all this band, while it was still dark, crept back to the town, each secretly carrying with her the arms, robes and insignia of the one who had possessed her.

When the morning broke and the sound of trumpets called each man to an appointed spot, direful was the outcry from the tents of all the chiefs, and though many heads were out-thrust in rage of indignation, no single person could be prevailed upon wholly to emerge. Only the lesser warriors, the slaves and the bearers of the loads moved freely to and fro and from between closed teeth and with fluttering eyelids tossed doubtful jests among themselves.

It was close upon the middle gong-stroke of the day when Ah-tang, himself clad in a shred torn from his tent (for in all the camp there did not remain a single garment bearing a sign of noble rank), got together a council of his chiefs. Some were clad in like attire, others carried a henchman's shield, a paper lantern or a branch of flowers; Tian alone displayed himself without reserve.

"There are moments," said Ah-tang, "when this person's admitted accomplishment of transfixing three foemen with a single javelin at a score of measured paces does not seem to provide a possible solution. Undoubtedly we are face to face with a crafty plan, and Ko'en Cheng has surely heard that Wu Sien is marching from the west. If we fail to knock upon the outer gate of Ti-foo at noon to-day Ko'en Cheng will say: 'My word returns. It is as naught.' If they who go are clad as underlings, Ko'en Cheng will cry: 'What slaves be these! Do men break plate with dogs? Our message was for six of

53

noble style. Ah—tang but mocks.'" He sat down again moodily. "Let others speak."

"Chieftain"—Tian threw forth his voice—"your word must be as iron—'Six captains shall attend.' There is yet another way."

"Speak on," Ah—tang commanded.

"The quality of Ah—tang's chiefs resides not in a cloak of silk nor in a silver—hilted sword, but in the sinews of their arms and the lightning of their eyes. If they but carry these they proclaim their rank for all to see. Let six attend taking neither sword nor shield, neither hat nor sandal, nor yet anything between. 'There are six thousand more,' shall be their taunt, 'but Ko'en Cheng's hospitality drew rein at six. He feared lest they might carry arms; behold they have come naked. Ti—foo need not tremble."

"It is well," agreed Ah—tang. "At least, nothing better offers. Let five accompany you."

Seated on a powerful horse Tian led the way. The others, not being of his immediate band, had not acquired the necessary control, so that they walked in a company. Coming to the Lantern Gate Tian turned his horse suddenly so that its angry hoof struck the gate. Looking back he saw the others following, with no great space between, and so passed in.

When the five naked captains reached the open gate they paused. Within stood a great concourse of the people, these being equally of both sexes, but they of the inner chambers pressing resolutely to the front. Through the throng of these their way must lead, and at the sight the hearts of all became as stagnant water in the sun.

"Tarry not for me, O brothers," said the one who led. "A thorn has pierced my foot. Take honourable precedence while I draw it forth."

"Never," declared the second of the band, "never shall it be cast abroad that Kang of the House of Ka failed his brother in necessity. I sustain thy shoulder, comrade."

"Alas!" exclaimed the third. "This person broke his fast on rhubarb stewed in fat. Inopportunely—" So he too turned aside.

"Have we considered well," said they who remained, "whether this be not a subtle snare, and while the camp is denuded of its foremost warriors a strong force—?"

Unconscious of these details, Tian went on alone. In spite of the absence of gravity on the part of the more explicit portion of the throng he suffered no embarrassment, partly because of his position, but chiefly through his inability to understand that his condition differed in any degree from theirs; for, owing to the piercing nature of his vision, they were to him as he to them. In this way he came to the open space known as the Space of the Eight Directions, where Ko'en Cheng and his nobles were assembled.

"One comes alone," they cried. "This guise is as a taunt." "Naked to a naked town—the analogy is plain." "Shall the mocker be suffered to return?"

Thus the murmur grew. Then one, more impetuous than the rest, swung clear his sword and drew it. For the first time Tian understood that treachery was afoot. He looked round for any of his band, but found that he was as a foam-tossed cork upon a turbulent Whang Hai. Cries of anger and derision filled the air; threatening arms waved encouragement to each other to begin. The one with drawn sword raised it above his head and made a step. Then Tian, recognizing that he was unarmed, and that a decisive moment had arrived, stooped low and tore a copper hoop from off his horse's foot. High he swung its polished brightness in the engaging sun, resolutely brought it down, so that it pressed over the sword-warrior's shattered head and hung about his neck. Having thus effected as much bloodshed as could reasonably be expected in the circumstances, Tian curved his feet about his horse's sides and imparting to it the virtue of his own condition they rose into the air together. When those who stood below were able to exert themselves a flight of arrows, spears and every kind of weapon followed, but horse and rider were by that time beyond their reach, and the only benevolent result attained was that many of their band were themselves transfixed by the falling shafts.

In such a manner Tian continued his progress from the town until he came above the Temple of Fire and Water Forces, where on a high tower a strong box of many woods was chained beneath a canopy, guarded by an incantation laid upon it by Leou, that no one should lift it down. Recognizing the contents as the object of his search, Tian brought his horse to rest upon the tower, and breaking the chains he bore the magic sheaths away, the charm (owing to Leou's superficial habits) being powerless against one who instead of lifting the box down carried it up.

In spite of this distinguished achievement it was many moons before Tian was able to lay the filial tribute of restored power at Ning's feet, for with shallow−witted obstinacy Ti−foo continued to hold out, and, scarcely less inept, Ah−tang declined to release Tian even to carry on so charitable a mission. Yet when the latter one ultimately returned and was, as the reward of his intrepid services, looking forward to a period of domestic reunion under the benevolent guidance of an affectionate father, it was but to point the seasoned proverb: "The fuller the cup the sooner the spill," for scarcely had Ning drawn on the recovered sheaths and with incautious joy repeated the magic sentence than he was instantly projected across vast space and into the trackless confines of the Outer Upper Paths. If this were an imagined tale, framed to entice the credulous, herein would its falseness cry aloud, but even in this age Ning may still be seen from time to time with a tail of fire in his wake, missing the path of his return as N'guk ordained.

Thus bereft, Tian was on the point of giving way to a seemly despair when a message concerned with Mu, the only daughter of Ko'en Cheng, reached him. It professed a high−minded regard for his welfare, and added that although the one who was inspiring the communication had been careful to avoid seeing him on the occasion of his entry into Ti−foo, it was impossible for her not to be impressed by the dignity of his bearing. Ko'en Cheng having become vastly wealthy as the result of entering into an arrangement with Ah−tang before Ti−foo was sacked, it did not seem unreasonable to Tian that Ning was in some way influencing his destiny from afar. On this understanding he ultimately married Mu, and thereby founded a prolific posterity who inherited a great degree of his powers. In the course of countless generations the attributes have faded, but even to this day the true descendants of the line of Ning are frequently vouchsafed dreams in which they stand naked and without shame, see gems or metals hidden or buried in the earth and float at will through space.

CHAPTER IV. The Inopportune Behaviour of the Covetous Li−loe

IT was upon the occasion of his next visit to the shutter in the wall that Kai Lung discovered the obtuse−witted Li−loe moving about the enclosure. Though docile and well−meaning on the whole, the stunted intelligence of the latter person made him a doubtful accomplice, and Kai Lung stood aside, hoping to be soon alone.

Li—loe held in his hand an iron prong, and with this he industriously searched the earth between the rocks and herbage. Ever since their previous encounter upon that same spot it had been impossible to erase from his deformed mind the conviction that a store of rare and potent wine lay somewhere concealed within the walls of the enclosure. Continuously he besought the story—teller to reveal the secret of its hiding—place, saying: "What an added bitterness will assail your noble throat if, when you are led forth to die, your eye closes upon the one who has faithfully upheld your cause lying with a protruded tongue panting in the noonday sun."

"Peace, witless," Kai Lung usually replied; "there is no such store."

"Nevertheless," the doorkeeper would stubbornly insist, "the cask cannot yet be empty. It is beyond your immature powers."

Thus it again befell, for despite Kai Lung's desire to escape, Li—loe chanced to look up suddenly and observed him.

"Alas, brother," he remarked reproachfully, when they had thus contended, "the vessel that returns whole the first time is chipped the second and broken at the third essay, and it will yet be too late between us. If it be as you claim, to what end did you boast of a cask of wine and of running among a company of goats with leaves entwined in your hair?"

"That," replied Kai Lung, "was in the nature of a classical allusion, too abstruse for your deficient wit. It concerned the story of Kiau Sun, who first attained the honour."

"Be that as it may," replied Li—loe, with mulish iteration, "five deficient strings of home—made cash are a meagre return for a friendship such as mine."

"There is a certain element of truth in what you claim," confessed Kai Lung, "but until my literary style is more freely recognized it will be impossible to reward you adequately. In anything not of a pecuniary nature, however, you may lean heavily upon my gratitude."

"In the meanwhile, then," demanded Li—loe, "relate to me the story to which reference has been made, thereby proving the truth of your assertion, and at the same time

57

affording an entertainment of a somewhat exceptional kind."

"The shadows lengthen," replied Kai Lung, "but as the narrative in question is of an inconspicuous span I will raise no barrier against your flattering request, especially as it indicates an awakening taste hitherto unsuspected."

"Proceed, manlet, proceed," said Li–loe, with a final probe among the surrounding rocks before selecting one to lean against. "Yet if this person could but lay his hand—"

The Story of Wong Pao and the Minstrel

To Wong Pao, the merchant, pleasurably immersed in the calculation of an estimated profit on a junk–load of birds' nests, sharks' fins and other seasonable delicacies, there came a distracting interruption occasioned by a wandering poet who sat down within the shade provided by Wong Pao's ornamental gate in the street outside. As he reclined there he sang ballads of ancient valour, from time to time beating a hollow wooden duck in unison with his voice, so that the charitable should have no excuse for missing the entertainment.

Unable any longer to continue his occupation, Wong Pao struck an iron gong.

"Bear courteous greetings to the accomplished musician outside our gate," he said to the slave who had appeared, "and convince him—by means of a heavily–weighted club if necessary—that the situation he has taken up is quite unworthy of his incomparable efforts."

When the slave returned it was with an entire absence of the enthusiasm of one who has succeeded in an enterprise.

"The distinguished mendicant outside disarmed the one who is relating the incident by means of an unworthy stratagem, and then struck him repeatedly on the head with the image of a sonorous wooden duck," reported the slave submissively.

Meanwhile the voice with its accompaniment continued to chant the deeds of bygone heroes.

"In that case," said Wong Pao coldly, "entice him into this inadequate chamber by words suggestive of liberal entertainment."

This device was successful, for very soon the slave returned with the stranger. He was a youth of studious appearance and an engaging openness of manner. Hung about his neck by means of a cord were a variety of poems suitable to most of the contingencies of an ordinary person's existence. The name he bore was Sun and he was of the house of Kiau.

"Honourable greeting, minstrel," said Wong Pao, with dignified condescension. "Why do you persist in exercising your illustrious talent outside this person's insignificant abode?"

"Because," replied Sun modestly, "the benevolent mandarin who has just spoken had not then invited me inside. Now, however, he will be able to hear to greater advantage the very doubtful qualities of my entertainment."

With these words Kiau Sun struck the duck so proficiently that it emitted a life–like call, and prepared to raise his voice in a chant.

"Restrain your undoubted capacity," exclaimed Wong Pao hastily. "The inquiry presented itself to you at an inaccurate angle. Why, to restate it, did you continue before this uninviting hovel when, under the external forms of true politeness, my slave endeavoured to remove you hence?"

"In the circumstances this person may have overlooked the delicacy of the message, for, as it is well written, 'To the starving, a blow from a skewer of meat is more acceptable than a caress from the hand of a maiden,'" said Kiau Sun. "Whereunto remember, thou two–stomached merchant, that although the house in question in yours, the street is mine."

"By what title?" demanded Wong Pao contentiously.

"By the same that confers this well–appointed palace upon you," replied Sun: "because it is my home."

"The point is one of some subtlety," admitted Wong Pao, "and might be pursued to an extreme delicacy of attenuation if it were argued by those whose profession it is to give a variety of meanings to the same thing. Yet even allowing the claim, it is none the less an unendurable affliction that your voice should disturb my peacefully conducted enterprise."

"As yours would have done mine, O concave–witted Wong Pao!"

"That," retorted the merchant, "is a disadvantage that you could easily have averted by removing yourself to a more distant spot."

"The solution is equally applicable to your own case, mandarin," replied Kiau Sun affably.

"Alas!" exclaimed Wong Pao, with an obvious inside bitterness, "it is a mistake to argue with persons of limited intelligence in terms of courtesy. This, doubtless, was the meaning of the philosopher Nhy–hi when he penned the observation, 'Death, a woman and a dumb mute always have the last word,' Why did I have you conducted hither to convince you dispassionately, rather than send an armed guard to force you away by violence?"

"Possibly," suggested the minstrel, "because my profession is a legally recognized one, and, moreover, under the direct protection of the exalted Mandarin Shen–y–ling."

"Profession!" retorted Wong Pao, stung by the reference to Shen–y–ling, for that powerful official's attitude was indeed the inner reason why he had not pushed violence to a keener edge against Kiau Sun, "an abject mendicancy, yielding two hands" grasp of copper cash a day on a stock composed of half a dozen threadbare odes."

"Compose me half a dozen better and one hand–count of cash shall be apportioned to you each evening," suggested Sun.

"A handful of cash for my labour!" exclaimed the indignant Wong Pao. "Learn, puny wayfarer, that in a single day the profit of my various enterprises exceeds a hundred taels of silver."

"That is less than the achievement of my occupation," said Kiau Sun.

"Less!" repeated the merchant incredulously. "Can you, O boaster, display a single tael?"

"Doubtless I should be the possessor of thousands if I made use of the attributes of a merchant—three hands and two faces. But that was not the angle of my meaning: your labour only compels men to remember; mine enables them to forget."

Thus they continued to strive, each one contending for the pre–eminence of his own state, regardless of the sage warning: "In three moments a labourer will remove an obstructing rock, but three moons will pass without two wise men agreeing on the meaning of a vowel"; and assuredly they would have persisted in their intellectual entertainment until the great sky–lantern rose and the pangs of hunger compelled them to desist, were it not for the manifestation of a very unusual occurrence.

The Emperor, N'ang Wei, then reigning, is now generally regarded as being in no way profound or inspired, but possessing the faculty of being able to turn the dissensions among his subjects to a profitable account, and other accomplishments useful in a ruler. As he passed along the streets of his capital he heard the voices of two raised in altercation, and halting the bearer of his umbrella, he commanded that the persons concerned should be brought before him and state the nature of their dispute.

"The rivalry is an ancient one," remarked the Emperor when each had made his claim. "Doubtless we ourselves could devise a judgment, but in this cycle of progress it is more usual to leave decision to the pronouncement of the populace—and much less exacting to our Imperial ingenuity. An edict will therefore be published, stating that at a certain hour Kiau Sun will stand upon the Western Hill of the city and recite one of his incomparable epics, while at the same gong–stroke Wong Pao will take his station on the Eastern Hill, let us say for the purpose of distributing pieces of silver among any who are able to absent themselves from the competing attraction. It will then be clearly seen which entertainment draws the greater number."

"Your mind, O all–wisest, is only comparable to the peacock's tail in its spreading brilliance!" exclaimed Wong Pao, well assured of an easy triumph.

Kiau Sun, however, remained silent, but he observed closely the benignly impartial expression of the Emperor's countenance.

When the indicated time arrived, only two persons could have been observed within the circumference of the Western Hill of the city—a blind mendicant who had lost his way and an extremely round–bodied mandarin who had been abandoned there by his carriers when they heard the terms of the edict. But about the Eastern Hill the throng was so great that for some time after it was unusual to meet a person whose outline had not been permanently altered by the occasion. Even Kiau Sun was present.

On a protected eminence stood N'ang Wei. Near him was Wong Pao, confidently awaiting the moment when the Emperor should declare himself. When, therefore, the all–wisest graciously made a gesture of command, Wong Pao hastened to his side, an unbecoming elation gilding the fullness of his countenance.

"Wong Pao," said the Illimitable, "the people are here in gratifying profusion. The moment has thus arrived for you to consummate your triumph over Kiau Sun."

"Omnipotence?" queried Wong Pao.

"The silver that you were to distribute freely to all who came. Doubtless you have a retinue of slaves in attendance with weighty sacks of money for the purpose?"

"But that was only in the nature of an imagined condition, Sublime Being, designed to test the trend of their preference," said Wong Pao, with an incapable feeling of no–confidence in the innermost seat of his self-esteem. "This abject person did not for a single breathing–space contemplate or provide for so formidable an outlay."

A shadow of inquiry appeared above the eyebrows of the Sublimest, although his refined imperturbability did not permit him to display any acute emotion.

"It is not entirely a matter of what you contemplated, merchant, but what this multitudinous and, as we now perceive, generally well–armed concourse imagined. Greatly do we fear that when the position has been explained to them, the breathing–space remaining, O Wong Pao, will not be in your body. What," continued the liberal-minded sovereign, turning to one of his attending nobles, "what was it that

62

happened to Ning—lo who failed to satisfy the lottery ticket holders in somewhat similar circumstances?"

"The scorpion vat, Serenest," replied the vassal.

"Ah," commented the Enlightened One, "for the moment we thought it was the burning sulphur plaster."

"That was Ching Yan, who lost approval in the inlaid coffin raffle, Benign Head," prompted the noble.

"True—there is a certain oneness in these cases. Well, Wong Pao, we are entirely surrounded by an expectant mob and their attitude, after much patient waiting, is tending towards a clearly—defined tragedy. By what means is it your intention to extricate us all from the position into which your insatiable vanity has thrust us?"

"Alas, Imperishable Majesty, I only appear to have three pieces of silver and a string of brass cash in my sleeve," confessed Wong Pao tremblingly.

"And that would not go very far—even if flung into the limits of the press," commented the Emperor. "We must look elsewhere for deliverance, then. Kiau Sun, stand forth and try your means."

Upon this invitation Sun appeared from the tent in which he had awaited the summons and advanced to the edge of the multitude. With no appearance of fear or concern, he stood before them, and bending his energies to the great task imposed upon him, he struck the hollow duck so melodiously that the note of expectancy vibrated into the farthest confines of the crowd. Then modulating his voice in unison Kiau Sun began to chant.

At first the narration was of times legendary, when dragons and demons moved about the earth in more palpable forms than they usually maintain to—day. A great mist overspread the Empire and men's minds were vaporous, nor was their purpose keen. Later, deities and well—disposed Forces began to exercise their powers. The mist was turned into a benevolent system of rivers and canals, and iron, rice and the silk—worm then appeared, Next, heroes and champions, whose names have been preserved, arose.

They fought the giants and an era of literature and peaceful tranquillity set in. After this there was the Great Invasion from the north, but the people rallied and by means of a war lasting five years, five moons and five days the land was freed again. This prefaced the Golden Age when chess was invented, printed books first made and the Examination System begun.

So far Kiau Sun had only sung of things that men knew dimly through a web of time, but the melody of his voice and the valours of the deeds he told had held their minds. Now he began skilfully to intertwine among the narration scenes and doings that were near to all—of the coming of Spring across the mountains that surround the capital; sunrise on the great lagoon, with the splash of oars and the cormorants in flight; the appearance of the blossom in the peach orchards; the Festival of Boats and of Lanterns, their daily task, and the reward each saw beyond. Finally he spoke quite definitely of the homes awaiting their return, the mulberry−tree about the gate, the fire then burning on the hearth, the pictures on the walls, the ancestral tablets, and the voices calling each. And as he spoke and made an end of speaking the people began silently to melt away, until none remained but Kiau, Wong Pao and the Emperor and his band.

"Kiau Sun," said the discriminating N'ang Wei, "in memory of this day the office of Chanter of Congratulatory Odes in the Palace ceremonial is conferred on you, together with the title 'Leaf−crowned' and the yearly allowance of five hundred taels and a jar of rice wine. And Wong Pao," he added thoughtfully—"Wong Pao shall be permitted to endow the post—also in memory of this day."

CHAPTER V. The Timely Intervention of the Mandarin Shan Tien's Lucky Day

WHEN Kai Lung at length reached the shutter, after the delay caused by Li−loe's inopportune presence, he found that Hwa−mei was already standing there beneath the wall.

"Alas!" he exclaimed, in an access of self−reproach, "is it possible that I have failed to greet your arriving footsteps? Hear the degrading cause of my—"

"Forbear," interrupted the maiden, with a magnanimous gesture of the hand that was not engaged in bestowing a gift of fruit. "There is a time to scatter flowers and a time to prepare the soil. To—morrow a further trial awaits you, for which we must conspire."

"I am in your large and all—embracing grasp," replied Kai Lung. "Proceed to spread your golden counsel."

"The implacable Ming—shu has deliberated with himself, and deeming it unlikely that you should a third time allure the imagination of the Mandarin Shan Tien by your art, he has ordered that you are again to be the first led out to judgment. On this occasion, however, he has prepared a cloud of witnesses who will, once they are given a voice, quickly overwhelm you in a flood of calumny."

"Even a silver trumpet may not prevail above a score of brazen horns," confessed the story—teller doubtfully. "Would it not be well to engage an even larger company who will outlast the first?"

"The effete Ming—shu has hired all there are," replied Hwa—mei, with a curbing glance. "Nevertheless, do not despair. At a convenient hour a trusty hand will let fall a skin of wine at their assembling place. Their testimony, should any arrive, will entail some conflict."

"I bow before the practical many—sidedness of your mind, enchanting one," murmured Kai Lung, in deep—felt admiration.

"To—morrow, being the first of the Month of Gathering—in, will be one of Shan Tien's lucky days," continued the maiden, her look acknowledging the fitness of the compliment, but at the same time indicating that the moment was not a suitable one to pursue the detail further. "After holding court the Mandarin will accordingly proceed to hazard his accustomed stake upon the chances of certain of the competitors in the approaching examinations. His mind will thus be alertly watchful for a guiding omen. The rest should lie within your persuasive tongue."

"The story of Lao Ting—" began Kai Lung.

"Enough," replied Hwa-mei, listening to a distant sound. "Already has this one strayed beyond her appointed limit. May your virtuous cause prevail!"

With this auspicious message the maiden fled, leaving Kai Lung more than ever resolved to conduct the enterprise in a manner worthy of her high regard.

On the following day, at the appointed hour, Kai Lung was again led before the Mandarin Shan Tien. To the alert yet downcast gaze of the former person it seemed as if the usually inscrutable expression of that high official was not wholly stern as it moved in his direction. Ming-shu, on the contrary, disclosed all his voracious teeth without restraint.

"Calling himself Kai Lung," began the detestable accuser, in a voice even more repulsive than its wont, "and claiming—"

"The name has a somewhat familiar echo," interrupted the Fountain of Justice, with a genial interest in what was going on, rare in one of his exalted rank. "Have we not seen the ill-conditioned thing before?"

"He has tasted of your unutterable clemency in the past," replied Ming-shu, "this being by no means his first appearance thus. Claiming to be a story-teller—"

"What," demanded the enlightened law-giver with leisurely precision, "is a story-teller, and how is he defined?"

"A story-teller, Excellence," replied the inscriber of his spoken word, with the concise manner of one who is not entirely grateful to another, "is one who tells stories. Having on—"

"The profession must be widely spread," remarked the gracious administrator thoughtfully. "All those who supplicate in this very average court practise it to a more or less degree."

"The prisoner," continued the insufferable Ming-shu, so lost to true refinement that he did not even relax his dignity at a remark handed down as gravity-removing from times immemorial, "has already been charged and made his plea. It only remains,

66

therefore, to call the witnesses and to condemn him."

"The usual band appears to be more retiring than their custom is," observed Shan Tien, looking around. "Their lack of punctual respect does not enlarge our sympathy towards their cause."

"They are all hard—striving persons of studious or commercial habits," replied Ming—shu, "and have doubtless become immersed in their various traffics."

"Should the immersion referred to prove to be so deep—"

"A speedy messenger has already gone, but his returning footsteps tarry," urged Ming—shu anxiously. "In this extremity, Excellence, I will myself—"

"High Excellence," appealed Kai Lung, as soon as Ming—shu's departing sandals were obscured to view, "out of the magnanimous condescension of your unworldly heart hear an added plea. Taught by the inoffensive example of that Lao Ting whose success in the literary competitions was brought about by a conjunction of miraculous omens—"

"Arrest the stream of your acknowledged oratory for a single breathing—space," commanded the Mandarin dispassionately, yet at the same time unostentatiously studying a list that lay within his sleeve. "What was the auspicious name of the one of whom you spoke?"

"Lao Ting, exalted; to whom at various periods were subjoined those of Li, Tzu, Sun, Chu, Wang and Chin."

"Assuredly. Your prayer for a fuller hearing will reach our lenient ears. In the meanwhile, in order to prove that the example upon which you base your claim is a worthy one, proceed to narrate so much of the story of Lao Ting as bears upon the means of his success."

The Story of Lao Ting and the Luminous Insect

If is of Lao Ting that the saying has arisen, "He who can grasp Opportunity as she slips by does not need a lucky dream."

So far, however, Lao Ting may be judged to have had neither opportunities nor lucky dreams. He was one of studious nature and from an early age had devoted himself to a veneration of the Classics. Yet with that absence of foresight on the part of the providing deities (for this, of course, took place during an earlier, and probably usurping, dynasty), which then frequently resulted in the unworthy and illiterate prospering, his sleeve was so empty that at times it seemed almost impossible for him to continue in his high ambition.

As the date of the examinations drew near, Lao Ting's efforts increased, and he grudged every moment spent away from books. His few available cash scarcely satisfied his ever-moving brush, and his sleeve grew so light that it seemed as though it might become a balloon and carry him into the Upper Air; for, as the Wisdom has it, "A well-filled purse is a trusty earth anchor." On food he spent even less, but the inability to procure light after the sun had withdrawn his benevolence from the narrow street in which he lived was an ever-present shadow across his hopes. On this extremity he patiently and with noiseless skill bored a hole through the wall into the house of a wealthy neighbour, and by this inoffensive stratagem he was able to distinguish the imperishable writings of the Sages far into the night. Soon, however, the gross hearted person in question discovered the device, owing to the symmetrical breathing of Lao Ting, and applying himself to the opening unperceived, he suddenly blew a jet of water through and afterwards nailed in a wooden skewer. This he did because he himself was also entering for the competitions, though he did not really fear Lao Ting.

Thus denied, Lao Ting sought other means to continue his study, if for only a few minutes longer daily, and it became his custom to leave his ill-equipped room when it grew dusk and to walk into the outer ways, always with his face towards the west, so that he might prolong the benefit of the great luminary to the last possible moment. When the time of no-light definitely arrived he would climb up into one of the high places to await the first beam of the great sky-lantern, and also in the reasonable belief that the nearer he got to it the more powerful would be its light.

It was upon such an occasion that Lao Ting first became aware of the entrancing presence of Chun Hoa–mi, and although he plainly recognized from the outset that the graceful determination with which she led a water–buffalo across the landscape by means of a slender cord attached to its nose was not conducive to his taking a high place in the competitions, he soon found that he was unable to withdraw himself from frequenting the spot at the same hour on each succeeding day. Presently, however, he decided that his previous misgiving was inaccurate, as her existence inspired him with an all–conquering determination to outdistance every other candidate in so marked a manner that his name would at once become famous throughout the province, to attain high office without delay, to lead a victorious army against the encroaching barbarian foe and thus to save the Empire in a moment of emergency, to acquire vast riches (in a not clearly defined manner), to become the intimate counsellor of the grateful Emperor, and finally to receive posthumous honours of unique distinction, the harmonious personality of Hoa–Mi being inextricably entwined among these achievements.

At other times, however, he became subject to a funereal conviction that he would fail discreditably in the examinations to an accompaniment of the ridicule and contempt of all who knew him, that he would never succeed in acquiring sufficient brass cash to ensure a meagre sustenance even for himself, and that he would probably end his lower existence by ignominious decapitation, so that his pale and hungry ghost would be unable to find its way from place to place and be compelled to remain on the same spot through all eternity. Yet so quickly did these two widely diverging vistas alternate in Lao Ting's mind that on many occasions he was under the influence of both presentiments at the same time.

It will thus be seen that Lao Ting was becoming involved in emotions of a many–sided hue, by which his whole future would inevitably be affected, when an event took place which greatly tended to restore his tranquillity of mind. He was, at the usual hour, lurking unseen on the path of Hoa–mi's approach when the water–buffalo, with the perversity of its kind, suddenly withdrew itself from the amiable control of its attendant's restraining hand and precipitated its resistless footsteps towards the long grass in which Lao Ting lay concealed. Recognizing that a decisive moment in the maiden's esteem lay before him, the latter, in spite of an incapable doubt as to the habits and manner of behaviour of creatures of this part, set out resolutely to subdue it. . . . At a later period, by clinging tenaciously to its tail, he undoubtedly impeded its progress, and thereby enabled Hoa–mi to greet him as one who had a claim upon her gratitude.

"The person who has performed this slight service is Ting, of the outcast line of Lao," said the student with an admiring bow in spite of a benumbing pain that involved all his lower attributes. "Having as yet achieved nothing, the world lies before him."

"She who speaks is Hoa–mi, her father's house being Chun," replied the maiden agreeably. "In addition to the erratic but now repentant animal that has thus, as it were, brought us within the same narrow compass, he possesses a wooden plough, two wheel–barrows, a red bow with three–score arrows, and a rice–field, and is therefore a person of some consequence."

"True," agreed Lao Ting, "though perhaps the dignity is less imposing than might be imagined in the eye of one who, by means of successive examinations, may ultimately become the Right hand of the Emperor."

"Is the contingency an impending one?" inquired Hoa–mi, with polite interest.

"So far," admitted Lao Ting, "it is more in the nature of a vision. There are, of necessity, many trials, and few can reach the ultimate end. Yet even the Yangtze–kiang has a source."

"Of your unswerving tenacity this person has already been witness," said the maiden, with a glance of refined encouragement.

"Your words are more inspiring than the example of the aged woman of Shang–li to the student Tsung," declared Lao Ting gratefully. "Unless the Omens are asleep they should tend to the same auspicious end."

"The exact instance of the moment escapes my recollection." Probably Hoa–mi was by no means willing that one of studious mind should associate her exclusively with water–buffaloes. "Is it related in the Classics?"

"Possibly, though in which actual masterpiece just now evades my grasp. The youth referred to was on the point of abandoning a literary career, appalled at the magnitude of the task before him, when he encountered an aged woman who was employed in laboriously rubbing away the surface of an iron crowbar on a block of stone. To his inquiry she cheerfully replied: 'The one who is thus engaged required a needle to complete a task. Being unable to procure one she was about to give way to an ignoble despair when chance put into her hands this bar, which only requires bringing down to the necessary size.' Encouraged by this painstaking example Tsung returned to his books and in due course became a high official."

"Doubtless in the time of his prosperity he retraced his footsteps and lavishly rewarded the one to whom he was thus indebted," suggested Hoa—mi gracefully.

"Doubtless," admitted Lao Ting, "but the detail is not pursued to so remote an extremity in the Classic. The delicate poise of the analogy is what is chiefly dwelt upon, the sign for a needle harmonizing with that for official, and there being a similar balance between crowbar and books."

"Your words are like a page written in vermilion ink," exclaimed Hoa—mi, with a sideway—expressed admiration.

"Alas!" he declared, with conscious humility, "my style is meagre and almost wholly threadbare. To remedy this, each day I strive to perfect myself in the correct formation of five new written signs. When equipped with a knowledge of every one there is I shall be competent to write so striking and original an essay on any subject that it will no longer be possible to exclude my name from the list of official appointments."

"It will be a day of well—achieved triumph for the spirits of your expectant ancestors," said Hoa—mi sympathetically.

"It will also have a beneficial effect on my own material prospects," replied Lao Ting, with a commendable desire to awaken images of a more specific nature in the maiden's imagination. "Where hitherto it has been difficult to support one, there will then be a lavish profusion for two. The moment the announcement is made, my impatient feet will carry me to this spot. Can it be hoped—?"

"It has long been this one's favourite resort also," confessed Hoa—mi, with every appearance of having adequately grasped Lao Ting's desired inference, "Yet to what number do the written signs in question stretch?"

"So highly favoured is our unapproachable language that the number can only be faintly conjectured. Some claim five–score thousand different written symbols; the least exacting agree to fourscore thousand."

"You are all–knowing," responded the maiden absently. With her face in an opposing direction her lips moved rapidly, as though she might be in the act of addressing some petition to a Power. Yet it is to be doubted if this accurately represents the nature of her inner thoughts, for when she again turned towards Lao Ting the engaging frankness of her expression had imperceptibly deviated, as she continued:

"In about nine and forty years, then, O impetuous one, our converging footsteps will doubtless again encounter upon this spot. In the meanwhile, however, this person's awaiting father is certainly preparing something against her tardy return which the sign for a crowbar would fittingly represent."

Then urging the water–buffalo to increased exertion she fled, leaving Lao Ting a prey to emotions of a very distinguished intensity.

In spite of the admittedly rough–edged nature of Hoa–mi's leave–taking, Lao Ting retraced his steps in an exalted frame of mind. He had spoken to the maiden and heard her incomparable voice. He now knew her name and the path leading to her father's house. It only remained for him to win a position worthy of her acceptance (if the Empire could offer such a thing), and their future happiness might be regarded as assured.

Thus engaged, Lao Ting walked on, seeing within his head the arrival of the bridal chair, partaking of the well–spread wedding feast, hearing the felicitations of the guests: "A hundred sons and a thousand grandsons!" Something white fluttering by the wayside recalled him to the realities of the day. He had reached the buildings of the outer city, and on a wall before him a printed notice was displayed.

It has already been set forth that the few solitary cash which from time to time fell into the student's sleeve were barely sufficient to feed his thirsty brush with ink. For the material on which to write and to practise the graceful curves essential to a style he was driven to various unworthy expedients. It had thus become his habit to lurk in the footsteps of those who affix public proclamations in the ways and spaces of the city, and when they had passed on to remove, as unostentatiously as possible, the more suitable pronouncements and to carry them to his own abode. For this reason he regarded every notice from a varying angle, being concerned less with what appeared upon it than with what did not appear. Accordingly he now crossed the way and endeavoured to secure the sheet that had attracted his attention. In this he was unsuccessful, however, for he could only detach a meagre fragment.

When Lao Ting reached his uninviting room the last pretence of daylight had faded. He recognized that he had lost many precious moments in Hoa—mi's engaging society, and although he would willingly have lost many more, there was now a deeper pang in his regret that he could not continue his study further into the night. As this was impossible, he drew his scanty night coverings around him and composed his mind for sleep, conscious of an increasing rigour in the air; for, as he found when the morning came, one who wished him well, passing in his absence, had written a lucky saying on a stone and cast it through the paper window.

When Lao Ting awoke it was still night, but the room was no longer entirely devoid of light. As his custom was, an open page lay on the floor beside him, ready to be caught up eagerly with the first gleam of day; above this a faint but sufficient radiance now hung, enabling him to read the written signs. At first the student regarded the surroundings with some awe, not doubting that this was in the nature of a visitation, but presently he discovered that the light was provided by a living creature, winged but docile, which carried a glowing lustre in its tail. When he had read to the end, Lao Ting endeavoured to indicate by a sign that he wished to turn the page. To his delight he found that the winged creature intelligently grasped the requirement and at once transferred its presence to the required spot. All through the night the youth eagerly read on, nor did this miraculously endowed visitor ever fail him. By dawn he had more than made up the time in which the admiration of Hoa—mi had involved him. If such a state of things could be assured for the future, the vista would stretch like a sunlit glade before his feet.

Early in the day he set out to visit an elderly monk, who lived in a cave on the mountain above. Before he went, however, he did not fail to procure a variety of leaves and herbs, and to display them about the room in order to indicate to his unassuming

73

companion that he had a continued interest in his welfare. The venerable hermit received him hospitably, and after inviting him to sit upon the floor and to partake of such food as he had brought with him, listened attentively to his story.

"Your fear that in this manifestation you may be the sport of a malicious Force, conspiring to some secret ill, is merely superstition," remarked Tzu–lu when Lao Ting had reached an end. "Although creatures such as you describe are unknown in this province, they undoubtedly exist in outer barbarian lands, as do apes with the tails of peacocks, ducks with their bones outside their skins, beings whose pale green eyes can discover the precious hidden things of the earth, and men with a hole through their chests so that they require no chair to carry them, but are transposed from spot to spot by means of poles."

"Your mind is widely opened, esteemed," replied Lao Ting respectfully. "Yet the omen must surely tend towards a definite course?"

"Be guided by the mature philosophy of the resolute Heng–ki, who, after an unfortunate augury, exclaimed to his desponding warriors: 'Do your best and let the Omens do their worst!' What has happened is as clear as the iridescence of a dragon's eye. In the past you have lent a sum of money to a friend who has thereupon passed into the Upper Air, leaving you unrequited."

"A friend receiving a sum of money from this person would have every excuse for passing away suddenly."

"Or," continued the accommodating recluse, "you have in some other way placed so formidable an obligation upon one now in the Beyond that his disturbed spirit can no longer endure the burden. For this reason it has taken the form of a luminous insect, and has thus returned to earth in order that it may assist you and thereby discharge the debt."

"The explanation is a convincing one," replied Lao Ting. "Might it not have been more satisfactory in the end, however, if the gracious person in question had clothed himself with the attributes of the examining chancellor or some high mandarin, so that he could have upheld my cause in any extremity?"

Without actually smiling, a form of entertainment that was contrary to his strict vow, the patriarchal anchorite moved his features somewhat at the youth's innocence.

"Do not forget that it is written: 'Though you set a monkey on horseback yet will his hands and feet remain hairy,'" he remarked. "The one whose conduct we are discussing may well be aware of his own deficiencies, and know that if he adopted such a course a humiliating exposure would await him. Do not have any fear for the future, however: thus protected, this person is inspired to prophesy that you will certainly take a high place in the examinations. . . . Indeed," he added thoughtfully, "it might be prudent to venture a string of cash upon your lucky number."

With this auspicious leave–taking Tzu–lu dismissed him, and Lao Ting returned to the city greatly refreshed in spirit by the encounter. Instead of retiring to his home he continued into the more reputable ways beyond, it then being about the hour at which the affixers of official notices were wont to display their energies.

So it chanced indeed, but walking with his feet off the ground, owing to the obliging solitary's encouragement, Lao Ting forgot his usual caution, and came suddenly into the midst of a band of these men at an angle of the paths.

"Honourable greetings," he exclaimed, feeling that if he passed them by unregarded his purpose might be suspected. "Have you eaten your rice?"

"How is your warmth and cold?" they replied courteously. "Yet why do you arrest your dignified footsteps to converse with outcasts so illiterate as ourselves?"

"The reason," admitted Lao Ting frankly, "need not be buried in a well. Had I avoided the encounter you might have said among yourselves: 'Here is one who shuns our gaze. This, perchance, is he who of late has lurked within the shadow of our backs to bear away our labour.' Not to create this unworthy suspicion I freely came among you, for, as the Ancient Wisdom says: 'Do not adjust your sandals while passing through a melon–field, nor yet arrange your hat beneath an orange–tree.'"

"Yet," said the leader of the band, "we were waiting thus in expectation of the one whom you describe. The incredible leper who rules our goings has, even at this hour and notwithstanding that now is the appointed day and time for the gathering together of the Harmonious Constellation of Paste Appliers and Long Brush Wielders, thrust within our hands a double task."

"May bats defile his Ancestral Tablets and goats propagate within his neglected tomb!" chanted the band in unison. "May the sinews of his hams snap suddenly in moments of achievement! May the principles of his warmth and cold never be properly adjusted but—"

"Thus positioned," continued the leader, indicating by a gesture that while he agreed with these sentiments the moment was not opportune for their full recital, "we await. If he who lurks in our past draws near he will doubtless accept from our hands that which he will assuredly possess behind our backs. Thus mutual help will lighten the toil of all."

"The one whom you require dwells beneath my scanty roof," said the youth. "He is now, however, absent on a secret mission. Entrust to me the burden of your harassment and I will answer, by the sanctity of the Four-eyed Image, that it shall reach his speedy hand."

When Lao Ting gained his own room, bowed down but rejoicing beneath the weight of his unexpected fortune, his eyes were gladdened by the soft light that hung about his books. Although it was not yet dark, the radiance of the glow seemed greater than before. Going to the spot the delighted student saw that in place of one there were now four, the grateful insect having meanwhile summoned others to his cause. All these stood in an expectant attitude awaiting his control, so that through the night he plied an untiring brush and leapt onward in the garden of similitudes.

From this time forward Lao Ting could not fail to be aware that the faces of those whom he familiarly encountered were changed towards him. Men greeted him as one worthy of their consideration, and he even heard his name spoken of respectfully in the society of learned strangers. More than once he found garlands of flowers hung upon his outer door, harmonious messages, and—once—a gift of food. Incredible as it seemed to him it had come to be freely admitted that the unknown scholar Lao Ting would take a very high place in the forthcoming competition, and those who were alert and watchful did not hesitate to place him first. To this general feeling a variety of portents had contributed. Doubtless the beginning was the significant fact, known to the few at first, that the miracle–working Tzu–lu had staked his inner garment on Lao Ting's success. Brilliant lights were seen throughout the night to be moving in the meagre dwelling (for the four efficacious creatures had by this time greatly added to their numbers), and the one within was credited with being assisted by the Forces. It is well said that that which passes out of one mouth passes into a hundred ears, and before dawn had become dusk all the early and astute were following the inspired hermit's example. They who conducted the lotteries, becoming suddenly aware of the burden of the hazard they incurred, thereat declared that upon the venture of Lao Ting's success there must be set two taels in return for one. Whereupon the desire of those who had refrained waxed larger than before, and thus the omens grew.

When the days that remained before the opening of the trial could be counted on the fingers of one hand, there came, at a certain hour, a summons on the outer door of Lao Ting's house, and in response to his spoken invitation there entered one, Sheng–yin, a competitor.

"Lao Ting," said this person, when they had exchanged formalities, "in spite of the flattering attentions of the shallow"—he here threw upon the floor a garland which he had conveyed from off Lao Ting's door—"it is exceedingly unlikely that at the first attempt your name will be among those of the chosen, and the possibility of it heading the list may be dismissed as vapid."

"Your experience is deep and wide," replied Lao Ting, the circumstance that Sheng–yin had already tried and failed three and thirty times adding an edge to the words; "yet if it is written it is written."

"Doubtless," retorted Sheng–yin no less capably; "but it will never be set to music. Now, until your inconsiderate activities prevailed, this person was confidently greeted as the one who would be first."

"The names of Wang–san and Yin Ho were not unknown to the expectant," suggested Lao Ting mildly.

"The mind of Wang–san is only comparable with a wastepaper basket," exclaimed the visitor harshly; "and Yin Ho is in reality as dull as split ebony. But in your case, unfortunately, there is nothing to go on, and, unlikely though it be, it is just possible

77

that this person's well–arranged ambitions may thereby be brought to a barren end. For that reason he is here to discuss this matter as between virtuous friends."

"Let your auspicious mouth be widely opened," replied Lao Ting guardedly. "My ears will not refrain."

"Is there not, perchance, some venerable relative in a distant part of the province whose failing eyes crave, at this juncture, to rest upon your wholesome features before he passes Upwards?"

"Assuredly some such inopportune person might be forthcoming," admitted Lao Ting. "Yet the cost of so formidable a journey would be far beyond this necessitous one's means."

"In so charitable a cause affluent friends would not be lacking. Depart on the third day and remain until the ninth and twenty taels of silver will glide imperceptibly into your awaiting sleeve."

"The prospect of not taking the foremost place in the competition—added to the pangs of those who have hazarded their store upon the unworthy name of Lao—is an ignoble one," replied the student, after a moment's thought. "The journey will be a costly task at this season of the rains; it cannot possibly be accomplished for less than fifty taels."

"It is well said, 'Do not look at robbers sharing out their spoil: look at them being executed,'" urged Sheng–yin. "Should you be so ill–destined as to compete, and, as would certainly be the case, be awarded a position of contempt, how unendurable would be your anguish when, amidst the execrations of the deluded mob, you remembered that thirty taels of the purest had slipped from your effete grasp."

"Should the Bridge of the Camel Back be passable, five and forty might suffice," mused Lao Tung to himself.

"Thirty–seven taels, five hundred cash, are the utmost that your obliging friends would hazard in the quest," announced Sheng–yin definitely. "On the day following that of the final competition the sum will be honourably—"

"By no means," interrupted the other, with unswerving firmness. "How thus is the journey to be defrayed? In advance, assuredly."

"The requirement is unusual. Yet upon satisfactory oaths being offered—"

"This person will pledge the repose of the spirits of his venerated ancestors practically back to prehistoric times," agreed Lao Ting readily. "From the third to the ninth day he will be absent from the city and will take no part in anything therein. Should he eat his words, may his body be suffocated beneath five cart–loads of books and his weary ghost chained to that of a leprous mule. It is spoken."

"Truly. But it may as well be written also." With this expression of narrow–minded suspicion Sheng–yin would have taken up one from a considerable mass of papers lying near at hand, had not Lao Ting suddenly restrained him.

"It shall be written with clarified ink on paper of a special excellence," declared the student. "Take the brush, Seng–yin, and write. It almost repays this person for the loss of a degree to behold the formation of signs so unapproachable as yours."

"Lao Ting," replied the visitor, pausing in his task, "you are occasionally inspired, but the weakness of your character results in a lack of caution. In this matter, therefore, be warned: 'The crocodile opens his jaws; the rat–trap closes his; keep yours shut.'"

When Lao Ting returned after a scrupulously observed six days of absence he could not fail to become aware that the city was in an uproar, and the evidence of this increased as he approached the cheap and lightly esteemed quarter in which those of literary ambitions found it convenient to reside. Remembering Sheng–yin's parting, he forbore to draw attention to himself by questioning any, but when he reached the door of his own dwelling he discovered the one of whom he was thinking, standing, as it were, between the posts.

"Lao Ting," exclaimed Sheng–yin, without waiting to make any polite reference to the former person's food or condition, "in spite of this calamity you are doubtless prepared to carry out the spirit of your oath?"

"Doubtless," replied Lao Ting affably. "Yet what is the nature of the calamity referred to, and how does it affect the burden of my vow?"

"Has not the tiding reached your ear? The examinations, alas! have been withheld for seven full days. Your journey has been in vain!"

"By no means!" declared the youth. "Debarred by your enticement from a literary career this person turned his mind to other aims, and has now gained a deep insight into the habits and behaviour of water–buffaloes."

"They who control the competitions from the Capital," continued Sheng–yin, without even hearing the other's words, "when all had been arranged, learned from the Chief Astrologer (may subterranean fires singe his venerable moustaches!) that a forgotten obscuration of the sun would take place on the opening day of the test. In the face of so formidable a portent they acted thus and thus."

"How then fares it that due warning of the change was not set forth?"

"The matter is as long as The Wall and as deep as seven wells," grumbled Sheng–yin, "and the Hoang Ho in flood is limpid by its side. Proclamations were sent forth, yet none appeared, and they entrusted with their wide disposal have a dragon–story of a shining lordly youth who ever followed in their steps. . . . Thus in a manner of expressing it, the spirit—"

"Sheng–yin," said Lao Ting, with courteous firmness, yet so moving the door so that while he passed in the former person remained outside, "you have sought, at the expenditure of thirty–seven taels five hundred cash, to deflect Destiny from her appointed line. The result has been lamentable to all—or nearly all—concerned. The lawless effort must not be repeated, for when heaven itself goes out of its way to set a correcting omen in the sky, who dare disobey?"

When the list and order of the competition was proclaimed, the name of Wang–san stood at the very head and that of Yin Ho was next. Lao Ting was the very last of those who were successful; Sheng–yin was the next, and was thus the first of those who were unsuccessful. It was as much as the youth had secretly dared to hope, and much better than he had generally feared. In Sheng–yin's case, however, it was infinitely worse than he had ever contemplated. Regarding Lao Ting as the cause of his disgrace he planned a sordid revenge. Waiting until night had fallen he sought the student's door-step and there took a potent drug, laying upon his ghost a strict injunction to devote itself to haunting and thwarting the ambitions of the one who dwelt within. But even in this he was inept, for the poison was less speedy than he thought, and Lao Ting returned in time to convey him to another door.

On the strength of his degree Lao Ting found no difficulty in earning a meagre competence by instructing others who wished to follow in his footsteps. He was also now free to compete for the next degree, where success would bring him higher honour and a slightly less meagre competence. In the meanwhile he married Hoa-mi, being able to display thirty-seven taels and nearly five hundred cash towards that end. Ultimately he rose to a position of remunerative ease, but it is understood that he attained this more by a habit of acting as the necessities of the moment required than by his literary achievements.

Over the door of his country residence in the days of his profusion he caused the image of a luminous insect to be depicted, and he engraved its semblance on his seal. He would also have added the presentment of a water-buffalo, but Hoa-mi deemed this inexpedient.

CHAPTER VI. The High-minded Strategy of the Amiable Hwa-mei

WARNED by the mischance attending his previous meeting with Hwa-mei, Kai Lung sought the walled enclosure at the earliest moment of his permitted freedom, and secreting himself among the interlacing growth he anxiously awaited the maiden's coming.

Presently a movement in the trees without betrayed a presence, and the story-teller was on the point of disclosing himself at the shutter when the approaching one displayed an unfamiliar outline. Instead of a maiden of exceptional symmetry and peach-like charm an elderly and deformed hag drew near. As she might be hostile to his cause, Kai Lung deemed it prudent to remain concealed; but in case she should prove to be an emissary from Hwa-mei seeking him, his purpose was to stand revealed. To combine these two attitudes until she should declare herself was by no means an easy task, but she looked neither near nor far in scrutiny until she stood, mumbling and infirm, beneath the shutter.

"It is well, minstrel," she called aloud. "She whom you await bid me greet you with a sign." At Kai Lung's feet there fell a crimson flower, growing on a thorny stem. "What word shall I in turn bear back? Speak freely, for her mind is as my open hand."

"Tell me rather," said Kai Lung, looking out, "how she fares and what averts her footsteps?"

"That will appear in due time," replied the aged one. "In the meanwhile I have her message to declare. Three times foiled in his malignant scheme the now obscene Ming-shu sets all the Axioms at naught. Distrusting you and those about your path, it is his sinister intention to call up for judgment Kai-moo, who lies within the women's cell beyond the Water Way."

"What is her crime and how will this avail him?"

"Charged with the murder of her man by means of the supple splinter her condemnation is assured. The penalty is piecemeal slicing, and in it are involved those of her direct line, in the humane effort to eradicate so treacherous a strain."

"That is but just," agreed Kai Lung.

"Truly. But on the slender ligament of a kindred name you will be joined with her in that end. Ming-shu will see to it that records of your kinship are not lacking. Being accused of no crime on your own behalf there will be nothing for you to appear against."

"It is written: 'Even leprosy may be cured, but the enmity of an official underling can never be dispelled,' and the malice of the persistent Ming-shu certainly points to the wisdom of the verse. Is the person of Kai-moo known to you, and where is the prison-house you speak of?"

To this the venerable creature replied that the cell in question was in a distant quarter of the city. Kai—moo, she continued, might be regarded as fashioned like herself, being deformed in shape and repellent in appearance. Furthermore, she was of deficient understanding, these things aiding Ming—shu's plan, as she would be difficult to reach and impossible to instruct when reached.

"The extremity is almost hopeless enough to be left to the ever—protecting spirits of one's all—powerful Ancestors," declared Kai Lung at length. "Did she from whom you come forecast any confidence?"

"She had some assurance in a certain plan, which it is my message to declare to you."

"Her wisdom is to be computed neither by a rule nor by a measure. Say on."

"The keeper of the women's prison—house lies within her hollowed hand, nor will silver be wanting to still any arising doubt. Wrapped in prison garb, and with her face disguised by art, she whose word I bear will come forth at the appointed call and, taking her place before Shan Tien, will play a fictitious part."

"Alas! dotard," interrupted Kai Lung impatiently, "it would be well if I spent my few remaining hours in kowtowing to the Powers whom I shall shortly meet. An aged and unsightly hag! Know you not, O venerable bat, that the smooth perfection of the one you serve would shine dazzling through a beaten mask of tempered steel? Her matchless hair, glossier than a starling's wing, floats like an autumn cloud. Her eyes strike fire from damp clay, or make the touch of velvet harsh and stubborn, according to her several moods. Peach—bloom held against her cheek withers incapably by comparison. Her feet, if indeed she has such commonplace attributes at all, are smaller—"

"Yet," interrupted the hag, in a changed and quite melodious voice, "if it is possible to delude the imagination of one whose longing eyes dwell so constantly on these threadbare charms, what then will be the position of the obtuse Ming—shu and the superficial Mandarin Shan Tien, burdened as they now are by outside cares?"

"There are times when the classical perfection of our graceful tongue is strangely inadequate to express emotion," confessed Kai Lung, colouring deeply, as Hwa—mei stood revealed before him. "It is truly said: 'The ingenuity of a guileless woman will undermine nine mountains.' You have cut off all the words of my misgivings."

"To that end have I wrought, for in this I also need your skill. Listen well and think deeply as I speak. Everywhere the outcome of the strife grows more uncertain day by day and no man really knows which side to favour yet. In this emergency each plays a double part. While visibly loyal to the Imperial cause, the Mandarin Shan Tien fans the whisper that in secret he upholds the rebellious banners. Ming—shu now openly avers that if this and that are thus and thus the rising has justice in its ranks, while at the same time he has it put abroad that this is but a cloak the better to serve the state. Thus every man maintains a double face in the hope that if the one side fails the other will preserve him, and as a band all pledge to save (or if need be to betray) each other."

"This is the more readily understood as it is the common case on every like occasion."

"Then doubtless there are instances waiting on your lips. Teach me such a story whereby the hope of those who are thus swayed may be engaged and leave the rest to my arranging hand."

On the following day at the appointed hour a bent and forbidding hag was brought before Shan Tien, and the nature of her offence proclaimed.

"It is possible to find an excuse for almost everything, regarding it from one angle or another," remarked the Mandarin impartially; "but the crime of destroying a husband—and by a means so unpleasantly insinuating—really seems to leave nothing to be said."

"Yet, imperishable, even a bad coin must have two sides," replied the hag. "That I should be guilty and yet innocent would be no more wonderful than the case of Weng Cho, who, when faced with the alternative of either defying the Avenging Societies or of opposing fixed authority found a way out of escaping both."

"That should be worth—that is to say, if you base your defence upon an existing case—"

84

"Providing the notorious thug Kai Lung is not thereby brought in," suggested the narrow—minded Ming—shu, who equally desired to learn the stratagem involved.

"Weng Cho was the only one concerned," replied the ancient obtusely—"he who escaped the consequences. Is it permitted to this one to make clear her plea?"

"If the fatigue is not more than your venerable personality can reasonably bear," replied Shan Tien courteously.

"To bear is the lot of every woman, be she young or old," replied the one before them. "I comply, omnipotence."

The Story of Weng Cho; or, the One Devoid of Name

There was peach—blossom in the orchards of Kien—fi, a blue sky above, and in the air much gladness; but in Wu Chi's yamen gloom hung like the herald of a thunderstorm. At one end of a table in the ceremonial hall sat Wu Chi, heaviness upon his brow, deceit in his eyes, and a sour enmity about the lines of his mouth; at the other end stood his son Weng, and between them, as it were, his whole life lay.

Wu Chi was an official of some consequence and had two wives, as became him. His union with the first had failed in its essential purpose; therefore he had taken another to carry on the direct line which alone could bring him contentment in this world and a reputable existence in the next. This degree of happiness was supplied by Weng's mother, yet she must ever remain but a "secondary wife," with no rights and a very insecure position. In the heart of the chief wife smouldered a most bitter hatred, but the hour of her ascendancy came, for after many years she also bore her lord a son. Thenceforward she was strong in her authority; but Weng's mother remained, for she was very beautiful, and despite all the arts of the other woman Wu Chi could not be prevailed upon to dismiss her. The easy solution of this difficulty was that she soon died—the "white powder death" was the shrewd comment of the inner chambers of Kien—fi.

Wu Chi put on no mourning, custom did not require it; and now that the woman had Passed Beyond he saw no necessity to honour her memory at the expense of his own domestic peace. His wife donned her gayest robes and made a feast. Weng alone stood apart, and in funereal sackcloth moved through the house like an accusing ghost. Each day his father met him with a frown, the woman whom alone he must regard as his mother with a mocking smile, but he passed them without any word of dutiful and submissive greeting. The period of all seemly mourning ended—it touched that allotted to a legal parent; still Weng cast himself down and made no pretence to hide his grief. His father's frown became a scowl, his mother's smile framed a biting word. A wise and venerable friend who loved the youth took him aside one day and with many sympathetic words counselled restraint.

"For," he said, "your conduct, though affectionate towards the dead, may be urged by the ill–disposed as disrespectful towards the living. If you have a deeper end in view, strive towards it by a less open path."

"You are subtle and esteemed in wisdom," replied Weng, "but neither of those virtues can restore a broken jar. The wayside fountain must one day dry up at its source, but until then not even a mountain placed upon its mouth can pen back its secret stores. So is it with unfeigned grief."

"The analogy may be exact," replied the aged friend, shaking his head, "but it is no less truly said: 'The wise tortoise keeps his pain inside.' Rest assured, on the disinterested advice of one who has no great experience of mountains and hidden springs, but a life–long knowledge of Wu Chi and of his amiable wife, that if you mourn too much you will have reason to mourn more."

His words were pointed to a sharp edge. At that moment Wu Chi was being confronted by his wife, who stood before him in his inner chamber. "Who am I?" she exclaimed vehemently, "that my authority should be denied before my very eyes? Am I indeed Che of the house of Meng, whose ancestors wore the Yellow Scabbard, or am I some nameless one? Or does my lord sleep, or has he fallen blind upon the side by which Weng approaches?"

"His heart is bad and his instincts perverted," replied Wu Chi dully. "He ignores the rites, custom, and the Emperor's example, and sets at defiance all the principles of domestic government. Do not fear that I shall not shortly call him to account with a very heavy call."

"Do so, my lord," said his wife darkly, "or many valiant champions of the House of Meng may press forward to make a cast of that same account. To those of our ancient line it would not seem a trivial thing that their daughter should share her rights with a purchased slave."

"Peace, cockatrice! the woman was well enough," exclaimed Wu Chi, with slow resentment. "But the matter of this obstinacy touches the dignity of my own authority, and before to-day has passed Weng shall bring up his footsteps suddenly before a solid wall."

Accordingly, when Weng returned at his usual hour he found his father awaiting him with curbed impatience. That Wu Chi should summon him into his presence in the great hall was of itself an omen that the matter was one of moment, but the profusion of lights before the Ancestral Tablets and the various symbols arranged upon the table showed that the occasion was to be regarded as one involving irrevocable issues.

"Weng Cho," said his father dispassionately, from his seat at the head of the table, "draw near, and first pledge the Ancient Ones whose spirits hover above their Tablets in a vessel of wine."

"I am drinking affliction and move under the compact of a solemn vow," replied Weng fixedly, "therefore I cannot do this; nor, as signs are given me to declare, will the forerunners of our line, who from their high places look down deep into the mind and measure the heart with an impartial rod, deem this an action of disrespect to their illustrious shades."

"It is well to be a sharer of their councils," said Wu Chi, with pointed insincerity. "But," he continued, in the same tone, "for whom can Weng Cho of the House of Wu mourn? His father is before him in his wonted health; in the inner chamber his mother plies an unfaltering needle; while from the Dragon Throne the supreme Emperor still rules the world. Haply, however, a thorn has pierced his little finger, or does he perchance bewail the loss of a favourite bird?"

"That thorn has sunk deeply into his existence, and the memory of that loss still dims his eyes with bitterness," replied Weng. "Bid the rain cease to fall when the clouds are heavy."

"The comparison is ill–chosen," cried Whu Chi harshly. "Rather should the allusion be to the evil tendency of a self–willed branch which, in spite of the continual watering of precept and affection, maintains its perverted course, and must henceforth either submit to be bound down into an appointed line, or be utterly cut off so that the tree may not suffer. Long and patiently have I marked your footsteps, Weng Cho, and they are devious. This is not a single offence, but it is no light one. Appointed by the Board of Ceremony, approved of by the Emperor, and observed in every loyal and high–minded subject are the details of the rites and formalities which alone serve to distinguish a people refined and humane from those who are rude and barbarous. By setting these observances at defiance you insult their framers, act traitorously towards your sovereign, and assail the foundations of your House; for your attitude is a direct reflection upon others; and if you render such a tribute to one who is incompetent to receive it, how will you maintain a seemly balance when a greater occasion arises?"

"When the earth that has nourished it grows cold the leaves of the branch fall—doubtless the edicts of the Board referred to having failed to reach their ears," replied Weng bitterly. "Revered father, is it not permitted that I should now depart? Behold I am stricken and out of place."

"You are evil and your heart is fat with presumptuous pride!" exclaimed Wu Chi, releasing the cords of his hatred and anger so that they leapt out from his throat like the sudden spring of a tiger from a cave. "Evil in birth, grown under an evil star and now come to a full maturity. Go you shall, Weng Cho, and that on a straight journey forthwith or else bend your knees with an acquiescent face." With these words he beat furiously on a gong, and summoning the entire household he commanded that before Weng should be placed a jar of wine and two glass vessels, and on the other side a staff and a pair of sandals. From an open shutter the face of the woman Che looked down in mocking triumph.

The alternatives thus presented were simple and irrevocable. On the one hand Weng must put from him all further grief, ignore his vows, and join in mirth and feast; on the other he must depart, never to return, and be deprived of every tie of kinship, relinquishing ancestry, possessions and name. It was a course severer than anything that Wu Chi had intended when he sent for his son, but resentment had distorted his eyesight. It was a greater test than Weng had anticipated, but his mind was clear, and his heart charged with fragrant memories of his loss. Deliberately but with silent dignity he poured the untasted wine upon the ground, drew his sword and touched the vessels lightly so that they broke, took from off his thumb the jade ring inscribed with the sign of the House of Wu, and putting on the sandals grasped the staff and prepared to leave the hall.

"Weng Cho, for the last time spoken of as of the House of Wu, now alienated from that noble line, and henceforth and for ever an outcast, you have made a choice and chosen as befits your rebellious life. Between us stretches a barrier wider and deeper than the Yellow Sea, and throughout all future time no sign shall pass from that distant shore to this. From every record of our race your name shall be cut out; no mention of it shall profane the Tablets, and both in this world and the next it shall be to us as though you have never been. As I break this bowl so are all ties broken, as I quench this candle so are all memories extinguished, and as, when you go, the space is filled with empty air, so shall it be."

"Ho, nameless stranger," laughed the woman from above, "here is food and drink to bear you on your way"; and from the grille she threw a withered fig and spat.

"The fruit is the cankered effort of a barren tree," cast back Weng over his shoulder. "Look to your own offspring, basilisk. It is given me to speak." Even as he spoke there was a great cry from the upper part of the house, the sound of many feet and much turmoil, but he went on his way without another word.

Thus it was that Weng Cho came to be cut off from the past. From his father's house he stepped out into the streets of Kien-fi a being without a name, destitute, and suffering the pangs of many keen emotions. Friends whom he encountered he saluted distantly, not desirous of sharing their affection until they should have learned his state; but there was one who stood in his mind as removed above the possibility of change, and to the summer-house of Tiao's home he therefore turned his steps.

Tiao was the daughter of a minor official, an unsuccessful man of no particular descent. He had many daughters, and had encouraged Weng's affection, with frequent professions that he regarded only the youth's virtuous life and discernment, and would otherwise have desired one not so highly placed. Tiao also had spoken of rice and contentment in a ruined pagoda. Yet as she listened to Weng's relation a new expression gradually revealed itself about her face, and when he had finished many paces lay between them.

"A breaker of sacred customs, a disobeyer of parents and an outcast! How do you disclose yourself!" she exclaimed wildly. "What vile thing has possessed you?"

"One hitherto which now rejects me," replied Weng slowly. "I had thought that here alone I might find a familiar greeting, but that also fails."

"What other seemly course presents itself?" demanded the maiden unsympathetically. "How degrading a position might easily become that of the one who linked her lot with yours if all fit and proper sequences are to be reversed! What menial one might supplant her not only in your affections but also in your Rites! He had defied the Principles!" she exclaimed, as her father entered from behind a screen.

"He has lost his inheritance," muttered the little old man, eyeing him contemptuously. "Weng Cho," he continued aloud, "you have played a double part and crossed our step with only half your heart. Now the past is past and the future an unwritten sheet."

"It shall be written in vermilion ink," replied Weng, regaining an impassive dignity; "and upon that darker half of my heart can now be traced two added names."

He had no aim now, but instinct drove him towards the mountains, the retreat of the lost and despairing. A three days' journey lay between. He went forward vacantly, without food and without rest. A falling leaf, as it is said, would have turned the balance of his destiny, and at the wayside village of Li—yong so it chanced. The noisome smell of burning thatch stung his face as he approached, and presently the object came into view. It was the bare cabin of a needy widow who had become involved in a lawsuit through the rapacity of a tax—gatherer. As she had the means neither to satisfy the tax nor to discharge the dues, the powerful Mandarin before whom she had been called ordered all her possessions to be seized, and that she should then be burned within her hut as a warning to others. This was the act of justice being carried out, and even as Weng heard the tale the Mandarin in question drew near, carried in his state chair to satisfy his eyes that his authority was scrupulously maintained. All those villagers who had not drawn off unseen at once fell upon their faces, so that Weng along remained standing, doubtful what course to take.

"Ill−nurtured dog!" exclaimed the Mandarin, stepping up to him, "prostrate yourself! Do you not know that I am of the Sapphire Button, and have fivescore bowmen at my yamen, ready to do my word?" And he struck the youth across the face with a jewelled rod.

"I have only one sword, but it is in my hand," cried Weng, reckless beneath the blow, and drawing it he at one stroke cut down the Mandarin before any could raise a hand. Then breaking in the door of the hovel he would have saved the woman, but it was too late, so he took the head and body and threw them into the fire, saying: "There, Mandarin, follow to secure justice. They shall not bear witness against you Up There in your absence."

The chair−carriers had fled in terror, but the villagers murmured against Weng as he passed through them. "It was a small thing that one house and one person should be burned; now, through this, the whole village will assuredly be consumed. He was a high official and visited justice impartially on us all. It was our affair, and you, who are a stranger, have done ill."

"I did you wrong, Mandarin," said Weng, resuming his journey; "you took me for one of them. I pass you the parting of the woman Che, burrowers in the cow−heap called Li−yong."

"Oi−ye!" exclaimed a voice behind, "but yonder earth−beetles haply have not been struck off the Tablets and found that a maiden with well−matched eyes can watch two ways at once, all of a morning: and thereby death through red spectacles is not that same death through blue spectacles. Things in their appointed places, noble companion."

"Greetings, wayfarer," said Weng, stopping. "The path narrows somewhat inconveniently hereabout. Take honourable precedence."

"The narrower the better to defend then," replied the stranger good−humouredly. "Whereto, also, two swords cut a larger slice than one. Without doubt fivescore valiant bowmen will soon be a−ranging when they hear that the enemy goes upon two feet, and then ill befall who knows not the passes." As he spoke an arrow, shot from a distance, flew above their heads.

"Why should you bear a part with me, and who are you who know these recent things?" demanded Weng doubtfully.

"I am one of many, we being a branch of that great spreading lotus the Triad, though called by the tillers here around the League of Tomb-Haunters, because we must be sought in secret places. The things I have spoken I know because we have many ears, and in our care a whisper passes from east to west and from north to south without a word being spilled."

"And the price of your sword is that I should join the confederacy?" asked Weng thoughtfully.

"I had set out to greet you before the estimable Mandarin who is now saluting his ancestors was so inopportune as to do so," replied the emissary. "Yet it is not to be denied that we offer an adequate protection among each other, while at the same time punishing guilt and administering a rigorous justice secretly."

"Lead me to your meeting-place, then," said Weng determinedly. "I have done with the outer things."

The guide pointed to a rock, shaped like a locusts head, which marked the highest point of the steep mountain before them. Soon the fertile lowlands ended and they passed beyond the limit of the inhabitable region. Still ascending they reached the Tiger's High Retreat, which defines the spot where even the animal kind turn back and where watercourses cease to flow. Beyond this the most meagre indication of vegetable sustenance came to an end, and thenceforward their passage was rendered more slow and laborious by frequent snow-storms, barriers of ice, and sudden tempests which strove to hurl them to destruction. Nevertheless, by about the hour of midnight they reached the rock shaped like a locust's head, which stood in the wildest and most inaccessible part of the mountain, and masked the entrance to a strongly-guarded cave. Here Weng suffered himself to be blindfolded, and being led forward he was taken into the innermost council. Closely questioned, he professed a spontaneous desire to be admitted into their band, to join in their dangers and share their honours; whereupon the oath was administered to him, the passwords and secret signs revealed, and he was bound from that time forth, under the bonds of a most painful death and torments in the afterworld, to submerge all passions save those for the benefit of their community, and to cherish no interests, wrongs or possessions that did not affect them all alike.

For the space of seven years Weng remained about the shadow of the mountain, carrying out, together with the other members of the band, the instructions which from time to time they received from the higher circles of the Society, as well as such acts of retributive justice as they themselves determined upon, and in this quiet and unostentatious manner maintaining peace and greatly purifying the entire province. In this passionless subservience to the principles of the Order none exceeded him; yet at no time have men been forbidden to burn joss-sticks to the spirit of the destinies, and who shall say?

At the end of seven years the first breath from out of the past reached Weng (or Thang, as he had announced himself to be when cast out nameless). One day he was summoned before the chief of their company and a mission laid upon him.

"You have proved yourself to be capable and sincere in the past, and this matter is one of delicacy," said the leader. "Furthermore, it is reported that you know something of the paths about Kien-fi?"

"There is not a forgotten turn within those paths by which I might stumble in the dark," replied Weng, striving to subdue his mind.

"See that out of so poignant a memory no more formidable barrier than a forgotten path arises," said the leader, observing him closely. "Know you, then a house bearing as a sign the figure of a golden ibis?"

"Truly; I have noted it," replied Weng, changing his position, so that he now leaned against a rock. "There dwelt an old man of some lower official rank, who had no son but many daughters."

"He has Passed, and one of those—Tiao by name," said the other, referring to a parchment—"has schemingly driven out the rest and held the patrimony. Crafty and ambitious, she has of late married a high official who has ever been hostile to ourselves. Out of a private enmity the woman seeks the lives of two who are under our most solemn protection, and now uses her husband's wealth and influence to that end.

It is on him that the blow must fall, for men kill only men, and she, having no son, will then be discredited and impotent."

"And concerning this official?" asked Weng.

"It has not been thought prudent to speak of him by name," replied the chief. "Stricken with a painful but not dangerous malady he has retired for a time to the healthier seclusion of his wife's house, and there he may be found. The woman you will know with certainty by a crescent scar—above the right eye."

"Beneath the eye," corrected Weng instantly.

"Assuredly, beneath: I misread the sign," said the head, appearing to consult the scroll. "Yet, out of a keen regard for your virtues, Thang, let me point a warning that it is antagonistic to our strict rule to remember these ancient scars too well. Further, in accordance with that same esteem, do not stoop too closely nor too long to identify the mark. By our pure and exacting standard no high attainment in the past can justify defection. The pains and penalties of failure you well know."

"I bow, chieftain," replied Weng acquiescently.

"It is well," said the chief. "Your strategy will be easy. To cure this lord's disorder a celebrated physician is even now travelling from the Capital towards Kien–fi. A day's journey from that place he will encounter obstacles and fall into the hands of those who will take away his robes and papers. About the same place you will meet one with a bowl on the roadside who will hail you, saying, 'Charity, out of your superfluity, noble mandarin coming from the north!' To him you will reply, 'Do mandarins garb thus and thus and go afoot? It is I who need a change of raiment and a chair; aye, by the token of the Locust's Head!' He will then lead you to a place where you will find all ready and a suitable chair with trusty bearers. The rest lies beneath your grinding heel. Prosperity!"

Weng prostrated himself and withdrew. The meeting by the wayside befell as he had received assurance—they who serve the Triad do not stumble—and at the appointed time he stood before Tiao's door and called for admission. He looked to the right and the left as one who examines a new prospect, and among the azalea flowers the

94

burnished roof of the summer–house glittered in the sun.

"Lucky omens attend your coming, benevolence," said the chief attendant obsequiously; "for since he sent for you an unpropitious planet has cast its influence upon our master, so that his power languishes."

"Its malignity must be controlled," said Weng, in a feigned voice, for he recognized the one before him. "Does any watch?"

"Not now," replied the attendant; "for he has slept since these two hours. Would your graciousness have speech with the one of the inner chamber?"

"In season perchance. First lead me to your lord's side and then see that we are undisturbed until I reappear. It may be expedient to invoke a powerful charm without delay."

In another minute Weng stood alone in the sick man's room, between them no more barrier than the silk–hung curtains of the couch. He slid down his right hand and drew a keen–edged knife; about his left he looped the even more fatal cord; then advancing with a noiseless step he pulled back the drapery and looked down. It was the moment for swift and silent action; nothing but hesitation and delay could imperil him, yet in that supreme moment he stepped back, released the curtain from his faltering grasp and, suffering the weapons to fall unheeded to the floor, covered his face with his hands, for lying before him he had seen the outstretched form, the hard contemptuous features, of his father.

Yet most solemnly alienated from him in every degree. By Wu Chi's own acts every tie of kinship had been effaced between them: the bowl had been broken, the taper blown out, empty air had filled his place. Wu Chi acknowledged no memory of a son; he could claim no reverence as a father. . . . Tiao's husband. . . . Then he was doubly childless. . . . The woman and her seed had withered, as he had prophesied.

On the one hand stood the Society, powerful enough to protect him in every extremity, yet holding failure as treason; most terrible and inexorable towards set disobedience. His body might find a painless escape from their earthly torments, but by his oaths his spirit lay in their keeping to be punished through all eternity.

That he was no longer Wu Chi's son, that he had no father—this conviction had been strong enough to rule him in every contingency of life save this. By every law of men and deities the ties between them had been dissolved, and they stood as a man and man; yet the salt can never be quite washed out of sea–water.

For a time which ceased to be hours or minutes, but seemed as a fragment broken off eternity, he stood, motionless but most deeply racked. With an effort he stooped to take the cord, and paused again; twice he would have seized the dagger, but doubt again possessed him. From a distant point of the house came the chant of a monk singing a prayer and beating upon a wooden drum. The rays of the sun falling upon the gilded roof in the garden again caught his eyes; nothing else stirred.

"These in their turn have settled great issues lightly," thought Weng bitterly. "Must I wait upon an omen?"

". . . submitting oneself to purifying scars," droned the voice far off; "propitiating if need be by even greater self–inflictions . . ."

"It suffices," said Weng dispassionately, and picking up the knife he turned to leave the room.

At the door he paused again, but not in an arising doubt. "I will leave a token for Tiao to wear as a jest," was the image that had sprung from his new abasement, and taking a sheet of parchment he quickly wrote thereon: "A wave has beat from that distant shore to this, and now sinks in the unknown depths."

Again he stepped noiselessly to the couch, drew the curtain and dropped the paper lightly on the form. As he did so his breath stopped; his fingers stiffened. Cautiously, on one knee, he listened intently, lightly touched the face; then recklessly taking a hand he raised the arm and suffered it to fall again. No power restrained it; no alertness of awakening life came into the dull face. Wu Chi had already Passed Beyond.

CHAPTER VII. Not Concerned with any Particular Attribute of Those who are Involved

UNENDURABLE was the intermingling of hopes and fears with which Kai Lung sought the shutter on the next occasion after the avowal of Hwa–mei's devoted strategy. While repeatedly assuring himself that it would have been better to submit to piecemeal slicing without a protesting word rather than that she should incur so formidable a risk, he was compelled as often to admit that when once her mind had formed its image no effort on his part would have held her back. Doubtless Hwa–mei readily grasped the emotion that would possess the one whose welfare was now her chief concern, for without waiting to gum her hair or to gild her lips she hastened to the spot beneath the wall at the earliest moment that Kai Lung could be there.

"Seven marble tombstones are lifted from off my chest!" exclaimed the story–teller when he could greet her. "How did your subterfuge proceed, and with what satisfaction was the history of Weng Cho received?"

"That," replied Hwa–mei modestly, "will provide the matter for an autumn tale, when seated around a pine–cone fire. In the meanwhile this protracted ordeal takes an ambiguous bend."

"To what further end does the malignity of the ill–made Ming–shu now shape itself? Should it entail a second peril to your head—"

"The one whom you so justly name fades for a moment out of our concern. Burdened with a secret mission he journeys to Hing–poo, nor does the Mandarin Shan Tien hold another court until the day of his return."

"That gives a breathing space of time to our ambitions?"

"So much is assured. Yet even in that a subtle danger lurks. Certain contingencies have become involved in the recital of your admittedly ingenious stories which the future unfolding of events may not always justify. For instance, the very speculative Shan Tien, casting his usual moderate limit to the skies, has accepted the Luminous Insect as a beckoning omen, and immersed himself deeply in the chances of every candidate bearing the name of Lao, Ting, Li, Tzu, Sung, Chu, Wang or Chin. Should all these fail incapably at the trials a very undignified period in the Mandarin's general manner of expressing himself may intervene."

"Had the time at the disposal of this person been sufficiently enlarged he would not have omitted the various maxims arising from the tale," admitted Kai Lung, with a shadow of remorse. "That suited to the need of a credulous and ill-balanced mind would doubtless be the proverb: 'He who believes in gambling will live to sell his sandals.' It is regrettable if the well-intending Mandarin took the wrong one. Fortunately another moon will fade before the results are known—"

"In the meantime," continued the maiden, indicating by a glance that what she had to relate was more essential to the requirements of the moment than anything he was saying: "Shan Tien is by no means indisposed towards your cause. Your unassuming attitude and deep research have enlarged your wisdom in his eyes. To-morrow he will send for you to lean upon your well-stored mind."

"Is the emergency one for which any special preparation is required?" questioned Kai Lung.

"That is the message of my warning. Of late a company of grateful friends has given the Mandarin an inlaid coffin to mark the sense of their indebtedness, the critical nature of the times rendering the gift peculiarly appropriate. Thus provided, Shan Tien has cast his eyes around to secure a burial robe worthy of the casket. The merchants proffer many, each endowed with all the qualities, but meanwhile doubts arise, and now Shan Tien would turn to you to learn what is the true and ancient essential of the garment, and wherein its virtue should reside."

"The call will not find me inept," replied Kai Lung. "The story of Wang Ho—"

"It is enough," exclaimed the maiden warningly. "The time for wandering together in the garden of the imagination has not yet arrived. Ming-shu's feet are on a journey, it is true, but his eyes are doubtless left behind. Until a like hour to-morrow gladdens our expectant gaze, farewell!"

On the following day, at about the stroke of the usual court, Li-loe approached Kai Lung with a grievous look.

"Alas, manlet," he exclaimed, "here is one direct from the presence of our high commander, requiring you against his thumb-signed bond. Go you must, and that alone, whether it be for elevation on a tree or on a couch. Out of an insatiable friendship this one would accompany you, were it possible, equally to hold your hand if you are to die or hold your cup if you are to feast. Yet touching that same cask of hidden wine there is still time—"

"Cease, mooncalf," replied Kai Lung reprovingly. "This is but an eddy on the surface of a moving stream. It comes, it goes; and the waters press on as before."

Then Kai Lung, neither bound nor wearing the wooden block, was led into the presence of Shan Tien, and allowed to seat himself upon the floor as though he plied his daily trade.

"Sooner or later it will certainly devolve upon this person to condemn you to a violent end," remarked the far—seeing Mandarin reassuringly. "In the ensuing interval, however, there is no need for either of us to dwell upon what must be regarded as an unpleasant necessity."

"Yet no crime has been committed, beneficence," Kai Lung ventured to protest; "nor in his attitude before your virtuous self has this one been guilty of any act of disrespect."

"You have shown your mind to be both wide and deep, and suitably lined," declared Shan Tien, dexterously avoiding the weightier part of the story—teller's plea. "A question now arises as to the efficacy of embroidered coffin cloths, and wherein their potent merit lies. Out of your well—stored memory declare your knowledge of this sort, conveying the solid information in your usual palatable way."

"I bow, High Excellence," replied Kai Lung. "This concerns the story of Wang Ho."

The Story of Wang Ho and the Burial Robe

There was a time when it did not occur to anyone in this pure and enlightened Empire to question the settled and existing order of affairs. It would have been well for the merchant Wang Ho had he lived in that happy era. But, indeed, it is now no unheard—of thing for an ordinary person to suggest that customs which have been established for centuries might with advantage be changed—a form of impiety which is in no degree removed from declaring oneself to be wiser or more profound than one's ancestors! Scarcely more seemly is this than irregularity in maintaining the Tablets or observing the Rites; and how narrow is the space dividing these delinquencies from the actual crimes of overturning images, counselling rebellion, joining in insurrection and resorting to indiscriminate piracy and bloodshed.

Certainly the merchant Wang Ho would be a thousand taels wealthier to–day if he had fully considered this in advance. Nor would Cheng Lin—but who attempts to eat an orange without first disposing of the peel, or what manner of a dwelling could be erected unless an adequate foundation be first provided?

Wang Ho, then, let it be stated, was one who had early in life amassed a considerable fortune by advising those whose intention it was to hazard their earnings in the State Lotteries as to the numbers that might be relied upon to be successful, or, if not actually successful, those at least that were not already predestined by malign influences to be absolutely incapable of success. These chances Wang Ho at first forecast by means of dreams, portents and other manifestations of an admittedly supernatural tendency, but as his name grew large and the number of his clients increased vastly, while his capacity for dreaming remained the same, he found it no less effective to close his eyes and to become inspired rapidly of numbers as they were thus revealed to him.

Occasionally Wang Ho was the recipient of an appropriate bag of money from one who had profited by his advice, but it was not his custom to rely upon this contingency as a source of income, nor did he in any eventuality return the amount which had been agreed upon (and invariably deposited with him in advance) as the reward of his inspired efforts. To those who sought him in a contentious spirit, inquiring why he did not find it more profitable to secure the prizes for himself, Wang Ho replied that his enterprise consisted in forecasting the winning numbers for State Lotteries and not in solving enigmas, writing deprecatory odes, composing epitaphs or conducting any of the other numerous occupations that could be mentioned. As this plausible evasion was accompanied by the courteous display of the many weapons which he always wore at different convenient points of his attire, the incident invariably ended in a manner satisfactory to Wang Ho.

Thus positioned Wang Ho prospered, and had in the course of years acquired a waist of honourable proportions, when the unrolling course of events influenced him to abandon his lucrative enterprise. It was not that he failed in any way to become as inspired as before; indeed, with increasing practice he attained a fluency that enabled him to outdistance every rival, so that on the occasion of one lottery he afterwards privately discovered that he had predicted the success of very possible combination of numbers, thus enabling those who followed his advice (as he did not fail to announce in inscriptions of vermilion assurance) to secure—among them—every variety of prize offered.

But, about this time, the chief wife of Wang Ho having been greeted with amiable condescension by the chief wife of a high official of the Province, and therefrom in an almost equal manner by the wives of even higher officials, the one in question began to abandon herself to a more rapidly outlined manner of existence than formerly, and to involve Wang Ho in a like attitude, so that presently this ill–considering merchant, who but a short time before would have unhesitatingly cast himself bodily to earth on the approach of a city magistrate, now acquired the habit of alluding to mandarins in casual conversation by names of affectionate abbreviation. Also, being advised of the expediency by a voice speaking in an undertone, he sought still further to extend beyond himself by suffering his nails to grow long and obliterating his name from the public announcements upon the city walls.

In spite of this ambitious sacrifice Wang Ho could not entirely shed from his habit a propensity to associate with those requiring advice on matters involving financial transactions. He could no longer conduct enterprises which entailed many clients and the lavish display of his name, but in the society of necessitous persons who were related to others of distinction he allowed it to be inferred that he was benevolently disposed and had a greater sufficiency of taels than he could otherwise make use of. He also involved himself, for the benefit of those whom he esteemed, in transactions connected with pieces of priceless jade, jars of wine of an especially fragrant character, and pictures of reputable antiquity. In the written manner of these transactions (for it is useless to conceal the fact that Wang Ho was incapable of tracing the characters of his own name) he employed a youth whom he never suffered to appear from beyond the background. Cheng Lin is thus brought naturally and unobtrusively into the narrative.

Had Cheng Lin come into the world when a favourably disposed band of demons was in the ascendant he would certainly have merited an earlier and more embellished appearance in this written chronicle. So far, however, nothing but omens of an ill—destined obscurity had beset his career. For many years two ambitions alone had contained his mind, both inextricably merged into one current and neither with any appearance of ever flowing into its desired end. The first was to pass the examination of the fourth degree of proficiency in the great literary competitions, and thereby qualify for a small official post where, in the course of a few years, he might reasonably hope to be forgotten in all beyond the detail of being allotted every third moon an unostentatious adequacy of taels. This distinction Cheng Lin felt to be well within his power of attainment could he but set aside three uninterrupted years for study, but to do this would necessitate the possession of something like a thousand taels of silver, and Lin might as well fix his eyes upon the great sky—lantern itself.

Dependent on this, but in no great degree removed from it, was the hope of being able to entwine into that future the actuality of Hsi Mean, a very desirable maiden whom it was Cheng Lin's practice to meet by chance on the river bank when his heavily—weighted duties for the day were over.

To those who will naturally ask why Cheng Lin, if really sincere in his determination, could not imperceptibly acquire even so large a sum as a thousand taels while in the house of the wealthy Wang Ho, immersed as the latter person was with the pursuit of the full face of high mandarins and further embarrassed by a profuse illiteracy, it should be sufficient to apply the warning: "Beware of helping yourself to corn from the manger of the blind mule."

In spite of his preoccupation Wang Ho never suffered his mind to wander when sums of money were concerned, and his inability to express himself by written signs only engendered in his alert brain an ever—present decision not to be entrapped by their use. Frequently, Cheng Lin found small sums of money lying in such a position as to induce the belief that they had been forgotten, but upon examining them closely he invariably found upon them marks by which they could be recognized if the necessity arose; he therefore had no hesitation in returning them to Wang Ho with a seemly reference to the extreme improbability of the merchant actually leaving money thus unguarded, and to the lack of respect which it showed to Cheng Lin himself to expect that a person of his integrity should be tempted by so insignificant an amount. Wang Ho always admitted the justice of the reproach, but he did not on any future occasion materially increase the sum in question, so that it is to be doubted if his heart was sincere.

It was on the evening of such an incident that Lin walked with Mean by the side of the lotus-burdened Hoang-keng expressing himself to the effect that instead of lilies her hair was worthy to be bound up with pearls of a like size, and that beneath her feet there should be spread a carpet not of verdure, but of the finest Chang-hi silk, embroidered with five-clawed dragons and other emblems of royal authority, nor was Mean in any way displeased by this indication of extravagant taste on her lover's part, though she replied:

"The only jewels that this person desires are the enduring glances of pure affection with which you, O my phoenix one, entwined the lilies about her hair, and the only carpet that she would crave would be the embroidered design created by the four feet of the two persons who are now conversing together for ever henceforth walking in uninterrupted harmony."

"Yet, alas!" exclaimed Lin, "that enchanting possibility seems to be more remotely positioned than ever. Again has the clay-souled Wang Ho, on the pretext that he can no longer make his in and out taels meet, sought to diminish the monthly inadequacy of cash with which he rewards this person's conscientious services."

"Undoubtedly that opaque-eyed merchant will shortly meet a revengeful fire-breathing vampire when walking alone on the edge of a narrow precipice," exclaimed Mean sympathetically. "Yet have you pressingly laid the facts before the spirits of your distinguished ancestors with a request for their direct intervention?"

"The expedient has not been neglected," replied Lin, "and appropriate sacrifices have accompanied the request. But even while in the form of an ordinary existence the venerable ones in question were becoming distant in their powers of hearing, and doubtless with increasing years the ineptitude has grown. It would almost seem that in the case of a person so obtuse as Wang Ho is, more direct means would have to be employed."

"It is well said," assented Mean, "that those who are unmoved by the thread of a vat of flaming sulphur in the Beyond, rend the air if they chance to step on a burning cinder here on earth."

"The suggestion is a timely one," replied Lin. "Wang Ho's weak spot lies between his hat and his sandals. Only of late, feeling the natural infirmities of time pressing about him, he has expended a thousand taels in the purchase of an elaborate burial robe, which he wears on every fit occasion, so that the necessity for its ultimate use may continue to be remote."

"A thousand taels!" repeated Mean. "With that sum you could—"

"Assuredly. The coincidence may embody something in the nature of an omen favourable to ourselves. At the moment, however, this person has not any clear-cut perception of how the benefit may be attained."

"The amount referred to has already passed into the hands of the merchant in burial robes?"

"Irrevocably. In the detail of the transference of actual sums of money Wang Ho walks hand in hand with himself from door to door. The pieces of silver are by this time beneath the floor of Shen Heng's inner chamber."

"Shen Heng?"

"The merchant in silk and costly fabrics, who lives beneath the sign of the Golden Abacus. It was from him—"

"Truly. It is for him that this person's sister Min works the finest embroideries. Doubtless this very robe—"

"It is of blue silk edged with sand pearls in a line of three depths. Felicitations on long life and a list of the most venerable persons of all times serve to remind the controlling deities to what length human endurance can proceed if suitably encouraged. These are designed in letters of threaded gold. Inferior spirits are equally invoked in characters of silver."

"The description is sharp-pointed. It is upon this robe that the one referred to has been ceaselessly engaged for several moons. On account of her narrow span of years, no less than her nimble-jointed dexterity, she is justly esteemed among those whose wares are guaranteed to be permeated with the spirit of rejuvenation."

"Thereby enabling the enterprising Shen Heng to impose a special detail into his account: 'For employing the services of one who will embroider into the fabric of the robe the vital principles of youth and long–life–to–come—an added fifty taels.' Did she of your house benefit to a proportionate extent?"

Mean indicated a contrary state of things by a graceful movement of her well–arranged eyebrows.

"Not only that," she added, "but the sordid–minded Shen Heng, on a variety of pretexts, has diminished the sum Min was to receive at the completion of the work, until that which should have required a full hand to grasp could be efficiently covered by two attenuated fingers. From this cause Min is vindictively inclined towards him and, steadfastly refusing to bend her feet in the direction of his workshop, she has, between one melancholy and another, involved herself in a dark distemper."

As Mean unfolded the position lying between her sister Min and the merchant Shen Heng, Lin grew thoughtful, and, although it was not his nature to express the changing degrees of emotion by varying the appearance of his face, he did not conceal from Mean that her words had fastened themselves upon his imagination.

"Let us rest here a while," he suggested presently. "That which you say, added to what I already know, may, under the guidance of a sincere mind, put a much more rainbow–like outlook on our combined future than hitherto appeared probable."

So they composed themselves about the bank of the river, while Lin questioned her more closely as to those things of which she had spoken. Finally, he laid certain injunctions upon her for her immediate guidance. Then, it being now the hour of middle light, they returned, Mean accompanying her voice to the melody of stringed wood, as she related songs of those who have passed through great endurances to a state of assured contentment. To Lin it seemed as though the city leapt forward to meet them, so narrow was the space of time involved in reaching it.

A few days later Wang Ho was engaged in the congenial occupation of marking a few pieces of brass cash before secreting them where Cheng Lin must inevitably displace them, when the person in question quietly stood before him. Thereupon Wang Ho returned the money to his inner sleeve, ineptly remarking that when the sun rose it was futile to raise a lantern to the sky to guide the stars.

"Rather is it said, 'From three things cross the road to avoid: a falling tree, your chief and second wives whispering in agreement, and a goat wearing a leopard's tail,'" replied Lin, thus rebuking Wang Ho, not only for his crafty intention, but also as to the obtuseness of the proverb he had quoted. "Nevertheless, O Wang Ho, I approach you on a matter of weighty consequence."

"To—morrow approaches," replied the merchant evasively. "If it concerns the detail of the reduction of your monthly adequacy, my word has become unbending iron."

"It is written: 'Cho Sing collected feathers to make a garment for his canary when it began to moult,'" replied Lin acquiescently. "The care of so insignificant a person as myself may safely be left to the Protecting Forces, esteemed. This matter touches your own condition."

"In that case you cannot be too specific." Wang Ho lowered himself into a reclining couch, thereby indicating that the subject was not one for hasty dismissal, at the same time motioning to Lin that he should sit upon the floor. "Doubtless you have some remunerative form of enterprise to suggest to me?"

"Can a palsied finger grasp a proffered coin? The matter strikes more deeply at your very existence, honoured chief."

"Alas!" exclaimed Wang Ho, unable to retain the usual colour of his appearance, "the attention of a devoted servant is somewhat like Tohen—hi Yang's spiked throne—it torments those whom it supports. However, the word has been spoken—let the sentence be filled in."

"The full roundness of your illustrious outline is as a display of coloured lights to gladden my commonplace vision," replied Lin submissively. "Admittedly of late, however, an element of dampness has interfered with the brilliance of the display."

"Speak clearly and regardless of polite evasion," commanded Wang Ho. "My internal organs have for some time suspected that hostile influences were at work. For how long have you noticed this, as it may be expressed, falling off?"

"My mind is as refined crystal before your compelling glance," admitted Lin. "Ever since it has been your custom to wear the funeral robe fashioned by Shen Heng has your noble shadow suffered erosion."

This answer, converging as it did upon the doubts that had already assailed the merchant's satisfaction, convinced him of Cheng Lin's discrimination, while it increased his own suspicion. He had for some little time found that after wearing the robe he invariably suffered pangs that could only be attributed to the influence of malign and obscure Beings. It is true that the occasions of his wearing the robe were elaborate and many-coursed feasts, when he and his guests had partaken lavishly of birds' nests, sharks' fins, sea snails and other viands of a rich and glutinous nature. But if he could not both wear the funeral robe and partake unstintingly of well-spiced food, the harmonious relation of things was imperilled; and, as it was since the introduction of the funeral robe into his habit that matters had assumed a more poignant phase, it was clear that the influence of the funeral robe was at the root of the trouble.

"Yet," protested Wang Ho, "the Mandarin Ling-ni boasts that he has already lengthened the span of his natural life several years by such an expedient, and my friend the high official T'cheng asserts that, while wearing a much less expensive robe than mine, he feels the essence of an increased vitality passing continuously into his being. Why, then, am I marked out for this infliction, Cheng Lin?"

"Revered," replied Lin, with engaging candour, "the inconveniences of living in a country so densely populated with demons, vampires, spirits, ghouls, dragons, omens, forces and influences, both good and bad, as our own unapproachably favoured Empire is, cannot be evaded from one end of life to the other. How much greater is the difficulty when the prescribed forms for baffling the ill-disposed among the unseen appear to have been wrongly angled by those framing the Rites!"

Wang Ho made a gesture of despair. It conveyed to Lin's mind the wise reminder of N'sy-hing: "When one is inquiring for a way to escape from an advancing tiger, flowers of speech assume the form of noisome bird—weed." He therefore continued:

"Hitherto it has been assumed that for a funeral robe to exercise its most beneficial force it should be the work of a maiden of immature years, the assumption being that, having a prolonged period of existence before her, the influence of longevity would pass through her fingers into the garment and in turn fortify the wearer."

"Assuredly," agreed Wang Ho anxiously. "Thus was the analogy outlined to me by one skilled in the devices, and the logic of it seems unassailable."

"Yet," objected Lin, with sympathetic concern in his voice, "how unfortunate must be the position of a person involved in a robe that has been embroidered by one who, instead of a long life, as been marked out by the Destinies for premature decay and an untimely death! For in that case the influence—"

"Such instances," interrupted Wang Ho, helping himself profusely to rice—spirit from a jar near at hand, "must providentially be of rare occurrence?"

"Esteemed head," replied Lin, helping Wang Ho to yet another superfluity of rice—spirit, "there are moments when it behoves each of us to maintain an unflaccid outline. Suspecting the true cause of your declining radiance, I have, at an involved expenditure of seven taels and three hand counts of brash cash, pursued this matter to its ultimate source. The robe in question owes its attainment to one Min, of the obscure house of Hsi, who recently ceased to have an existence while her years yet numbered short of a score. Not only was it the last work upon which she was engaged, but so closely were the two identified that her abrupt Passing Beyond must certainly exercise a corresponding effect upon any subsequent wearer."

"Alas!" exclaimed Wang Ho, feeling many of the symptoms of contagion already manifesting themselves about his body. "Was the infliction of a painless nature?"

"As to whether it was leprosy, the spotted plague, or acute demoniacal possession, the degraded Shen Heng maintains an unworthy silence. Indeed, at the mention of Hsi Min's name he wraps his garment about his head and rolls upon the floor—from which the worst may be inferred. They of Min's house, however, are less capable of guile, and for an adequate consideration, while not denying that Shen Heng has paid them to maintain a stealthy silence, they freely admit that the facts are as they have been stated."

"In that case, Shen Heng shall certainly return the thousand taels in exchange for this discreditable burial robe," exclaimed Wang Ho vindictively.

"Venerated personality," said Lin, with unabated loyalty, "the essential part of the development is to safeguard your own incomparable being against every danger. Shen Heng may be safely left to the avenging demons that are ever lying in wait for the contemptible."

"The first part of your remark is inspired," agreed Wang Ho, his incapable mind already beginning to assume a less funereal forecast. "Proceed, regardless of all obstacles."

"Consider the outcome of publicly compelling Shen Heng to undo the transaction, even if it could be legally achieved! Word of the calamity would pass on heated breath, each succeeding one becoming more heavily embroidered than the robe itself. The yamens and palaces of your distinguished friends would echo with the once honoured name of Wang Ho, now associated with every form of malignant distemper and impending fate. All would hasten to withdraw themselves from the contagion of your overhanging end."

"Am I, then," demanded Wang Ho, "to suffer the loss of a thousand taels and retain an inadequate and detestable burial robe that will continue to exercise its malign influence over my being?"

"By no means," replied Lin confidently. "But be warned by the precept: 'Do not burn down your house in order to inconvenience even your chief wife's mother.' Sooner or later a relation of Shen Heng's will turn his steps towards your inner office. You can then, without undue effort, impose on him the thousand taels that you have suffered loss from those of his house. In the meantime a device must be sought for exchanging your dangerous but imposing–looking robe for one of proved efficiency."

"It begins to assume a definite problem in this person's mind as to whether such a burial robe exists," declared Wang Ho stubbornly.

"Yet it cannot be denied, when a reliable system is adopted in the fabrication," protested Lin. "For a score and five years the one to whom this person owes his being has worn such a robe."

"To what age did your venerated father attain?" inquired the merchant, with courteous interest.

"Fourscore years and three parts of yet another score."

"And the robe in question eventually accompanied him when he Passed Beyond?"

"Doubtless it will. He is still wearing it," replied Lin, as one who speaks of casual occurrences.

"Is he, then, at so advanced an age, in the state of an ordinary existence?"

"Assuredly. Fortified by the virtue emanating from the garment referred to, it is his deliberate intention to continue here for yet another score of years at least."

"But if such robes are of so dubious a nature how can reliance be placed on any one?"

"Esteemed," replied Lin, "it is a matter that has long been suspected among the observant. Unfortunately, the Ruby Buttons of the past mistakenly formulated that the essence of continuous existence was imparted to a burial robe through the hands of a young maiden—hence so many deplorable experiences. The proper person to be so employed is undoubtedly one of ripe attainment, for only thereby can the claim to possess the vital principle be assured."

"Was the robe which has so effectively sustained your meritorious father thus constructed?" inquired Wang Ho, inviting Lin to recline himself upon a couch by a gesture as of one who discovers for the first time that an honoured guest has been overlooked.

"It is of ancient make, and thereby in the undiscriminating eye perhaps somewhat threadbare; but to the desert-traveller all wells are sparkling," replied Lin. "A venerable woman, inspired of certain magic wisdom, which she wove into the texture,

110

to the exclusion of the showier qualities, designed it at the age of threescore years and three short of another score. She was engaged upon its fabrication yet another seven, and finally Passed Upwards at an attainment of three hundred and thirty-three years, three moons, and three days, thus conforming to all the principles of allowed witchcraft."

"Cheng Lin," said Wang Ho amiably, pouring out for the one whom he addressed a full measure of rice-spirit, "the duty that an obedient son owes even to a grasping and self-indulgent father has in the past been pressed to a too-conspicuous front, at the expense of the harmonious relation that should exist between a comfortably-positioned servant and a generous and broad-minded master. Now in the matter of these two coffin cloths—"

"My ears are widely opened towards your auspicious words, benevolence," replied Lin.

"You, Cheng Lin, are still too young to be concerned with the question of Passing Beyond; your imperishable father is, one is compelled to say, already old enough to go. As regards both persons, therefore, the assumed virtue of one burial robe above another should be merely a matter of speculative interest. Now if some arrangement should be suggested, not unprofitable to yourself, by which one robe might be imperceptibly substituted for another—and, after all, one burial robe is very like another—"

"The prospect of deceiving a trustful and venerated sire is so ignoble that scarcely any material gain would be a fitting compensation—were it not for the fact that an impending loss of vision renders the deception somewhat easy to accomplish. Proceed, therefore, munificence, towards a precise statement of your open-handed prodigality.

*

Indescribable was the bitterness of Shen Heng's throat when Cheng Lin unfolded his burden and revealed the Wang Ho thousand-tael burial robe, with an unassuming request for the return of the purchase money, either in gold or honourable paper, as the article was found unsuitable. Shen Heng shook the rafters of the Golden Abacus with indignation, and called upon his domestic demons, the spirits of eleven generations of embroidering ancestors, and the illuminated tablets containing the High Code and

111

Authority of the Distinguished Brotherhood of Coffin Cloth and Burial Robe Makers in protest against so barbarous an innovation.

Bowing repeatedly and modestly expressing himself to the effect that it was incredible that he was not justly struck dead before the sublime spectacle of Shen Heng's virtuous indignation, Cheng Lin carefully produced the written lines of the agreement, gently directing the Distinguished Brother's fire–kindling eyes to an indicated detail. It was a provision that the robe should be returned and the purchase money restored if the garment was not all that was therein stipulated: with his invariable painstaking loyalty Lin had insisted upon this safeguard when he drew up the form, although, probably from a disinclination to extol his own services, he had omitted mentioning the fact to Wang Ho in their recent conversation.

With deprecating firmness Lin directed Shen Heng's reluctant eyes to another line—the unfortunate exaction of fifty taels in return for the guarantee that the robe should be permeated with the spirit of rejuvenation. As the undoubted embroiderer of the robe—one Min of the family of Hsi—had admittedly Passed Beyond almost with the last stitch, it was evident that she could only have conveyed by her touch an entirely contrary emanation. If, as Shen Heng never ceased to declare, Min was still somewhere alive, let her be produced and a fitting token of reconciliation would be forthcoming; otherwise, although with the acutest reluctance, it would be necessary to carry the claim to the court of the chief District Mandarin, and (Cheng Lin trembled at the sacrilegious thought) it would be impossible to conceal the fact that Shen Heng employed persons of inauspicious omen, and the high repute of coffin cloths from the Golden Abacus would be lost. The hint arrested Shen Heng's fingers in the act of tearing out a handful of his beautiful pigtail. For the first time he noticed, with intense self–reproach, that Lin was not reclining on a couch.

The amiable discussion that followed, conducted with discriminating dignity by Shen Heng and conscientious humility on the part of Cheng Lin, extended from one gong–stroke before noon until close upon the time for the evening rice. The details arrived at were that Shen Heng should deliver to Lin eight–hundred and seventy–five taels against the return of the robe. He would also press upon that person a silk purse with an onyx clasp, containing twenty–five taels, as a deliberate mark of his individual appreciation and quite apart from anything to do with the transaction on hand. All suggestions of anything other than the strictest high–mindedness were withdrawn from both sides. In order that the day should not be wholly destitute of sunshine at the Golden Abacus, Lin declared his intention of purchasing, at a price not exceeding three taels and a half, the oldest and most unattractive burial robe that the stock contained. So moved was Shen Heng by this delicate consideration that he refused to accept more than two taels and three–quarters. Moreover, he added for Lin's acceptance a small jar of crystallized limpets.

To those short–sighted ones who profess to discover in the conduct of Cheng Lin (now an official of the seventeenth grade and drawing his quarterly sufficiency of taels in a distant province) something not absolutely honourably arranged, it is only necessary to display the ultimate end as it affected those persons in any way connected.

Wang Ho thus obtained a burial robe in which he was able to repose absolute confidence. Doubtless it would have sustained him to an advanced age had he not committed self–ending, in the ordinary way of business, a few years later.

Shen Heng soon disposed of the returned garment for two thousand taels to a person who had become prematurely wealthy owing to the distressed state of the Empire. In addition he had sold, for more than two taels, a robe which he had no real expectation of ever selling at all.

Min, made welcome at the house of Mean and Lin, removed with them to that distant province. There she found that the remuneration for burial robe embroidery was greater than she had ever obtained before. With the money thus amassed she was able to marry an official of noble rank.

The father of Cheng Lin had passed into the Upper Air many years before the incidents with which this related narrative concerns itself. He is thus in no way affected. But Lin did not neglect, in the time of his prosperity, to transmit to him frequent sacrifices of seasonable delicacies suited to his condition.

CHAPTER VIII. The Timely Disputation among Those of an Inner Chamber of Yu–Ping

FOR the space of three days Ming—shu remained absent from Yu—pin, and the affections of Kai Lung and Hwa—mei prospered. On the evening of the third day the maiden stood beneath the shutter with a more definite look, and Kai Lung understood that a further period of unworthy trial was now at hand.

"Behold!" she explained, "at dawn the corrupt Ming—shu will pass within our gates again, nor is it prudent to assume that his enmity has lessened."

"On the contrary," replied Kai Lung, "like that unnatural reptile that lives on air, his malice will have grown upon the voidness of its cause. As the wise Ling—kwang remarks: 'He who plants a vineyard with one hand—'"

"Assuredly, beloved," interposed Hwa—mei dexterously. "But our immediate need is less to describe Ming—shu's hate in terms of classical analogy than to find a potent means of baffling its vevom."

"You are all—wise as usual," confessed Kai Lung, with due humility. "I will restrain my much too verbose tongue."

"The invading Banners from the north have for the moment failed and those who drew swords in their cause are flying to the hills. In Yu—ping, therefore, loyalty wears a fully round face and about the yamen of Shan Tien men speak almost in set terms. While these conditions prevail, justice will continue to be administered precisely as before. We have thus nothing to hope in that direction."

"Yet in the ideal state of purity aimed at by the illustrious founders of our race—" began Kai Lung, and ceased abruptly, remembering.

"As it is, we are in the state of Tsin in the fourteenth of the heaven—sent Ching," retorted Hwa—mei capably. "The insatiable Ming—shu will continue to seek your life, calling to his aid every degraded subterfuge. When the nature of these can be learned somewhat in advance, as the means within my power have hitherto enabled us to do, a trusty shield is raised in your defence."

Kai Lung would have spoken of the length and the breadth of his indebtedness, but she who stood below did not encourage this.

"Ming-shu's absence makes this plan fruitless here to-day, and as a consequence he may suddenly disclose a subtle snare to which your feet must bend. In this emergency my strategy has been towards safeguarding your irreplaceable life to-morrow at all hazard. Should this avail, Ming-shu's later schemes will present no baffling veil."

"Your virtuous little finger is as strong as Ming-shu's offensive thumb," remarked Kai Lung. "This person has no fear."

"Doubtless," acquiesced Hwa-mei. "But she who has spun the thread knows the weakness of the net. Heed well to the end that no ineptness may arise. Shan Tien of late extols your art, claiming that in every circumstance you have a story fitted to the need."

"He measures with a golden rule," agreed Kai Lung. "Left to himself, Shan Tien is a just, if superficial, judge."

The knowledge of this boast, Hwa-mei continued to relate, had spread to the inner chambers of the yamen, where the lesser ones vied with each other in proclaiming the merit of the captive minstrel. Amid this eulogy Hwa-mei moved craftily and played an insidious part, until she who was their appointed head was committed to the claim. Then the maiden raised a contentious voice.

"Our lord's trout were ever salmon," she declared, "and lo! here is another great and weighty fish! Assuredly no living man is thus and thus; or are the T'ang epicists returned to earth? Truly our noble one is easily pleased—in many ways!" With these well-fitted words she fixed her eyes upon the countenance of Shan Tien's chief wife and waited.

"The sun shines through his words and the moon adorns his utterances," replied the chief wife, with unswerving loyalty, though she added, no less suitably: "That one should please him easily and another therein fail, despite her ceaseless efforts, is as the Destinies provide."

"You are all-seeing," admitted Hwa-mei generously; "nor is a locked door any obstacle to your discovering eye. Let this arisement be submitted to a facile test. Dependent from my ill-formed ears are rings of priceless jade that have ever tinged your thoughts, while about your shapely neck is a crystal charm, to which an unclouded background would doubtless give some lustre. I will set aside the rings and thou shalt set aside the charm. Then, at a chosen time, this vaunted one shall attend before us here, and I having disclosed the substance of a theme, he shall make good the claim. If he so does, capably and without delay, thou shalt possess the jewels. But if, in the judgment of these around, he shall fail therein, then are both jewels mine. Is it so agreed?"

"It is agreed!" cried those who were the least concerned, seeing some entertainment to themselves. "Shall the trial take place at once?"

"Not so," replied Hwa—mei. "A sufficient space must be allowed for this one wherein to select the matter of the test. To—morrow let it be, before the hour of evening rice. And thou?"

"Inasmuch as it will enlarge the prescience of our lord in minds that are light and vaporous, I also do consent," replied the chief wife. "Yet must he too be of our company, to be witness of the upholding of his word and, if need be, to cast a decisive voice."

"Thus," continued Hwa—mei, as she narrated these events, "Shan Tien is committed to the trial and thereby he must preserve you until that hour. Tell me now the answer to the test, that I may frame the question to agree."

Kai Lung thought a while, then said:

"There is the story of Chang Tao. It concerns one who, bidden to do an impossible task, succeeded though he failed, and shows how two identically similar beings may be essentially diverse. To this should be subjoined the apophthegm that that which we are eager to obtain may be that which we have striven to avoid."

"It suffices," agreed Hwa—mei. "Bear well your part."

"Still," suggested Kai Lung, hoping to detain her retiring footsteps for yet another span, "were it not better that I should fall short at the test, thus to enlarge your word before your fellows?"

"And in so doing demean yourself, darken the face of Shan Tien's present regard, and alienate all those who stand around! O most obtuse Kai Lung!"

"I will then bare my throat," confessed Kai Lung. "The barbed thought had assailed my mind that perchance the rings of precious jade lay coiled around your heart. Thus and thus I spoke."

"Thus also will I speak," replied Hwa—mei, and her uplifted eyes held Kai Lung by the inner fibre of his being. "Did I value them as I do, and were they a single hair of my superfluous head, the whole head were freely offered to a like result."

With these noticeable words, which plainly testified the strength of her emotion, the maiden turned and hastened on her way, leaving Kai Lung gazing from the shutter in a very complicated state of disquietude.

The Story of Chang Tao, Melodious Vision and the Dragon

After Chang Tao had reached the age of manhood his grandfather took him apart one day and spoke of a certain matter, speaking as a philosopher whose mind has at length overflowed.

"Behold!" he said, when they were at a discreet distance aside, "your years are now thus and thus, but there are still empty chairs where there should be occupied cradles in your inner chamber, and the only upraised voice heard in this spacious residence is that of your esteemed father repeating the Analects. The prolific portion of the tree of our illustrious House consists of its roots; its existence onwards narrows down to a single branch which as yet has put forth no blossoms."

"The loftiest tower rises from the ground," remarked Chang Tao evasively, not wishing to implicate himself on either side as yet.

"Doubtless; and as an obedient son it is commendable that you should close your ears, but as a discriminating father there is no reason by I should not open my mouth," continued the venerable Chang in a voice from which every sympathetic modulation was withdrawn. "It is admittedly a meritorious resolve to devote one's existence to explaining the meaning of a single obscure passage of one of the Odes, but if the detachment necessary to the achievement results in a hitherto carefully-preserved line coming to an incapable end, it would have been more satisfactory to the dependent shades of our revered ancestors that the one in question should have collected street garbage rather than literary instances, or turned somersaults in place of the pages of the Classics, had he but given his first care to providing you with a wife and thereby safeguarding our unbroken continuity."

"My father is all-wise," ventured Chang Tao dutifully, but observing the nature of the other's expression he hastened to add considerately, "but my father's father is even wiser."

"Inevitably," assented the one referred to; "not merely because he is the more mature by a generation, but also in that he is thereby nearer to the inspired ancients in whom the Cardinal Principles reside."

"Yet, assuredly, there must be occasional exceptions to this rule of progressive deterioration?" suggested Chang Tao, feeling that the process was not without a definite application to himself.

"Not in our pure and orthodox line," replied the other person firmly. "To suggest otherwise is to admit the possibility of a son being the superior of his own father, and to what a discordant state of things would that contention lead! However immaturely you may think at present, you will see the position at its true angle when you have sons of your own."

"The contingency is not an overhanging one," said Chang Tao. "On the last occasion when I reminded my venerated father of my age and unmarried state, he remarked that, whether he looked backwards or forwards, extinction seemed to be the kindest destiny to which our House could be subjected."

"Originality, carried to the length of eccentricity, is a censurable accomplishment in one of official rank," remarked the elder Chang coldly. "Plainly it is time that I should lengthen the authority of my own arm very perceptibly. If a father is so neglectful of his duty, it is fitting that a grandfather should supply his place. This person will himself procure a bride for you without delay."

"The function might perhaps seem an unusual one," suggested Chang Tao, who secretly feared the outcome of an enterprise conducted under these auspices.

"So, admittedly, are the circumstances. What suitable maiden suggests herself to your doubtless better–informed mind? Is there one of the house of Tung?"

"There are eleven," replied Chang Tao, with a gesture of despair, "all reputed to be untiring with their needle, skilled in the frugal manipulation of cold rice, devout, discreet in the lines of their attire, and so sombre of feature as to be collectively known to the available manhood of the city as the Terror that Lurks for the Unwary. Suffer not your discriminating footsteps to pause before that house, O father of my father! Now had you spoken of Golden Eyebrows, daughter of Kuo Wang—"

"It would be as well to open a paper umbrella in a thunderstorm as to seek profit from an alliance with Kuo Wang. Crafty and ambitious, he is already deep in questionable ventures, and high as he carries his head at present, there will assuredly come a day when Kuo Wang will appear in public with his feet held even higher than his crown."

"The rod!" exclaimed Chang Tao in astonishment. "Can it really be that one who is so invariably polite to me is not in every way immaculate?"

"Either bamboo will greet his feet or hemp adorn his neck," persisted the other, with a significant movement of his hands in the proximity of his throat. "Walk backwards in the direction of that house, son of my son. Is there not one Ning of the worthy line of Lo, dwelling beneath the emblem of a Sprouting Aloe?"

"Truly," agreed the youth, "but at an early age she came under the malign influence of a spectral vampire, and in order to deceive the creature she was adopted to the navigable portion of the river here, and being announced as having Passed Above was henceforth regarded as a red mullet."

"Yet in what detail does that deter you?" inquired Chang, for the nature of his grandson's expression betrayed an acute absence of enthusiasm towards the maiden thus concerned.

"Perchance the vampire was not deceived after all. In any case this person dislikes red mullet," replied the youth indifferently.

The venerable shook his head reprovingly.

"It is imprudent to be fanciful in matters of business," he remarked. "Lo Chiu, her father, is certainly the possessor of many bars of silver, and, as it is truly written: 'With wealth one may command demons; without it one cannot summon even a slave.'"

"It is also said: 'When the tree is full the doubtful fruit remains upon the branch,'" retorted Chang Tao. "Are not maidens in this city as the sand upon a broad seashore? If one opens and closes one's hands suddenly out in the Ways on a dark night, the chances are that three or four will be grasped. A stone cast at a venture—"

"Peace!" interrupted the elder. "Witless spoke thus even in the days of this person's remote youth—only the virtuous did not then open and close their hands suddenly in the Ways on dark nights. Is aught reported of the inner affairs of Shen Yi, a rich philosopher who dwells somewhat remotely on the Stone Path, out beyond the Seven Terraced Bridge?"

Chang Tao looked up with a sharply awakening interest.

"It is well not to forget that one," he replied. "He is spoken of as courteous but reserved, in that he drinks tea with few though his position is assured. Is not his house that which fronts on a summer–seat domed with red copper?"

"It is the same," agreed the other. "Speak on."

"What I recall is meagre and destitute of point. Nevertheless, it so chanced that some time ago this person was proceeding along the further Stone Path when an aged female mendicant, seated by the wayside, besought his charity. Struck by her destitute appearance he bestowed upon her a few unserviceable broken cash, such as one retains for the indigent, together with an appropriate blessing, when the hag changed abruptly into the appearance of a young and alluring maiden, who smilingly extended to this one her staff, which had meanwhile become a graceful branch of flowering lotus. The manifestation was not sustained, however, for as he who is relating the incident would have received the proffered flower he found that his hand was closing on the neck of an expectant serpent, which held in its mouth an agate charm. The damsel had likewise altered, imperceptibly merging into the form of an overhanging fig–tree, among whose roots the serpent twined itself. When this person would have eaten one of the ripe fruit of the tree he found that the skin was filled with a bitter dust, whereupon he withdrew, convinced that no ultimate profit was likely to result from the encounter. His departure was accompanied by the sound of laughter, mocking yet more melodious than a carillon of silver gongs hung in a porcelain tower, which seemed to proceed from the summer–seat domed with red copper."

"Some omen doubtless lay within the meeting," said the elder Chang. "Had you but revealed the happening fully on your return, capable geomancers might have been consulted. In this matter you have fallen short."

"It is admittedly easier to rule a kingdom than to control one's thoughts," confessed Chang Tao frankly. "A great storm of wind met this person on his way back, and when he had passed through it, all recollection of the incident had, for the time, been magically blown from his mind."

"It is now too late to question the augurs. But in the face of so involved a portent it would be well to avert all thought from Melodious Vision, wealthy Shen Yi's incredibly attractive daughter."

"It is unwise to be captious in affairs of negotiation," remarked the young man thoughtfully. "Is the smile of the one referred to such that at the vision of it the internal organs of an ordinary person begin to clash together, beyond the power of all control?"

"Not in the case of the one who is speaking," replied the grandfather of Chang Tao, "but a very illustrious poet, whom Shen Yi charitably employed about his pig–yard, certainly described it as a ripple on the surface of a dark lake of wine, when the moon reveals the hidden pearls beneath; and after secretly observing the unstudied grace of her movements, the most celebrated picture–maker of the province burned the implements of his craft, and began life anew as a trainer of performing elephants. But when maidens are as numerous as the grains of sand—"

"Esteemed," interposed Chang Tao, with smooth determination, "wisdom lurks in the saying: 'He who considers everything decides nothing.' Already this person has spent an unprofitable score of years through having no choice in the matter; at this rate he will spend yet another score through having too much. Your timely word shall be his beacon. Neither the disadvantage of Shen Yi's oppressive wealth nor the inconvenience of Melodious Vision's excessive beauty shall deter him from striving to fulfil your delicately expressed wish."

"Yet," objected the elder Chang, by no means gladdened at having the decision thus abruptly lifted from his mouth, "so far, only a partially formed project—"

"To a thoroughly dutiful grandson half a word from your benevolent lips carries further than a full-throated command does from a less revered authority."

"Perchance. This person's feet, however, are not liable to a similar acceleration, and a period of adequate consideration must intervene before they are definitely moving in the direction of Shen Yi's mansion. 'Where the road bends abruptly take short steps,' Chang Tao."

"The necessity will be lifted from your venerable shoulders, revered," replied Chang Tao firmly. "Fortified by your approving choice, this person will himself confront Shen Yi's doubtful countenance, and that same bend in the road will be taken at a very sharp angle and upon a single foot."

"In person! It is opposed to the Usages!" exclaimed the venerable; and at the contemplation of so undignified a course his voice prudently withdrew itself, though his mouth continued to open and close for a further period.

"'As the mountains rise, so the river winds,'" replied Chang Tao, and with unquenchable deference he added respectfully as he took his leave, "Fear not, eminence; you will yet remain to see five generations of stalwart he-children, all pressing forward to worship your imperishable memory."

In such a manner Chang Tao set forth to defy the Usages and—if perchance it might be—to speak to Shen Yi face to face of Melodious Vision. Yet in this it may be that the youth was not so much hopeful of success by his own efforts as that he was certain of failure by the elder Chang's. And in the latter case the person in question might then irrevocably contract him to a maiden of the house of Tung, or to another equally forbidding. Not inaptly is it written: "To escape from fire men will plunge into boiling water."

Nevertheless, along the Stone Path many doubts and disturbances arose within Chang Tao's mind. It was not in this manner that men of weight and dignity sought wives. Even if Shen Yi graciously overlooked the absence of polite formality, would not the romantic imagination of Melodious Vision be distressed when she learned that she had been approached with so indelicate an absence of ceremony? "Here, again," said Chang Tao's self-reproach accusingly, "you have, as usual, gone on in advance of both your feet and of your head. 'It is one thing to ignore the Rites: it is quite another to expect the gods to ignore the Penalties.' Assuredly you will suffer for it."

It was at this point that Chang Tao was approached by one who had noted his coming from afar, and had awaited him, for passers-by were sparse and remote.

"Prosperity attend your opportune footsteps," said the stranger respectfully. "A misbegotten goat-track enticed this person from his appointed line by the elusive semblance of an avoided li. Is there, within your enlightened knowledge, the house of one Shen Yi, who makes a feast to-day, positioned about this inauspicious region? It is further described as fronting on a summer-seat domed with red copper."

"There is such a house as you describe, at no great distance to the west," replied Chang Tao. "But that he marks the day with music had not reached these superficial ears."

"It is but among those of his inner chamber, this being the name-day of one whom he would honour in a refined and at the same time inexpensive manner. To that end am I bidden."

"Of what does your incomparable exhibition consist?" inquired Chang Tao.

"Of a variety of quite commonplace efforts. It is entitled 'Half-a-gong-stroke among the No-realities; or Gravity-removing devoid of Inelegance.' Thus, borrowing the neck-scarf of the most dignified-looking among the lesser ones assembled I will at once discover among its folds the unsuspected presence of a family of tortoises; from all parts of the person of the roundest-bodied mandarin available I will control the appearance of an inexhaustible stream of copper cash, and beneath the scrutinizing eyes of all a bunch of paper chrysanthemums will change into the similitude of a crystal bowl in whose clear depth a company of gold and silver carp glide from side to side."

"These things are well enough for the immature, and the sight of an unnaturally stout official having an interminable succession of white rabbits produced from the various recesses of his waistcloth admittedly melts the austerity of the superficial of both sexes. But can you, beneath the undeceptive light of day, turn a sere and unattractive hag into the substantial image of a young and beguiling maiden, and by a further complexity into a fruitful fig-tree; or induce a serpent so far to forsake its natural instincts as to poise on the extremity of its tail and hold a charm within its mouth?"

"None of these things lies within my admitted powers," confessed the stranger. "To what end does your gracious inquiry tend?"

"It is in the nature of a warning, for within the shadow of the house you seek manifestations such as I describe pass almost without remark. Indeed it is not unlikely that while in the act of displaying your engaging but simple skill you may find yourself transformed into a chameleon or saddled with the necessity of finishing your gravity-removing entertainment under the outward form of a Manchurian ape."

"Alas!" exclaimed the other. "The eleventh of the moon was ever this person's unlucky day, and he would have done well to be warned by a dream in which he saw an unsuspecting kid walk into the mouth of a voracious tiger."

"Undoubtedly the tiger was an allusion to the dangers awaiting you, but it is not yet too late for you to prove that you are no kid," counselled Chang Tao. "Take this piece of silver so that the enterprise of the day may not have been unfruitful and depart with all speed on a homeward path. He who speaks is going westward, and at the lattice of Shen Yi he will not fail to leave a sufficient excuse for your no-appearance."

"Your voice has the compelling ring of authority, beneficence," replied the stranger gratefully. "The obscure name of the one who prostrates himself is Wo, that of his degraded father being Weh. For this service he binds his ghost to attend your ghost

124

through three cycles of time in the After."

"It is remitted," said Chang Tao generously, as he resumed his way. "May the path be flattened before your weary feet."

Thus, unsought as it were, there was placed within Chang Tao's grasp a staff that might haply bear his weight into the very presence of Melodious Vision herself. The exact strategy of the undertaking did not clearly yet reveal itself, but "When fully ripe the fruit falls of its own accord," and Chang Tao was content to leave such detail to the guiding spirits of his destinies. As he approached the outer door he sang cheerful ballads of heroic doings, partly because he was glad, but also to reassure himself.

"One whom he expects awaits," he announced to the keeper of the gate. "The name of Wo, the son of Weh, should suffice."

"It does not," replied the keeper, swinging his roomy sleeve specifically. "So far it has an empty, short—stopping sound. It lacks sparkle; it has no metallic ring. . . . He sleeps."

"Doubtless the sound of these may awaken him," said Chang Tao, shaking out a score of cash.

"Pass in munificence. Already his expectant eyes rebuke the unopen door."

Although he had been in a measure prepared by Wo, Chang Tao was surprised to find that three persons alone occupied the chamber to which he was conducted. Two of these were Shen Yi and a trusted slave; at the sight of the third Chang Tao's face grew very red and the deficiencies of his various attributes began to fill his mind with dark forebodings, for this was Melodious Vision and no man could look upon her without her splendour engulfing his imagination. No record of her pearly beauty is preserved beyond a scattered phrase or two; for the poets and minstrels of the age all burned what they had written, in despair at the inadequacy of words. Yet it remains that whatever a man looked for, that he found, and the measure of his requirement was not stinted.

"Greeting," said Shen Yi, with easy—going courtesy. He was a more meagre man than Chang Tao had expected, his face not subtle, and his manner restrained rather than oppressive. "You have come on a long and winding path; have you taken your rice?"

"Nothing remains lacking," replied Chang Tao, his eyes again elsewhere. "Command your slave, Excellence."

"In what particular direction do your agreeable powers of leisure–beguiling extend?"

So far Chang Tao had left the full consideration of this inevitable detail to the inspiration of the moment, but when the moment came the prompting spirits did not disclose themselves. His hesitation became more elaborate under the expression of gathering enlightenment that began to appear in Melodious Vision's eyes.

"An indifferent store of badly sung ballads," he was constrained to reply at length, "and—perchance—a threadbare assortment of involved questions and replies."

"Was it your harmonious voice that we were privileged to hear raised beneath our ill–fitting window a brief space ago?" inquired Shen Yi.

"Admittedly at the sight of this noble palace I was impelled to put my presumptuous gladness into song."

"Then let it fain be the other thing," interposed the maiden, with decision. "Your gladness came to a sad end, minstrel."

"Involved questions are by no means void of divertisement," remarked Shen Yi, with conciliatory mildness in his voice. "There was one, turning on the contradictory nature of a door which under favourable conditions was indistinguishable from an earthenware vessel, that seldom failed to baffle the unalert in the days before the binding of this person's hair."

"That was the one which it had been my feeble intention to propound," confessed Chang Tao.

"Doubtless there are many others equally enticing," suggested Shen Yi helpfully.

"Alas," admitted Chang Tao with conscious humiliation; "of all those wherein I retain an adequate grasp of the solution, the complication eludes me at the moment, and thus in a like but converse manner with the others."

"Esteemed parent," remarked Melodious Vision, without emotion, "this is neither a minstrel nor one in any way entertaining. It is merely Another."

"Another!" exclaimed Chang Tao in refined bitterness. "Is it possible that after taking so extreme and unorthodox a course as to ignore the Usages and advance myself in person I am to find that I have not even the mediocre originality of being the first, as a recommendation?"

"If the matter is thus and thus, so far from being the first, you are only the last of a considerable line of worthy and enterprising youths who have succeeded in gaining access to the inner part of this not really attractive residence on one pretext or another," replied the tolerant Shen Yi. "In any case you are honourably welcome. From the position of your various features I now judge you to be Tao, only son of the virtuous house of Chang. May you prove more successful in your enterprise than those who have preceded you."

"The adventure appears to be tending in unforeseen directions," said Chang Tao uneasily. "Your felicitation, benign, though doubtless gold at heart, is set in a doubtful frame."

"It is for your stalwart endeavour to assure a happy picture," replied Shen Yi, with undisturbed cordiality. "You bear a sword."

"What added involvement is this?" demanded Chang Tao. "This one's thoughts and intention were not turned towards savagery and arms, but in the direction of a pacific union of two distinguished lines."

"In such cases my attitude has invariably been one of sympathetic unconcern," declared Shen Yi. "The weight of either side produces an atmosphere of absolute poise that cannot fail to give full play to the decision of the destinies."

"But if this attitude is maintained on your part how can the proposal progress to a definite issue?" inquired Chang Tao.

"So far, it never has so progressed," admitted Shen Yi. "None of the worthy and hard-striving young men—any of whom I should have been overjoyed to greet as a son-in-law had my inopportune sense of impartiality permitted it—has yet returned from the trial to claim the reward."

"Even the Classics become obscure in the dark. Clear your throat of all doubtfulness, O Shen Yi, and speak to a definite end."

"That duty devolves upon this person, O would-be propounder of involved questions," interposed Melodious Vision. Her voice was more musical than a stand of hanging jewels touched by a rod of jade, and each word fell like a separate pearl. "He who ignores the Usages must expect to find the Usages ignored. Since the day when K'ung-tsz framed the Ceremonies much water has passed beneath the Seven Terraced Bridge, and that which has overflowed can never be picked up again. It is no longer enough that you should come and thereby I must go; that you should speak and I be silent; that you should beckon and I meekly obey. Inspired by the uprisen sisterhood of the outer barbarian lands, we of the inner chambers of the Illimitable Kingdom demand the right to express ourselves freely on every occasion and on every subject, whether the matter involved is one that we understand or not."

"Your clear-cut words will carry far," said Chang Tao deferentially, and, indeed, Melodious Vision's voice had imperceptibly assumed a penetrating quality that justified the remark. "Yet is it fitting that beings so superior in every way should be swayed by the example of those who are necessarily uncivilized and rude?"

"Even a mole may instruct a philosopher in the art of digging," replied the maiden, with graceful tolerance. "Thus among those uncouth tribes it is the custom, when a valiant youth would enlarge his face in the eyes of a maiden, that he should encounter forth and slay dragons, to the imperishable glory of her name. By this beneficent habit not only are the feeble and inept automatically disposed of, but the difficulty of choosing one from among a company of suitors, all apparently possessing the same superficial attributes, is materially lightened."

"The system may be advantageous in those dark regions," admitted Chang Tao reluctantly, "but it must prove unsatisfactory in our more favoured land."

"In what detail?" demanded the maiden, pausing in her attitude of assured superiority.

"By the essential drawback that whereas in those neglected outer parts there really are no dragons, here there really are. Thus—"

"Doubtless there are barbarian maidens for those who prefer to encounter barbarian dragons, then," exclaimed Melodious Vision, with a very elaborately sustained air of no-concern.

"Doubtless," assented Chang Tao mildly. "Yet having set forth in the direction of a specific Vision it is this person's intention to pursue it to an ultimate end."

"The quiet duck puts his foot on the unobservant worm," murmured Shen Yi, with delicate encouragement, adding "This one casts a more definite shadow than those before."

"Yet," continued the maiden, "to all, my unbending word is this: he who would return for approval must experience difficulties, overcome dangers and conquer dragons. Those who do not adventure on the quest will pass outward from this person's mind."

"And those who do will certainly Pass Upward from their own bodies," ran the essence of the youth's inner thoughts. Yet the network of her unevadable power and presence was upon him; he acquiescently replied:

"It is accepted. On such an errand difficulties and dangers will not require any especial search. Yet how many dragons slain will suffice to win approval?"

"Crocodile-eyed one!" exclaimed Melodious Vision, surprised into wrathfulness. "How many—" Here she withdrew in abrupt vehemence.

"Your progress has been rapid and profound," remarked Shen Yi, as, with flattering attention, he accompanied Chang Tao some part of the way towards the door. "Never before has that one been known to leave a remark unsaid; I do not altogether despair of seeing her married yet. As regards the encounter with the dragon—well, in the case of the one whispering in your ear there was the revered mother of the one whom he sought. After all, a dragon is soon done with—one way or the other."

In such a manner Chang Tao set forth to encounter dragons, assured that difficulties and dangers would accompany him on either side. In this latter detail he was inspired, but as the great light faded and the sky–lantern rose in interminable succession, while the unconquerable li ever stretched before his expectant feet, the essential part of the undertaking began to assume a dubious facet. In the valleys and fertile places he learned that creatures of this part now chiefly inhabited the higher fastnesses, such regions being more congenial to their wild and intractable natures. When, however, after many laborious marches he reached the upper peaks of pathless mountains the scanty crag–dwellers did not vary in their assertion that the dragons had for some time past forsaken those heights for the more settled profusion of the plains. Formerly, in both places they had been plentiful, and all those whom Chang Tao questioned spoke openly of many encounters between their immediate forefathers and such Beings.

It was in the downcast frame of mind to which the delays in accomplishing his mission gave rise that Chang Tao found himself walking side by side with one who bore the appearance of an affluent merchant. The northernward way was remote and solitary, but seeing that the stranger carried no outward arms Chang Tao greeted him suitably and presently spoke of the difficulty of meeting dragons, or of discovering their retreats from dwellers in that region.

"In such delicate matters those who know don't talk, and those who talk don't know," replied the other sympathetically. "Yet for what purpose should one who would pass as a pacific student seek to encounter dragons?"

"For a sufficient private reason it is necessary that I should kill a certain number," replied Chang Tao freely. "Thus their absence involves me in much ill–spared delay."

At this avowal the stranger's looks became more sombre, and he breathed inwards several times between his formidable teeth before he made reply.

"This is doubtless your angle, but there is another; nor is it well to ignore the saying, 'Should you miss the tiger be assured that he will not miss you,'" he remarked at length.

"Have you sufficiently considered the eventuality of a dragon killing you?"

"It is no less aptly said: 'To be born is in the course of nature, but to die is according to the decree of destiny.'"

"That is a two-edged weapon, and the dragon may be the first to apply it."

"In that case this person will fall back upon the point of the adage: 'It is better to die two years too soon than to live one year too long,'" replied Chang Tao. "Should he fail in the adventure and thus lose all hope of Melodious Vision, of the house of Shen, there will be no further object in prolonging a wearisome career."

"You speak of Melodious Vision, she being of the house of Shen," said the stranger, regarding his companion with an added scrutiny. "Is the unmentioned part of her father's honourable name Yi, and is his agreeable house so positioned that it fronts upon a summer-seat domed with red copper?"

"The description is exact," admitted Chang Tao. "Have you, then, in the course of your many-sided travels, passed that way?"

"It is not unknown to me," replied the other briefly. "Learn now how incautious had been your speech, and how narrowly you have avoided the exact fate of which I warned you. The one speaking to you is in reality a powerful dragon, his name being Pe-lung, from the circumstance that the northern limits are within his sway. Had it not been for a chance reference you would certainly have been struck dead at the parting of our ways."

"If this is so it admittedly puts a new face upon the matter," agreed Chang Tao. "Yet how can reliance be spontaneously placed upon so incredible a claim? You are a man of moderate cast, neither diffident nor austere, and with no unnatural attributes. All the dragons with which history is concerned possess a long body and a scaly skin, and have, moreover, the power of breathing fire at will."

"That is easily put to the test." No sooner had Pe-lung uttered these words than he faded, and in his place appeared a formidable monster possessing all the terror-inspiring characteristics of his kind. Yet in spite of his tree-like eyebrows,

131

fiercely–moving whiskers and fire–breathing jaws, his voice was mild and pacific as he continued: "What further proof can be required? Assuredly, the self–opinionated spirit in which you conduct your quest will bring you no nearer to a desired end."

"Yet this will!" exclaimed Chang Tao, and suddenly drawing his reliable sword he drove it through the middle part of the dragon's body. So expertly was the thrust weighted that the point of the weapon protruded on the other side and scarred the earth. Instead of falling lifeless to the ground, however, the Being continued to regard its assailant with benignant composure, whereupon the youth withdrew the blade and drove it through again, five or six times more. As this produced no effect beyond rendering the edge of the weapon unfit for further use, and almost paralysing the sinews of his own right arm, Chang Tao threw away the sword and sat down on the road in order to recall his breath. When he raised his head again the dragon had disappeared and Pe–lung stood there as before.

"Fortunately it is possible to take a broad–minded view of your uncourteous action, owing to your sense of the fitnesses being for the time in abeyance through allegiance to so engaging a maiden as Melodious Vision," said Pe–lung in a voice not devoid of reproach. "Had you but confided in me more fully I should certainly have cautioned you in time. As it is, you have ended by notching your otherwise capable weapon beyond repair and seriously damaging the scanty cloak I wear"—indicating the numerous rents that marred his dress of costly fur. "No wonder dejection sits upon your downcast brow."

"Your priceless robe is a matter of profuse regret and my self–esteem can only be restored by your accepting in its place this threadbare one of mine. My rust–eaten sword is unworthy of your second thought. But certainly neither of these two details is the real reason of my dark despair."

"Disclose yourself more openly," urged Pe–lung.

"I now plainly recognize the futility of my well–intentioned quest. Obviously it is impossible to kill a dragon, and I am thus the sport either of Melodious Vision's deliberate ridicule or of my own ill–arranged presumption."

"Set your mind at rest upon that score: each blow was competently struck and convincingly fatal. You may quite fittingly claim to have slain half a dozen dragons at the least—none of the legendary champions of the past has done more."

"Yet how can so arrogant a claim be held, seeing that you stand before me in the unimpaired state of an ordinary existence?"

"The explanation is simple and assuring. It is, in reality, very easy to kill a dragon, but it is impossible to keep him dead. The reason for this is that the Five Essential Constituents of fire, water, earth, wood and metal are blended in our bodies in the Sublime or Indivisible proportion. Thus although it is not difficult by extreme violence to disturb the harmonious balance of the Constituents, and so bring about the effect of no—existence, they at once re—tranquillize again, and all effect of the ill usage is spontaneously repaired."

"That is certainly a logical solution, but it stands in doubtful stead when applied to the familiar requirements of life; nor is it probable that one so acute—witted as Melodious Vision would greet the claim with an acquiescent face," replied Chang Tao. "Not unnaturally is it said: 'He who kills tigers does not wear rat—skin sleeves.' It would be one thing to make a boast of having slain six dragons; it would be quite another to be bidden to bring in their tails."

"That is a difficulty which must be considered," admitted Pe—lung, "but a path round it will inevitably be found. In the meantime night is beginning to encircle us, and many dark Powers will be freed and resort to these inaccessible slopes. Accompany me, therefore, to my bankrupt hovel, where you will be safe until you care to resume your journey."

To this agreeable proposal Chang Tao at once assented. The way was long and laborious, "For," remarked Pe—lung, "in an ordinary course I should fly there in a single breath of time; but to seize an honoured guest by the body—cloth and thus transfer him over the side of a mountain is toilsome to the one and humiliating to the other."

To beguile the time he spoke freely of the hardships of his lot.

"We dragons are frequently objects of envy at the hands of the undiscriminating, but the few superficial privileges we enjoy are heavily balanced by the exacting scope of our duties. Thus to-night it is my degraded task to divert the course of the river flowing below us, so as to overwhelm the misguided town of Yang, wherein swells a sordid outcast who has reviled the Sacred Claw. In order to do this properly it will be my distressing part to lie across the bed of the stream, my head resting upon one bank and my tail upon the other, and so remain throughout the rigour of the night.

As they approached the cloudy pinnacle whereon was situated the dragon's cave, one came forth at a distance to meet them. As she drew near, alternating emotions from time to time swayed Chang Tao's mind. From beneath a well-ruled eyebrow Pe-lung continued to observe him closely.

"Fuh-sang, the unattractive daughter of my dwindling line," remarked the former person, with refined indifference. "I have rendered you invisible, and she, as her custom is, would advance to greet me."

"But this enchanting apparition is Melodious Vision!" exclaimed Chang Tao. "What new bewilderment is here?"

"Since you have thus expressed yourself, I will now throw off the mask and reveal fully why I have hitherto spared your life, and for what purpose I have brought you to these barren heights," replied Pe-lung. "In the past Shen Yi provoked the Deities, and to mark their displeasure it was decided to take away his she-child and to substitute for it one of demoniac birth. Accordingly Fuh-sang, being of like age, was moulded to its counterpart, and an attendant gnome was despatched with her secretly to make the change. Becoming overwhelmed with the fumes of rice-spirit, until then unknown to his simple taste, this clay-brained earth-pig left the two she-children alone for a space while he slept. Discovering each other to be the creature of another part, they battled together and tore from one another the signs of recognition. When the untrustworthy gnome recovered from his stupor he saw what he had done, but being terror-driven he took up one of the she-children at a venture and returned with a pliant tale. It was not until a few moons ago that while in a close extremity he confessed his crime. Meanwhile Shen Yi had made his peace with those Above and the order being revoked the she-children had been exchanged again. Thus the matter rests."

"Which, then, of the twain is she inherent of your house and which Melodious Vision?" demanded Chang Tao in some concern. "The matter can assuredly not rest thus."

"That," replied Pe-lung affably, "it will be your engaging task to unravel, and to this end will be your opportunity of closely watching Fuh-sang's unsuspecting movements in my absence through the night."

"Yet how should I, to whom the way of either maiden is as yet no more than the title-page of a many-volumed book, succeed where the father native to one has failed?"

"Because in your case the incentive will be deeper. Destined, as you doubtless are, to espouse Melodious Vision, the Forces connected with marriage and its Rites will certainly endeavour to inspire you. This person admittedly has no desire to nurture one who should prove to be of merely human seed, but your objection to propagating a race of dragonets turns on a keener edge. Added to all, a not unnatural disinclination to be dropped from so great a height as this into so deep and rocky a valley as that will conceivably lend wings to your usually nimble-footed mind."

While speaking to Chang Tao in this encouraging strain, Pe-lung was also conversing suitably with Fuh-sang, who had by this time joined them, warning her of his absence until the dawn, and the like. When he had completed his instruction he stroked her face affectionately, greeting Chang Tao with a short but appropriate farewell, and changing his form projected himself downwards into the darkness of the valley below. Recognizing that the situation into which he had been drawn possessed no other outlet, Chang Tao followed Fuh-sang on her backward path, and with her passed unsuspected into the dragon's cave.

Early as was Pe-lung's return on the ensuing morning, Chang Tao stood on a rocky eminence to greet him, and the outline of his face, though not altogether free of doubt, was by no means hopeless. Pe-lung still retained the impressive form of a gigantic dragon as he cleft the Middle Air, shining and iridescent, each beat of his majestic wings being as a roll of thunder and the skittering of sand and water from his crepitant scales leaving blights and rain-storms in his wake. When he saw Chang Tao he drove an earthward angle and alighting near at hand considerably changed into the semblance of an affluent merchant as he approached.

"Greeting," he remarked cheerfully. "Did you find your early rice?"

"It has sufficed," replied Chang Tao. "How is your own incomparable stomach?"

Pe–lung pointed to the empty bed of the deflected river and moved his head from side to side as one who draws an analogy to his own condition. "But of your more pressing enterprise," he continued, with sympathetic concern: "have you persevered to a fruitful end, or will it be necessary—?" And with tactful feeling he indicated the gesture of propelling an antagonist over the side of a precipice rather than allude to the disagreeable contingency in spoken words.

"When the oil is exhausted the lamp goes out," admitted Chang Tao, "but my time is not yet come. During the visionary watches of the night my poising mind was sustained by Forces as you so presciently foretold, and my groping hand was led to an inspired solution of the truth."

"This points to a specific end. Proceed," urged Pe–lung, for Chang Tao had hesitated among his words as though their import might not be soothing to the other's mind.

"Thus it is given me to declare: she who is called Melodious Vision is rightly of the house of Shen, and Fuh–sang is no less innate of your exalted tribe. The erring gnome, in spite of his misdeed, was but a finger of the larger hand of destiny, and as it is, it is."

"This assurance gladdens my face, no less for your sake than for my own," declared Pe–lung heartily. "For my part, I have found a way to enlarge you in the eyes of those whom you solicit. It is a custom with me that every thousand years I should discard my outer skin—not that it requires it, but there are certain standards to which we better–class dragons must conform. These sloughs are hidden beneath a secret stone, beyond the reach of the merely vain or curious. When you have disclosed the signs by which I shall have securance of Fuh–sang's identity I will pronounce the word and the stone being thus released you shall bear away six suits of scales in token of your prowess."

136

Then replied Chang Tao: "The signs, Assuredly. Yet, omnipotence, without your express command the specific detail would be elusive to my respectful tongue."

"You have the authority of my extended hand," conceded Pe-lung readily, raising it as he spoke. "Speak freely."

"I claim the protection of its benignant shadow," said Chang Tao, with content. "You, O Pe-lung, are one who has mingled freely with creatures of every kind in all the Nine Spaces. Yet have you not, out of your vast experience thus gained, perceived the essential wherein men and dragons differ? Briefly and devoid of graceful metaphor, every dragon, esteemed, would seem to possess a tail; beings of my part have none."

For a concise moment the nature of Pe-lung's reflection was clouded in ambiguity, though the fact that he became entirely enveloped in a dense purple vapour indicated feelings of more than usual vigour. When this cleared away it left his outer form unchanged indeed, but the affable condescension of his manner was merged into one of dignified aloofness.

"Certainly all members of our enlightened tribe have tails," he replied, with distant precision, "nor does this one see how any other state is possible. Changing as we constantly do, both male and female, into Beings, Influences, Shadows and unclothed creatures of the lower parts, it is essential for our mutual self-esteem that in every manifestation we should be thus equipped. At this moment, though in the guise of a substantial trader, I possess a tail—small but adequate. Is it possible that you and those of your insolvent race are destitute?"

"In this particular, magnificence, I and those of my threadbare species are most lamentably deficient. To the proving of this end shall I display myself?"

"It is not necessary," said Pe-lung coldly. "It is inconceivable that, were it otherwise, you would admit the humiliating fact."

"Yet out of your millenaries of experience you must already—"

"It is well said that after passing a commonplace object a hundred times a day, at nightfall its size and colour are unknown to one," replied Pe-lung. "In this matter, from motives which cannot have been otherwise than delicate, I took too much for granted it would seem. . . . Then you—all—Shen Yi, Melodious Vision, the military governor of this province, even the sublime Emperor—all—?"

"All tailless," admitted Chang Tao, with conscious humility. "Nevertheless there is a tradition that in distant aeons—"

"Doubtless on some issue you roused the High Ones past forgiveness and were thus deprived as the most signal mark of their displeasure."

"Doubtless," assented Chang Tao, with unquenchable politeness.

"Coming to the correct attitude that you have maintained throughout, it would appear that during the silent gong–strokes of the night, by some obscure and indirect guidance it was revealed to you that Fuh—that any Being of my superior race was, on the contrary—" The menace of Pe–lung's challenging eye, though less direct and assured than formerly, had the manner of being uncertainly restrained by a single much–frayed thread, but Chang Tao continued to meet it with respectful self–possession.

"The inference is unflinching," he replied acquiescently. "I prostrate myself expectantly."

"You have competently performed your part," admitted Pe–lung, although an occasional jet of purple vapour clouded his upper person and the passage of his breath among his teeth would have been distasteful to one of sensitive refinement. "Nothing remains but the fulfilling of my iron word."

Thereupon he pronounced a mystic sign and revealing the opening to a cave he presently brought forth six sets of armoured skin. Binding these upon Chang Tao's back, he dismissed him, yet the manner of his parting was as of one who is doubtful even to the end.

Thus equipped—

But who having made a distant journey into Outer Land speaks lengthily of the level path of his return, or of the evening glow upon the gilded roof of his awaiting home?

Thus, this limit being reached in the essential story of Chang Tao, Melodious Vision and the Dragon, he who relates their commonplace happenings bows submissively.

Nevertheless it is true that once again in a later time Chang Tao encountered in the throng one whom he recognized. Encouraged by the presence of so many of his kind, he approached the other and saluted him.

"Greeting, O Pe–lung," he said, with outward confidence. "What bends your footsteps to this busy place of men?"

"I come to buy an imitation pig–tail to pass for one," replied Pe–lung, with quiet composure. "Greeting, valorous champion! How fares Melodious Vision?"

"Agreeably so," admitted Chang Tao, and then, fearing that so far his reply had been inadequate, he added: "Yet, despite the facts, there are moments when this person almost doubts if he did not make a wrong decision in the matter after all."

"That is a very common complaint," said Pe–lung, becoming most offensively amused.

CHAPTER IX. The Propitious Dissension between Two whose General Attributes have already been sufficiently Described

WHEN Kai Lung had related the story of Chang Tao and had made an end of speaking, those who were seated there agreed with an undivided voice that he had competently fulfilled his task. Nor did Shan Tien omit an approving word, adding:

"On one point the historical balance of a certain detail seemed open to contention. Accompany me, therefore, to my own severe retreat, where this necessarily flat and unentertaining topic can be looked at from all round."

When they were alone together the Mandarin unsealed a jar of wine, apportioned melon seeds, and indicated to Kai Lung that he should sit upon the floor at a suitable distance from himself.

"So long as we do not lose sight of the necessity whereby my official position will presently involve me in condemning you to a painful death, and your loyal subjection will necessitate your whole-hearted co-operation in the act, there is no reason why the flower of literary excellence should wither for lack of mutual husbandry," remarked the broad-minded official tolerantly.

"Your enlightened patronage is a continual nourishment to the soil of my imagination," replied the story teller.

"As regards the doings of Chang Tao and of the various other personages who unite with him to form the fabric of the narrative, would not a strict adherence to the fable in its classical simplicity require the filling in of certain details which under your elusive tongue seemed, as you proceeded, to melt imperceptibly into a discreet background?"

"Your voice is just," confessed Kai Lung, "and your harmonious ear corrects the deficiencies of my afflicted style. Admittedly in the story of Chang Tao there are here and there analogies which may be fittingly left to the imagination as the occasion should demand. Is it not rightly said: 'Discretion is the handmaiden of Truth'? and in that spacious and well-appointed palace there is every kind of vessel, but the meaner are not to be seen in the more ceremonial halls. Thus he who tells a story prudently suits his furnishing to the condition of his hearers."

"Wisdom directs your course," replied Shan Tien, "and propriety sits beneath your supple tongue. As the necessity for this very seemly expurgation is now over, I would myself listen to your recital of the fullest and most detailed version—purely, let it be freely stated, in order to judge whether its literary qualities transcend those of the other."

"I comply, benevolence," replied Kai Lung. "This rendering shall be to the one that has gone before as a spreading banyan-tree overshadowing an immature shrub."

"Forbear!" exclaimed a discordant voice, and the sour-eyed Ming-shu revealed his inopportune presence from behind a hanging veil. "Is it meet, O eminence, that in this person's absence you should thus consort on terms of fraternity with tomb-riflers and grain-thieves?"

"The reproach is easily removed," replied Shan Tien hospitably. "Join the circle of our refined felicity and hear at full length by what means the ingenious Chang Tao—"

"There are moments when one despairs before the spectacle of authority thus displayed," murmured Ming–shu, his throat thickening with acrimony. "Understand, pre–eminence," he continued more aloud, "that not this one's absence but your own presence is the distressing feature, as being an obstacle in the path of that undeviating justice in which our legal system is embedded. From the first moment of our encountering it had been my well–intentioned purpose that loyal confidence should be strengthened and rebellion cowed by submitting this opportune but otherwise inoffensive stranger to a sordid and degrading end. Yet how shall this beneficent example be attained if on every occasion—"

"Your design is a worthy and enlightened one," interposed the Mandarin, with dignity. "What you have somewhat incapably overlooked, Ming–shu, is the fact that I never greet this intelligent and painstaking young man without reminding him of the imminence of his fate and of his suitability for it."

"Truth adorns your lips and accuracy anoints your palate," volunteered Kai Lung.

"Be this as the destinies permit, there is much that is circuitous in the bending of events," contended Ming–shu stubbornly. "Is it by chance or through some hidden tricklage that occasion always finds Kai Lung so adequately prepared?"

"It is, as the story of Chang Tao has this day justified, and as this discriminating person has frequently maintained, that the one in question has a story framed to meet the requirement of every circumstance," declared Shan Tien.

"Or that each requirement is subtly shaped to meet his preparation," retorted Ming–shu darkly. "Be that as it shall perchance ultimately appear, it is undeniable that your admitted weaknesses—"

"Weaknesses!" exclaimed the astonished Mandarin, looking around the room as though to discover in what crevice the unheard–of attributes were hidden. "This person's weaknesses? Can the sounding properties of this ill–constructed roof thus pervert one word into the semblance of another? If not, the bounds set to the admissable from the taker–down of the spoken word, Ming–shu, do not in their most elastic moods extend to calumny and distortion. . . . The one before you has no weaknesses. . . . Doubtless before another moon has changed you will impute to him actual faults!"

"Humility directs my gaze," replied Ming–shu, with downcast eyes, and he plainly recognized that his presumption had been too maintained. "Yet," he added, with polished irony, "there is a well–timed adage that rises to the lips: 'Do not despair; even Yuen Yan once cast a missile at the Tablets!'"

"Truly," agreed Shan Tien, with smooth concurrence, "the line is not unknown to me. Who, however, was the one in question and under what provocation did he so behave?"

"That is beyond the province of the saying," replied Ming–shu. "Nor is it known to my remembrance."

"Then out of your own mouth a fitting test is set, which if Kai Lung can agreeably perform will at once demonstrate a secret and a guilty confederacy between you both. Proceed, O story–teller, to incriminate Ming–shu together with yourself!"

"I proceed, High Excellence, but chiefly to the glorification of your all–discerning mind," replied Kai Lung.

The Story of Yuen Yan, of the Barber Chou–hu, and His Wife Tsae–che

"Do not despair; even Yuen Yan once cast a missile at the Tablets," is a proverb of encouragement well worn throughout the Empire; but although it is daily on the lips of some it is doubtful if a single person could give an intelligent account of the Yuen Yan in question beyond repeating the outside facts that he was of a humane and consistent disposition and during the greater part of his life possessed every desirable attribute of wealth, family and virtuous esteem. If more closely questioned with reference to the specific incident alluded to, these persons would not hesitate to assert that the proverb was not to be understood in so superficial a sense, protesting, with much indignation, that Yuen Yan was of too courteous and lofty a nature to be guilty of so unseemly an action, and contemptuously inquiring what possible reason one who enjoyed every advantage in this world and every prospect of an unruffled felicity in The Beyond could have for behaving in so outrageous a manner. This explanation by no means satisfied the one who now narrates, and after much research he has brought to light the forgotten story of Yuen Yan's early life, which may be thus related.

At the period with which this part of the narrative is concerned, Yuen Yan dwelt with his mother in one of the least attractive of the arches beneath the city wall. As a youth it had been his intention to take an exceptionally high place in the public examinations, and, rising at once to a position of responsible authority, to mark himself out for continual promotion by the exercise of unfailing discretion and indomitable zeal. Having saved his country in a moment of acute national danger, he contemplated accepting a title of unique distinction and retiring to his native province, where he would build an adequate palace which he had already planned out down to the most trivial detail. There he purposed spending the remainder of his life, receiving frequent tokens of regard from the hand of the gratified Emperor, marrying an accomplished and refined wife who would doubtless be one of the princesses of the Imperial House, and conscientiously regarding The Virtues throughout. The transition from this sumptuously contrived residence to a damp arch in the city wall, and from the high destiny indicated to the occupation of leading from place to place a company of sightless mendicants, had been neither instantaneous nor painless, but Yuen Yan had never for a moment wavered from the enlightened maxims which he had adopted as his guiding principles, nor did he suffer unending trials to lessen his reverence for The Virtues. "Having set out with the full intention of becoming a wealthy mandarin, it would have been a small achievement to have reached that position with unshattered ideals," he frequently remarked; "but having thus set out it is a matter for more than ordinary congratulation to have fallen to the position of leading a string of blind beggars about the city and still to retain unimpaired the ingenuous beliefs and aspirations of youth."

"Doubtless," replied his aged mother, whenever she chanced to overhear this honourable reflection, "doubtless the foolish calf who innocently puts his foot into the jelly finds a like consolation. This person, however, would gladly exchange the most illimitable moral satisfaction engendered by acute poverty for a few of the material comforts of a sordid competence, nor would she hesitate to throw into the balance all the aspirations and improving sayings to be found within the Classics."

"Esteemed mother," protested Yan, "more than three thousand years ago the royal philosopher Nin-hyo made the observation: 'Better an earth-lined cave from which the stars are visible than a golden pagoda roofed over with iniquity,' and the saying has stood the test of time."

"The remark would have carried a weightier conviction if the broad-minded sovereign had himself first stood the test of lying for a few years with enlarged joints and afflicted bones in the abode he so prudently recommended for others," replied his mother, and without giving Yuen Yan any opportunity of bringing forward further proof of their highly-favoured destiny she betook herself to her own straw at the farthest end of the arch.

Up to this period of his life Yuen Yan's innate reverence and courtesy of manner had enabled him to maintain an impassive outlook in the face of every discouragement, but now he was exposed to a fresh series of trials in addition to the unsympathetic attitude which his mother never failed to unroll before him. It has already been expressed that Yuen Yan's occupation and the manner by which he gained his livelihood consisted in leading a number of blind mendicants about the streets of the city and into the shops and dwelling-places of those who might reasonably be willing to pay in order to be relieved of their presence. In this profession Yan's venerating and custom-regarding nature compelled him to act as leaders of blind beggars had acted throughout all historical times and far back into the dim recesses of legendary epochs and this, in an era when the leisurely habits of the past were falling into disuse, and when rivals and competitors were springing up on all sides, tended almost daily to decrease the proceeds of his labour and to sow an insidious doubt even in his unquestioning mind.

In particular, among those whom Yan regarded most objectionably was one named Ho. Although only recently arrived in the city from a country beyond the Bitter Water, Ho was already known in every quarter both to the merchants and stallkeepers, who trembled at his approaching shadow, and to the competing mendicants who now counted their cash with two fingers where they had before needed both hands. This distressingly active person made no secret of his methods and intention; for, upon his arrival, he plainly announced that his object was to make the foundations of benevolence vibrate like the strings of a many-toned lute, and he compared his general progress through the haunts of the charitably disposed to the passage of a highly-charged firework through an assembly of meditative turtles. He was usually

144

known, he added, as "the rapidly-moving person," or "the one devoid of outline," and it soon became apparent that he was also quite destitute of all dignified restraint. Selecting the place of commerce of some wealthy merchant, Ho entered without hesitation and thrusting aside the waiting customers he continued to strike the boards impatiently until he gained the attention of the chief merchant himself. "Honourable salutations," he would say, "but do not entreat this illiterate person to enter the inner room, for he cannot tarry to discuss the movements of the planets or the sublime Emperor's health. Behold, for half-a-tael of silver you may purchase immunity from his discreditable persistence for seven days; here is the acknowledgement duly made out and attested. Let the payment be made in pieces of metal and not in paper obligations." Unless immediate compliance followed Ho at once began noisily to cast down the articles of commerce, to roll bodily upon the more fragile objects, to become demoniacally possessed on the floor, and to resort to a variety of expedients until all the customers were driven forth in panic.

In the case of an excessively stubborn merchant he had not hesitated to draw a formidable knife and to gash himself in a superficial but very imposing manner; then he had rushed out uttering cries of terror, and sinking down by the door had remained there for the greater part of the day, warning those who would have entered to be upon their guard against being enticed in and murdered, at the same time groaning aloud and displaying his own wounds. Even this seeming disregard of time was well considered, for when the tidings spread about the city other merchants did not wait for Ho to enter and greet them, but standing at their doors money in hand they pressed it upon him the moment he appeared and besought him to remove his distinguished presence from their plague-infected street. To the ordinary mendicants of the city this stress of competition was disastrous, but to Yuen Yan it was overwhelming. Thoroughly imbued with the deferential systems of antiquity, he led his band from place to place with a fitting regard for the requirements of ceremonial etiquette and a due observance of leisurely unconcern. Those to whom he addressed himself he approached with obsequious tact, and in the face of refusal to contribute to his store his most violent expedient did not go beyond marshalling his company of suppliants in an orderly group upon the shop floor, where they sang in unison a composed chant extolling the fruits of munificence and setting forth the evil plight which would certainly attend the flinty-stomached in the Upper Air. In this way Yuen Yan had been content to devote several hours to a single shop in the hope of receiving finally a few pieces of brass money; but now his persecutions were so mild that the merchants and vendors rather welcomed him by comparison with the intolerable Ho, and would on no account pay to be relieved of the infliction of his presence. "Have we not disbursed in one day to the piratical Ho thrice the sum which we had set by to serve its purpose for a hand–count of moons; and do we possess the Great Secret?" they cried. "Nevertheless, dispose your engaging band of mendicants about the place freely until it suits your refined convenience to proceed elsewhere, O meritorious Yuen Yan, for your unassuming qualities have won our consistent regard; but an insatiable sponge has already been laid upon the well–spring of our benevolence and the tenacity of our closed hand is inflexible."

Even the passive mendicants began to murmur against his leadership, urging him that he should adopt some of the simpler methods of the gifted Ho and thereby save them all from an otherwise inevitable starvation. The Emperor Kai–tsing, said the one who led their voices (referring in his malignant bitterness to a sovereign of the previous dynasty), was dead, although the fact had doubtless escaped Yuen Yan's deliberate perception. The methods of four thousand years ago were becoming obsolete in the face of a strenuous competition, and unless Yuen Yan was disposed to assume a more highly–coiled appearance they must certainly address themselves to another leader.

It was on this occasion that the incident took place which has passed down in the form of an inspiriting proverb. Yuen Yan had conscientiously delivered at the door of his abode the last of his company and was turning his footsteps towards his own arch when he encountered the contumelious Ho, who was likewise returning at the close of a day's mendicancy—but with this distinction: that, whereas Ho was followed by two stalwart attendants carrying between them a sack full of money, Yan's share of his band's enterprise consisted solely of one base coin of a kind which the charitable set aside for bestowing upon the blind and quite useless for all ordinary purposes of exchange. A few paces farther on Yan reached the Temple of the Unseen Forces and paused for a moment, as his custom was, to cast his eyes up to the tablets engraved with The Virtues, before which some devout person nightly hung a lantern. Goaded by a sudden impulse, Yan looked each way about the deserted street, and perceiving that he was alone he deliberately extended his out–thrust tongue towards the inspired precepts. Then taking from an inner sleeve the base coin he flung it at the inscribed characters and observed with satisfaction that it struck the verse beginning, "The Rewards of a Quiescent and Mentally–introspective Life are Unbounded—"

When Yan entered his arch some hours later his mother could not fail to perceive that a subtle change had come over his manner of behaving. Much of the leisurely dignity had melted out of his footsteps, and he wore his hat and outer garments at an angle which plainly testified that he was a person who might be supposed to have a marked objection to returning home before the early hours of the morning. Furthermore, as he entered he was chanting certain melodious words by which he endeavoured to convey the misleading impression that his chief amusement consisted in defying the official watchers of the town, and he continually reiterated a claim to be regarded as "one of the beardless goats." Thus expressing himself, Yan sank down in his appointed corner and would doubtlessly soon have been floating peacefully in the Middle Distance had not the door been again thrown open and a stranger named Chou-hu entered.

"Prosperity!" said Chou-hu courteously, addressing himself to Yan's mother. "Have you eaten your rice? Behold, I come to lay before you a very attractive proposal regarding your son."

"The flower attracts the bee, but when he departs it is to his lips that the honey clings," replied the woman cautiously; for after Yan's boastful words on entering she had a fear lest haply this person might be one on behalf of some guardian of the night whom her son had flung across the street (as he had specifically declared his habitual treatment of them to be) come to take him by stratagem.

"Does the pacific lamb become a wolf by night?" said Chou-hu, displaying himself reassuringly. "Wrap your ears well round my words, for they may prove very remunerative. It cannot be a matter outside your knowledge that the profession of conducting an assembly of blind mendicants from place to place no longer yields the wage of even a frugal existence in this city. In the future, for all the sympathy that he will arouse, Yan might as well go begging with a silver bowl. In consequence of his speechless condition he will be unable to support either you or himself by any other form of labour, and your line will thereupon become extinct and your standing in the Upper Air be rendered intolerable."

"It is a remote contingency, but, as the proverb says, 'The wise hen is never too old to dread the Spring,'" replied Yan's mother, with commendable prudence. "By what means, then, may this calamity be averted?"

147

"The person before you," continued Chou-hu, "is a barber and embellisher of pig-tails from the street leading to the Three-tiered Pagoda of Eggs. He has long observed the restraint and moderation of Yan's demeanour and now being in need of one to assist him his earliest thought turns to him. The affliction which would be an insuperable barrier in all ordinary cases may here be used to advantage, for being unable to converse with those seated before him, or to hear their salutations, Yan will be absolved from the necessity of engaging in diffuse and refined conversation, and in consequence he will submit at least twice the number of persons to his dexterous energies. In that way he will secure a higher reward than this person could otherwise afford and many additional comforts will doubtless fall into the sleeve of his engaging mother."

At this point the woman began to understand that the sense in which Chou-hu had referred to Yan's speechless condition was not that which she had at the time deemed it to be. It may here be made clear that it was Yuen Yan's custom to wear suspended about his neck an inscribed board bearing the words, "Speechless, and devoid of the faculty of hearing," but this originated out of his courteous and deferential nature (for to his self-obliterative mind it did not seem respectful that he should appear to be better endowed than those whom he led), nor could it be asserted that he wilfully deceived even the passing stranger, for he would freely enter into conversation with anyone whom he encountered. Nevertheless an impression had thus been formed in Chou-hu's mind and the woman forbore to correct it, thinking that it would be scarcely polite to assert herself better informed on any subject than he was, especially as he had spoken of Yan thereby receiving a higher wage. Yan himself would certainly have revealed something had he not been otherwise employed. Hearing the conversation turn towards his afflictions, he at once began to search very industriously among the straw upon which he lay for the inscribed board in question; for to his somewhat confused imagination it seemed at the time that only by displaying it openly could he prove to Chou-hu that he was in no way deficient. As the board was found on the following morning nailed to the great outer door of the Hall of Public Justice (where it remained for many days owing to the official impression that so bold and undeniable a pronouncement must have received the direct authority of the sublime Emperor), Yan was not unnaturally engaged for a considerable time, and in the meanwhile his mother contrived to impress upon him by an unmistakable sign that he should reveal nothing, but leave the matter in her hands.

Then said Yan's mother: "Truly the proposal is not altogether wanting in alluring colours, but in what manner will Yan interpret the commands of those who place themselves before him, when he has attained sufficient proficiency to be entrusted with the knife and the shearing irons?"

"The objection is a superficial one," replied Chou-hu. "When a person seats himself upon the operating stool he either throws back his head, fixing his eyes upon the upper room with a set and resolute air, or inclines it slightly forward as in a reverent tranquillity. In the former case he requires his uneven surfaces to be made smooth; in the latter he is desirous that his pig-tail should be drawn out and trimmed. Do not doubt Yan's capability to conduct himself in a discreet and becoming manner, but communicate to him, by the usual means which you adopt, the offer thus laid out, and unless he should be incredibly obtuse or unfilial to a criminal degree he will present himself at the Sign of the Gilt Thunderbolt at an early hour to-morrow."

There is a prudent caution expressed in the proverb, "The hand that feeds the ox grasps the knife when it is fattened: crawl backwards from the presence of a munificent official." Chou-hu, in spite of his plausible pretext, would have experienced no difficulty in obtaining the services of one better equipped to assist him than was Yuen Yan, so that in order to discover his real object it becomes necessary to look underneath his words. He was indeed, as he had stated, a barber and an embellisher of pig-tails, and for many years he had grown rich and round-bodied on the reputation of being one of the most skilful within his quarter of the city. In an evil moment, however, he had abandoned the moderation of his past life and surrounded himself with an atmosphere of opium smoke and existed continually in the mind-dimming effects of rice-spirit. From this cause his custom began to languish; his hand no longer swept in the graceful and unhesitating curves which had once been the admiration of all beholders, but displayed on the contrary a very disconcerting irregularity of movement, and on the day of his visit he had shorn away the venerable moustaches of the baker Heng-cho under a mistaken impression as to the reality of things and a wavering vision of their exact position. Now the baker had been inordinately proud of his long white moustaches and valued them above all his possessions, so that, invoking the spirits of his ancestors to behold his degradation and to support him in his resolve, and calling in all the passers-by to bear witness to his oath, he had solemnly bound himself either to cut down Chou-hu fatally, or, should that prove too difficult an accomplishment, to commit suicide within his shop. This twofold danger thoroughly

149

stupefied Chou-hu and made him incapable of taking any action beyond consuming further and more unstinted portions of rice-spirit and rending article after article of his apparel until his wife Tsae-che modestly dismissed such persons as loitered, and barred the outer door.

"Open your eyes upon the facts by which you are surrounded, O contemptible Chou-hu," she said, returning to his side and standing over him. "Already your degraded instincts have brought us within measurable distance of poverty, and if you neglect your business to avoid Heng-cho, actual want will soon beset us. If you remain openly within his sight you will certainly be removed forcibly to the Upper Air, leaving this inoffensive person destitute and abandoned, and if by the exercise of unfailing vigilance you escape both these dangers, you will be reserved to an even worse plight, for Heng-cho in desperation will inevitably carry out the latter part of his threat, dedicating his spirit to the duty of continually haunting you and frustrating your ambitions here on earth and calling to his assistance myriads of ancestors and relations to torment you in the Upper Air."

"How attractively and in what brilliantly-coloured outlines do you present the various facts of existence!" exclaimed Chou-hu, with inelegant resentment. "Do not neglect to add that, to-morrow being the occasion of the Moon Festival, the inexorable person who owns this residence will present himself to collect his dues, that, in consequence of the rebellion in the south, the sagacious viceroy has doubled the price of opium, that some irredeemable outcast has carried away this person's blue silk umbrella, and then doubtless the alluring picture of internal felicity around the Ancestral Altar of the Gilt Thunderbolt will be complete."

"Light words are easily spoken behind barred doors," said his wife scornfully. "Let my lord, then, recline indolently upon the floor of his inner chamber while this person sumptuously lulls him into oblivion with the music of her voice, regardless of the morrow and of the fate in which his apathy involves us both."

"By no means!" exclaimed Chou-hu, rising hastily and tearing away much of his elaborately arranged pigtail in his uncontrollable rage; "there is yet a more pleasurable alternative than that and one which will ensure to this person a period of otherwise unattainable domestic calm and at the same time involve a detestable enemy in confusion. Anticipating the dull-witted Heng-cho this one will now proceed across the street and, committing suicide within his door, will henceforth enjoy the honourable satisfaction of haunting his footsteps and rending his bakehouses and ovens untenable." With this assurance Chou-hu seized one of his most formidable business weapons and caused it to revolve around his head with great rapidity, but at the same time with extreme carefulness.

"There is a ready saying: 'The new-born lamb does not fear a tiger, but before he becomes a sheep he will flee from a wolf,'" said Tsae-che without in any way deeming it necessary to arrest Chou-hu's hand. "Full confidently will you set out, O Chou-hu, but to reach the shop of Heng-cho it is necessary to pass the stall of the dealer in abandoned articles, and next to it are enticingly spread out the wares of Kong, the merchant in distilled spirits. Put aside your reliable scraping iron while you still have it, and this not ill-disposed person will lay before you a plan by which you may even yet avoid all inconveniences and at the same time regain your failing commerce."

"It is also said: 'The advice of a wise woman will ruin a walled city,'" replied Chou-hu, somewhat annoyed at his wife so opportunely comparing him to a sheep, but still more concerned to hear by what possible expedient she could successfully avert all the contending dangers of his position. "Nevertheless, proceed."

"In one of the least reputable quarters of the city there dwells a person called Yuen Yan," said the woman. "He is the leader of a band of sightless mendicants and in this position he has frequently passed your open door, though—probably being warned by the benevolent—he has never yet entered. Now this Yuen Yan, save for one or two unimportant details, is the reflected personification of your own exalted image, nor would those most intimate with your form and outline be able to pronounce definitely unless you stood side by side before them. Furthermore, he is by nature unable to hear any remark addressed to him, and is incapable of expressing himself in spoken words. Doubtless by these indications my lord's locust-like intelligence will already have leapt to an inspired understanding of the full project?"

"Assuredly," replied Chou-hu, caressing himself approvingly. "The essential details of the scheme are built about the ease with which this person could present himself at the abode of Yuen Yan in his absence and, gathering together that one's store of wealth unquestioned, retire with it to a distant and unknown spot and thereby elude the implacable Heng-cho's vengeance."

151

"Leaving your menial one in the 'walled city' referred to, to share its fate, and, in particular, to undertake the distressing obligation of gathering up the atrocious Heng–cho after he has carried his final threat into effect? Truly must the crystal stream of your usually undimmed intelligence have become vaporized. Listen well. Disguising your external features slightly so that the resemblance may pass without remark, present yourself openly at the residence of the Yuen Yan in question—"

"First learning where it is situated?" interposed Chou–hu, with a desire to grasp the details competently.

"Unless a person of your retrospective taste would prefer to leave so trivial a point until afterwards," replied his wife in a tone of concentrated no–sincerity. "In either case, however, having arrived there, bargain with the one who has authority over Yuen Yan's movements, praising his demeanour and offering to accept him into the honours and profits of your craft. The words of acquiescence should spring to meet your own, for the various branches of mendicancy are languishing, and Yuen Yan can have no secret store of wealth. Do not hesitate to offer a higher wage than you would as an affair of ordinary commerce, for your safety depends upon it. Having secured Yan, teach him quickly the unpolished outlines of your business and then clothing him in robes similar to your own let him take his stand within the shop and withdraw yourself to the inner chamber. None will suspect the artifice, and Yuen Yan is manifestly incapable of betraying it. Heng–cho, seeing him display himself openly, will not deem it necessary to commit suicide yet, and, should he cut down Yan fatally, the officials of the street will seize him and your own safety will be assured. Finally, if nothing particular happens, at least your prosperity will be increased, for Yuen Yan will prove industrious, frugal, not addicted to excesses and in every way reliable, and towards the shop of so exceptional a barber customers will turn in an unending stream."

"Alas!" exclaimed Chou–hu, "when you boasted of an inspired scheme this person for a moment foolishly allowed his mind to contemplate the possibility of your having accidentally stumbled upon such an expedient haply, but your suggestion is only comparable with a company of ducks attempting to cross an ice–bound stream—an excessive outlay of action but no beneficial progress. Should Yuen Yan freely present himself here on the morrow, pleading destitution and craving to be employed, this person will consider the petition with an open head, but it is beneath his dignity to wait upon so low–class an object." Affecting to recollect an arranged meeting of some

152

importance, Chou-hu then clad himself in other robes, altered the appearance of his face, and set out to act in the manner already described, confident that the exact happening would never reach his lesser one's ears.

On the following day Yuen Yan presented himself at the door of the Gilt Thunderbolt, and quickly perfecting himself in the simpler methods of smoothing surfaces and adorning pig-tails he took his stand within the shop and operated upon all who came to submit themselves to his embellishment. To those who addressed him with salutations he replied by a gesture, tactfully bestowing an agreeable welcome yet at the same time conveying the impression that he was desirous of remaining undisturbed in the philosophical reflection upon which he was engaged. In spite of this it was impossible to lead his mind astray from any weighty detail, and those who, presuming upon his absorbed attitude, endeavoured to evade a just payment on any pretext whatever invariably found themselves firmly but courteously pressed to the wall by the neck, while a highly polished smoothing blade was flashed to and fro before their eyes with an action of unmistakable significance. The number of customers increased almost daily, for Yan quickly proved himself to be expert above all comparison, while others came from every quarter of the city to test with their own eyes and ears the report that had reached them, to the effect that in the street leading to the Three-tiered Pagoda of Eggs there dwelt a barber who made no pretence of elegant and refined conversation and who did not even press upon those lying helpless in his power miraculous ointments and infallible charm-waters. Thus Chou-hu prospered greatly, but Yan still obeyed his mother's warning and raised a mask before his face so that Chou-hu and his wife never doubted the reality of his infirmities. From this cause they did not refrain from conversing together freely before him on subjects of the most poignant detail, whereby Yan learned much of their past lives and conduct while maintaining an attitude of impassive unconcern.

Upon a certain evening in the month when the grass-blades are transformed into silk-worms Yan was alone in the shop, improving the edge and reflecting brilliance of some of his implements, when he head the woman exclaim from the inner room: "Truly the air from the desert is as hot and devoid of relief as the breath of the Great Dragon. Let us repose for the time in the outer chamber." Whereupon they entered the shop and seating themselves upon a couch resumed their occupations, the barber fanning himself while he smoked, his wife gumming her hair and coiling it into the semblance of a bird with outstretched wings.

"The necessity for the elaborate caution of the past no longer exists," remarked Chou–hu presently. "The baker Heng–cho is desirous of becoming one of those who select the paving–stones and regulate the number of hanging lanterns for the district lying around the Three–tiered Pagoda. In this ambition he is opposed by Kong, the distilled–spirit vendor, who claims to be a more competent judge of paving–stones and hanging lanterns and one who will exercise a lynx–eyed vigilance upon the public outlay and especially devote himself to curbing the avarice of those bread–makers who habitually mix powdered white earth with their flour. Heng–cho is therefore very concerned that many should bear honourable testimony of his engaging qualities when the day of trial arrives, and thus positioned he has inscribed and sent to this person a written message offering a dignified reconciliation and adding that he is convinced of the necessity of an enactment compelling all persons to wear a smooth face and a neatly braided pig–tail."

"It is a creditable solution of the matter," said Tsae–che, speaking between the ivory pins which she held in her mouth. "Henceforth, then, you will take up your accustomed stand as in the past?"

"Undoubtedly," replied Chou–hu. "Yuen Yan is painstaking, and has perhaps done as well as could be expected of one of his shallow intellect, but the absence of suave and high–minded conversation cannot fail to be alienating the custom of the more polished. Plainly it is a short–sighted policy for a person to try and evade his destiny. Yan seems to have been born for the express purpose of leading blind beggars about the streets of the city and to that profession he must return."

"O distressingly superficial Chou–hu!" exclaimed his wife, "do men turn willingly from wine to partake of vinegar, or having been clothed in silk do they accept sackcloth without a struggle? Indeed, your eyes, which are large to regard your own deeds and comforts, grow small when they are turned towards the attainments of another. In no case will Yan return to his mendicants, for his band is by this time scattered and dispersed. His sleeve being now well lined and his hand proficient in every detail of his craft, he will erect a stall, perchance even directly opposite or next to ourselves, and by subtlety, low charges and diligence he will draw away the greater part of your custom."

"Alas!" cried Chou-hu, turning an exceedingly inferior yellow, "there is a deeper wisdom in the proverb, 'Do not seek to escape from a flood by clinging to a tiger's tail,' than appears at a casual glance. Now that this person is contemplating gathering again into his own hands the execution of his business, he cannot reasonably afford to employ another, yet it is an intolerable thought that Yan should make use of his experience to set up a sign opposed to the Gilt Thunderbolt. Obviously the only really safe course out of an unpleasant dilemma will be to slay Yan with as little delay as possible. After receiving continuous marks of our approval for so long it is certainly very thoughtless of him to put us to so unpardonable an inconvenience."

"It is not an alluring alternative," confessed Tsae-che, crossing the room to where Yan was seated in order to survey her hair to greater advantage in a hanging mirror of three sides composed of burnished copper; "but there seems nothing else to be done in the difficult circumstances."

"The street is opportunely empty and there is little likelihood of anyone approaching at this hour," suggested Chou-hu. "What better scheme could be devised than that I should indicate to Yan by signs that I would honour him, and at the same time instruct him further in the correct pose of some of the recognized attitudes, by making smooth the surface of his face? Then during the operation I might perchance slip upon an overripe whampee lying unperceived upon the floor; my hand—"

"Ah-ah!" cried Tsae-che aloud, pressing her symmetrical fingers against her gracefully-proportioned ears; "do not, thou dragon-headed one, lead the conversation to such an extremity of detail, still less carry the resolution into effect before the very eyes of this delicately-susceptible person. Now to-morrow, after the midday meal, she will be journeying as far as the street of the venders of woven fabrics in order to procure a piece of silk similar to the pearl-grey robe which she is wearing. The opportunity will be a favourable one, for to-morrow is the weekly occasion on which you raise the shutters and deny customers at an earlier hour; and it is really more modest that one of my impressionable refinement should be away from the house altogether and not merely in the inner chamber when that which is now here passes out."

"The suggestion is well timed," replied Chou-hu. "No interruption will then be possible."

"Furthermore," continued his wife, sprinkling upon her hair a perfumed powder of gold which made it sparkle as it engaged the light at every point with a most entrancing lustre, "would it not be desirable to use a weapon less identified with your own hand? In the corner nearest to Yan there stands a massive and heavily knotted club which could afterwards be burned. It would be an easy matter to call the simple Yan's attention to some object upon the floor and then as he bent down suffer him to Pass Beyond."

"Assuredly," agreed Chou–hu, at once perceiving the wisdom of the change; "also, in that case, there would be less—"

"Ah!" again cried the woman, shaking her upraised finger reprovingly at Chou–hu (for so daintily endowed was her mind that she shrank from any of the grosser realities of the act unless they were clothed in the very gilded flowers of speech). "Desist, O crimson–minded barbarian! Let us now walk side by side along the river bank and drink in the soul–stirring melody of the musicians who at this hour will be making the spot doubly attractive with the concord of stringed woods and instruments of brass struck with harmonious unison."

The scheme for freeing Chou–hu from the embarrassment of Yan's position was not really badly arranged, nor would it have failed in most cases, but the barber was not sufficiently broad–witted to see that many of the inspired sayings which he used as arguments could be taken in another light and conveyed a decisive warning to himself. A pleasantly devised proverb has been aptly compared to a precious jewel, and as the one has a hundred light–reflecting surfaces, so has the other a diversity of applications, until it is not infrequently beyond the comprehension of an ordinary person to know upon which side wisdom and prudence lie. On the following afternoon Yan was seated in his accustomed corner when Chou–hu entered the shop with uneven feet. The barriers against the street had been raised and the outer door was barred so that none might intrude, while Chou–hu had already carefully examined the walls to ensure that no crevices remained unsealed. As he entered he was seeking, somewhat incoherently, to justify himself by assuring the deities that he had almost changed his mind until he remembered the many impious acts on Yan's part in the past, to avenge which he felt himself to be their duly appointed instrument. Furthermore, to convince them of the excellence of his motive (and also to protect himself against the influence of evil spirits) he advanced repeating the words of an invocation which in his youth he had been accustomed to say daily in the temple, and thereupon Yan knew that the moment was at hand.

"Behold, master!" he exclaimed suddenly, in clearly expressed words, "something lies at your feet."

Chou–hu looked down to the floor and lying before him was a piece of silver. To his dull and confused faculties it sounded an inaccurate detail of his pre–arranged plan that Yan should have addressed him, and the remark itself seemed dimly to remind him of something that he had intended to say, but he was too involved with himself to be able to attach any logical significance to the facts and he at once stooped greedily to possess the coin. Then Yan, who had an unfaltering grasp upon the necessities of each passing second, sprang agilely forward, swung the staff, and brought it so proficiently down upon Chou–hu's lowered head that the barber dropped lifeless to the ground and the weapon itself was shattered by the blow. Without a pause Yan clothed himself with his master's robes and ornaments, wrapped his own garment about Chou–hu instead, and opening a stone door let into the ground rolled the body through so that it dropped down into the cave beneath. He next altered the binding of his hair a little, cut his lips deeply for a set purpose, and then reposing upon the couch of the inner chamber he took up one of Chou–hu's pipes and awaited Tsae–che's return.

"It is unendurable that they of the silk market should be so ill–equipped," remarked Tsae–che discontentedly as she entered. "This pitiable one has worn away the heels of her sandals in a vain endeavour to procure a suitable embroidery, and has turned over the contents of every stall to no material end. How have the events of the day progressed with you, my lord?"

"To the fulfilling of a written destiny. Yet in a measure darkly, for a light has gone out," replied Yuen Yan.

"There was no unanticipated divergence?" inquired the woman with interest and a marked approval of this delicate way of expressing the operation of an unpleasant necessity.

"From detail to detail it was as this person desired and contrived," said Yan.

"And, of a surety, this one also?" claimed Tsae-che, with an internal emotion that something was insidiously changed in which she had no adequate part.

"The language may be fully expressed in six styles of writing, but who shall read the mind of a woman?" replied Yan evasively. "Nevertheless, in explicit words, the overhanging shadow has departed and the future is assured."

"It is well," said Tsae-che. "Yet how altered is your voice, and for what reason do you hold a cloth before your mouth?"

"The staff broke and a splinter flying upwards pierced my lips," said Yan, lowering the cloth. "You speak truly, for the pain attending each word is by no means slight, and scarcely can this person recognize his own voice."

"Oh, incomparable Chou-hu, how valiantly do you bear your sufferings!" exclaimed Tsae-che remorsefully. "And while this heedless one has been passing the time pleasantly in handling rich brocades you have been lying here in anguish. Behold now, without delay she will prepare food to divert your mind, and to mark the occasion she had already purchased a little jar of gold-fish gills, two eggs branded with the assurance that they have been earth-buried for eleven years, and a small serpent preserved in oil."

When they had eaten for some time in silence Yuen Yan again spoke. "Attend closely to my words," he said, "and if you perceive any disconcerting oversight in the scheme which I am about to lay before you do not hesitate to declare it. The threat which Heng-cho the baker swore he swore openly, and many reputable witnesses could be gathered together who would confirm his words, while the written message of reconciliation which he sent will be known to none. Let us therefore take that which lies in the cave beneath and clothing it in my robes bear it unperceived as soon as the night has descended and leave it in the courtyard of Heng-cho's house. Now Heng-cho has a fig plantation outside the city, so that when he rises early, as his custom is, and finds the body, he will carry it away to bury it secretly there, remembering his impetuous words and well knowing the net of entangling circumstances which must otherwise close around him. At that moment you will appear before him, searching for your husband, and suspecting his burden raise an outcry that may draw the neighbours to your side if necessary. On this point, however, be discreetly observant, for if the tumult calls down the official watch it will go evilly with Heng–cho, but we shall profit little. The greater likelihood is that as soon as you lift up your voice the baker will implore you to accompany him back to his house so that he may make a full and honourable compensation. This you will do, and hastening the negotiation as much as is consistent with a seemly regard for your overwhelming grief, you will accept not less than five hundred taels and an undertaking that a suitable funeral will be provided."

"O thrice–versatile Chou–hu!" exclaimed Tsae–che, whose eyes had reflected an ever–increasing sparkle of admiration as Yan unfolded the details of his scheme, "how insignificant are the minds of others compared with yours! Assuredly you have been drinking at some magic well in this one's absence, for never before was your intellect so keen and lustreful. Let us at once carry your noble stratagem into effect, for this person's toes vibrate to bear her on a project of such remunerative ingenuity."

Accordingly they descended into the cave beneath and taking up Chou–hu they again dressed him in his own robes. In his inner sleeve Yan placed some parchments of slight importance; he returned the jade bracelet to his wrist and by other signs he made his identity unmistakable; then lifting him between them, when the night was well advanced, they carried him through unfrequented ways and left him unperceived within Heng–cho's gate.

"There is yet another precaution which will ensure to you the sympathetic voices of all if it should become necessary to appeal openly," said Yuen Yan when they had returned. "I will make out a deed of final intention conferring all I possess upon Yuen Yan as a mark of esteem for his conscientious services, and this you can produce if necessary in order to crush the niggard baker in the wine–press of your necessitous destitution." Thereupon Yan drew up such a document as he had described, signing it with Chou–hu's name and sealing it with his ring, while Tsae–che also added her sign and attestation. He then sent her to lurk upon the roof, strictly commanding her to keep an undeviating watch upon Heng–cho's movements.

It was about the hour before dawn when Heng–cho appeared, bearing across his back a well–filled sack and carrying in his right hand a spade. His steps were turned towards the fig orchard of which Yan had spoken, so that he must pass Chou–hu's house, but before he reached it Tsae–che had glided out and with loosened hair and trailing robes she sped along the street. Presently there came to Yuen Yan's waiting ear a long-drawn cry and the sounds of many shutters being flung open and the tread of hurrying feet. The moments hung about him like the wings of a dragon-dream, but a prudent restraint chained him to the inner chamber.

It was fully light when Tsae-che returned, accompanied by one whom she dismissed before she entered. "Felicity," she explained, placing before Yan a heavy bag of silver. "Your word has been accomplished."

"It is sufficient," replied Yan in a tone from which every tender modulation was absent, as he laid the silver by the side of the parchment which he had drawn up. "For what reason is the outer door now barred and they who drink tea with us prevented from entering to wish Yuen Yan prosperity?"

"Strange are my lord's words, and the touch of his breath is cold to his menial one," said the woman in doubting reproach.

"It will scarcely warm even the roots of Heng-cho's fig-trees," replied Yuen Yan with unveiled contempt. "Stretch across your hand."

In trembling wonder Tsae-che laid her hand upon the ebony table which stood between them and slowly advanced it until Yan seized it and held it firmly in his own. For a moment he held it, compelling the woman to gaze with a soul-crushing dread into his face, then his features relaxed somewhat from the effort by which he had controlled them, and at the sight Tsae-che tore away her hand and with a scream which caused those outside to forget the memory of every other cry they had ever heard, she cast herself from the house and was seen in the city no more.

These are the pages of the forgotten incident in the life of Yuen Yan which this narrator has sought out and discovered. Elsewhere, in the lesser Classics, it may be read that the person in question afterwards lived to a venerable age and finally Passed Above surrounded by every luxury, after leading an existence consistently benevolent and marked by an even exceptional adherence to the principles and requirements of The Virtues.

CHAPTER X. The Incredible Obtuseness of Those who had Opposed the Virtuous Kai Lung

IT was later than the appointed hour that same day when Kai Lung and Hwa–mei met about the shutter, for the Mandarin's importunity had disturbed the harmonious balance of their fixed arrangement. As the story–teller left the inner chamber a message of understanding, veiled from those who stood around, had passed between their eyes, and so complete was the sympathy that now directed them that without a spoken word their plans were understood. Li–loe's acquiescence had been secured by the bestowal of a flask of wine (provided already by Hwa–mei against such an emergency), and though the door–keeper had indicated reproach by a variety of sounds, he forbore from speaking openly of any vaster store.

"Let the bitterness of this one's message be that which is first spoken, so that the later and more enduring words of our remembrance may be devoid of sting. A star has shone across my mediocre path which now an envious cloud has conspired to obscure. This meeting will doubtless be our last."

Then replied Kai Lung from the darkness of the space above, his voice unhurried as its wont:

"If this is indeed the end, then to the spirits of the destinies I prostrate myself in thanks for those golden hours that have gone before, and had there been no others to recall then would I equally account myself repaid in life and death by this."

"My words ascend with yours in a pale spiral to the bosom of the universal mother," Hwa–mei made response. "I likewise am content, having tasted this felicity."

"There is yet one other thing, esteemed, if such a presumption is to be endured," Kai Lung ventured to request. "Each day a stone has been displaced from off the wall and these now lie about your gentle feet. If you should inconvenience yourself to the extent of standing upon the mound thus raised, and would stretch up your hand, I, leaning forth, could touch it with my finger–tips."

"This also will I dare to do and feel it no reproach," replied Hwa—mei; thus for the first time their fingers met.

"Let me now continue the ignoble message that my unworthy lips must bear," resumed the maiden, with a gesture of refined despair. "Ming—shu and Shan Tien, recognizing a mutual need in each, have agreed to forego their wordy strife and have entered upon a common cause. To mark this reconciliation the Mandarin to—morrow night will make a feast of wine and song in honour of Ming—shu and into this assembly you will be led, bound and wearing the wooden cang, to contribute to their offensive mirth. To this end you will not be arraigned to—morrow, but on the following morning at a special court swift sentence will be passed and carried out, neither will Shan Tien suffer any interruption nor raise an arresting hand."

The darkness by this time encompassed them so that neither could see the other's face, but across the scent—laden air Hwa—mei was conscious of a subtle change, as of a poise or the tightening of a responsive cord.

"This is the end?" she whispered up, unable to sustain. "Ah, is it not the end?"

"In the high wall of destiny that bounds our lives there is ever a hidden gap to which the Pure Ones may guide our unconscious steps perchance, if they see fit to intervene. . . . So that to—morrow, being the eleventh of the Moon of Gathering—in, is to be celebrated by the noble Mandarin with song and wine? Truly the nimble—witted Ming—shu must have slumbered by the way!"

"Assuredly he has but now returned from a long journey."

"Haply he may start upon a longer. Have the musicians been commanded yet?"

"Even now one goes to inform the leader of their voices and to bid him hold his band in readiness."

"Let it be your continual aim that nothing bars their progress. Where does that just official dwell of whom you lately spoke?"

"The Censor K'o—yih, he who rebuked Shan Tien's ambitions and made him mend his questionable life? His yamen is about the Three—eyed Gate of Tai, a half—day's journey to the south."

"The lines converge and the issues of Shan Tien, Ming—shu and we who linger here will presently be brought to a very decisive point where each must play a clear—cut part. To that end is your purpose firm?"

"Lay your commands," replied Hwa—mei steadfastly, "and measure not the burden of their weight."

"It is well," agreed Kai Lung. "Let Shan Tien give the feast and the time of acquiescence will have passed. . . . The foothold of to—morrow looms insecure, yet a very pressing message must meanwhile reach your hands."

"At the feast?"

"Thus: about the door of the inner hall are two great jars of shining brass, one on either side, and at their approach a step. Being led, at that step I shall stumble. . . . the message you will thereafter find in the jar from which I seek support."

"It shall be to me as your spoken word. Alas! the moment of recall is already here."

"Doubt not; we stand on the edge of an era that is immeasurable. For that emergency I now go to consult the spirits who have so far guided us."

On the following day at an evening hour Kai Lung received an imperious summons to accompany one who led him to the inner courts. Yet neither the cords about his arms nor the pillory around his neck could contain the gladness of his heart. From within came the sounds of instruments of wood and string with the measured beating of a drum; nothing had fallen short, for on that forbidden day, incredibly blind to the depths of his impiety, the ill—starred Mandarin Shan Tien was having music!

"Gall of a misprocured she—mule!" exclaimed the unsympathetic voice of the one who had charge of him, and the rope was jerked to quicken his loitering feet. In an effort to comply Kai Lung missed the step that crossed his path and stumbling blindly forward

163

would have fallen had he not struck heavily against a massive jar of lacquered brass, one of two that flanked the door.

"Thy province is to tell a tale rather than to dance a grotesque, as I understand the matter," said the attendant, mollified by the amusement. "In any case, restrain thy admitted ardour for a while; the call is not yet for us."

From a group that stood apart some distance from the door one moved forth and leisurely crossed the hall. Kai Lung's wounded head ceased to pain him.

"What slave is this," she demanded of the other in a slow and level tone, "and wherefore do the two of you intrude on this occasion?"

"The exalted lord commands that this one of the prisoners should attend here thus, to divert them with his fancies, he having a certain wit of the more foolish kind. Kai Lung, the dog's name is."

"Approach yet nearer to the inner door," enjoined the maiden, indicating the direction; "so that when the message comes there shall be no inept delay." As they moved off to obey she stood in languid unconcern, leaning across the opening of a tall brass vase, one hand swinging idly in its depths, until they reached their station. Kai Lung did not need his eyes to know.

Presently the music ceased, and summoned to appear in turn, Kai Lung stood forth among the guests. On the right hand of the Mandarin reclined the base Ming–shu, his mind already vapoury with the fumes of wine, the secret malice of his envious mind now boldly leaping from his eyes.

"The overrated person now about to try your refined patience to its limit is one who calls himself Kai Lung," declared Ming–shu offensively. "From an early age he has combined minstrelsy with other and more lucrative forms of crime. It is the boast of this contumacious mendicant that he can recite a story to fit any set of circumstances, this, indeed, being the only merit claimed for his feeble entertainment. The test selected for your tolerant amusement on this very second–rate occasion is that he relates the story of a presuming youth who fixes his covetous hopes upon one so far above his degraded state that she and all who behold his uncouth efforts are consumed by helpless laughter. Ultimately he is to be delivered to a severe but well—earned death by a conscientious official whose leisurely purpose is to possess the maiden for himself. Although occasionally bordering on the funereal, the details of the narrative are to be of a light and gravity—removing nature on the whole. Proceed."

The story—teller made obeisance towards the Mandarin, whose face meanwhile revealed a complete absence of every variety of emotion.

"Have I your genial permission to comply, nobility?" he asked.

"The word is spoken," replied Shan Tien unwillingly. "Let the vaunt be justified."

"I obey, High Excellence. This involves the story of Hien and the Chief Examiner."

The Story of Hien and the Chief Examiner

In the reign of the Emperor K'ong there lived at Ho Chow an official named Thang—li, whose degree was that of Chief Examiner of Literary Competitions for the district. He had an only daughter, Fa Fei, whose mind was so liberally stored with graceful accomplishments as to give rise to the saying that to be in her presence was more refreshing than to sit in a garden of perfumes listening to the wisdom of seven elderly philosophers, while her glossy floating hair, skin of crystal lustre, crescent nails and feet smaller and more symmetrical than an opening lotus made her the most beautiful creature in all Ho Chow. Possessing no son, and maintaining an open contempt towards all his nearer relations, it had become a habit for Thang—li to converse with his daughter almost on terms of equality, so that she was not surprised on one occasion, when, calling her into his presence, he graciously commanded her to express herself freely on whatever subject seemed most important in her mind.

"The Great Middle Kingdom in which we live is not only inhabited by the most enlightened, humane and courteous—minded race, but is itself fittingly the central and most desirable point of the Universe, surrounded by other less favoured countries peopled by races of pig—tailless men and large—footed women, all destitute of refined intelligence," replied Fa Fei modestly. "The sublime Emperor is of all persons the wisest, purest and—"

"Undoubtedly," interrupted Thang–li. "These truths are of gem–like brilliance, and the ears of a patriotic subject can never be closed to the beauty and music of their ceaseless repetition. Yet between father and daughter in the security of an inner chamber there not unnaturally arise topics of more engrossing interest. For example, now that you are of a marriageable age, have your eyes turned in the direction of any particular suitor?"

"Oh, thrice–venerated sire!" exclaimed Fa Fei, looking vainly round for some attainable object behind which to conceal her honourable confusion, "should the thoughts of a maiden dwell definitely on a matter of such delicate consequence?"

"They should not," replied her father; "but as they invariably do, the speculation is one outside our immediate concern. Nor, as it is your wonted custom to ascend upon the outside roof at a certain hour of the morning, is it reasonable to assume that you are ignorant of the movements of the two young men who daily contrive to linger before this in no way attractive residence without any justifiable pretext."

"My father is all–seeing," replied Fa Fei in a commendable spirit of dutiful acquiescence, and also because it seemed useless to deny the circumstance.

"It is unnecessary," said Thang–li. "Surrounded, as he is, by a retinue of eleven female attendants, it is enough to be all–hearing. But which of the two has impressed you in the more favourable light?"

"How can the inclinations of an obedient daughter affect the matter?" said Fa Fei evasively. "Unless, O most indulgent, it is your amiable intention to permit me to follow the inspiration of my own unfettered choice?"

"Assuredly," replied the benevolent Thang–li. "Provided, of course, that the choice referred to should by no evil mischance run in a contrary direction to my own maturer judgment."

"Yet if such an eventuality did haply arise?" persisted Fa Fei.

"None but the irredeemably foolish spend their time in discussing the probable sensation of being struck by a thunderbolt," said Thang–li more coldly. "From this day forth, also, be doubly guarded in the undeviating balance of your attitude. Restrain the swallow–like flights of your admittedly brilliant eyes, and control the movements of your expressive fan within the narrowest bounds of necessity. This person's position between the two is one of exceptional delicacy and he has by no means yet decided which to favour.

"In such a case," inquired Fa Fei, caressing his pig–tail persuasively, "how does a wise man act, and by what manner of omens is he influenced in his decision?"

"In such a case," replied Thang–li, "a very wise man does not act; but maintaining an impassive countenance, he awaits the unrolling of events until he sees what must inevitably take place. It is thus that his reputation for wisdom is built up."

"Furthermore," said Fa Fei hopefully, "the ultimate pronouncement rests with the guarding deities?"

"Unquestionably," agreed Thang–li. "Yet, by a venerable custom, the esteem of the maiden's parents is the detail to which the suitors usually apply themselves with the greatest diligence."

*

Of the two persons thus referred to by Thang–li, one, Tsin Lung, lived beneath the sign of the Righteous Ink Brush. By hereditary right Tsin Lung followed the profession of copying out the more difficult Classics in minute characters upon parchments so small that an entire library could be concealed among the folds of a garment, in this painstaking way enabling many persons who might otherwise have failed at the public examination, and been driven to spend an idle and perhaps even dissolute life, to pass with honourable distinction to themselves and widespread credit to his resourceful system. One gratified candidate, indeed, had compared his triumphal passage through the many grades of the competition to the luxurious ease of being carried in a sedan–chair, and from that time Tsin Lung was jestingly referred to as a "sedan–chair."

It might reasonably be thought that a person enjoying this enviable position would maintain a loyal pride in the venerable traditions of his house and suffer the requirements of his craft to become the four walls of his ambition. Alas! Tsin Lung must certainly have been born under the influence of a very evil planet, for the literary quality of his profession did not entice his imagination at all, and his sole and frequently-expressed desire was to become a pirate. Nothing but the necessity of obtaining a large sum of money with which to purchase a formidable junk and to procure the services of a band of capable and bloodthirsty outlaws bound him to Ho Chow, unless, perchance, it might be the presence there of Fa Fei after he had once cast his piratical eye upon her overwhelming beauty.

The other of the two persons was Hien, a youth of studious desires and unassuming manner. His father had been the chief tax-collector of the Chunling mountains, beyond the town, and although the exact nature of the tax and the reason for its extortion had become forgotten in the process of interminable ages, he himself never admitted any doubt of his duty to collect it from all who passed over the mountains, even though the disturbed state of the country made it impossible for him to transmit the proceeds to the capital. To those who uncharitably extended the envenomed tongue of suspicion towards the very existence of any Imperial tax, the father of Hien replied with unshaken loyalty that in such a case the sublime Emperor had been very treacherously served by his advisers, as the difficulty of the paths and the intricate nature of the passes rendered the spot peculiarly suitable for the purpose, and as he was accompanied by a well-armed and somewhat impetuous band of followers, his arguments were inevitably successful. When he Passed Beyond, Hien accepted the leadership, but solely out of a conscientious respect for his father's memory, for his heart was never really in the occupation. His time was almost wholly taken up in reading the higher Classics, and even before he had seen Fa Fei his determination had been taken that when once he had succeeded in passing the examination for the second degree and thereby become entitled to an inferior mandarinship he would abandon his former life forever. From this resolution the entreaties of his devoted followers could not shake him, and presently they ceased to argue, being reassured by the fact that although Hien presented himself unfailingly for every examination his name appeared at the foot of each successive list with unvarying frequency. It was at this period that he first came under the ennobling spell of Fa Fei's influence and from that time forth he redoubled his virtuous efforts.

After conversing with her father, as already related, Fa Fei spent the day in an unusually thoughtful spirit. As soon as it was dark she stepped out from the house and veiling her purpose under the pretext of gathering some herbs to complete a charm she presently entered a grove of overhanging cedars where Hien had long been awaiting her footsteps.

"Rainbow of my prosaic existence!" he exclaimed, shaking hands with himself courteously, "have you yet carried out your bold suggestion?" and so acute was his anxiety for her reply that he continued to hold his hand unconsciously until Fa Fei turned away her face in very becoming confusion.

"Alas, O my dragon–hearted one," she replied at length, "I have indeed dared to read the scroll, but how shall this person's inelegant lips utter so detestable a truth?"

"It is already revealed," said Hien, striving to conceal from her his bitterness. "When the list of competitors at the late examination is publicly proclaimed to–morrow at the four gates of the city, the last name to be announced will again, and for the eleventh time, be that of the degraded Hien."

"Beloved," exclaimed Fa Fei, resolved that as she could not honourably deny that her Hien's name was again indeed the last one to appear she would endeavour to lead his mind subtly away to the contemplation of more pleasurable thoughts, "it is as you have said, but although your name is the last, it is by far the most dignified and romantic–sounding of all, nor is there another throughout the list which can be compared to it for the ornamental grace of its flowing curves."

"Nevertheless," replied Hien, in a violent access of self–contempt, "it is a name of abandoned omen and is destined only to reach the ears of posterity to embellish the proverb of scorn, 'The lame duck should avoid the ploughed field.' Can there—can there by no chance have been some hope–inspiring error?"

"Thus were the names inscribed on the parchment which after the public announcement will be affixed to the Hall of Ten Thousand Lustres," replied Fa Fei. "With her own unworthy eyes this incapable person beheld it."

"The name 'Hien' is in no way striking or profound," continued the one in question, endeavouring to speak as though the subject referred to some person standing at a considerable distance away. "Furthermore, so commonplace and devoid of character are its written outlines that it has very much the same appearance whichever way up it is looked at. . . . The possibility that in your graceful confusion you held the list in such a position that what appeared to be the end was in reality the beginning is remote in the extreme, yet—"

In spite of an absorbing affection Fa Fei could not disguise from herself that her feelings would have been more pleasantly arranged if her lover had been inspired to accept his position unquestioningly. "There is a detail, hitherto unrevealed, which disposes of all such amiable suggestions," she replied. "After the name referred to, someone in authority had inscribed the undeniable comment 'As usual.'"

"The omen is a most encouraging one," exclaimed Hien, throwing aside all his dejection. "Hitherto this person's untiring efforts had met with no official recognition whatever. It is now obvious that far from being lost in the crowd he is becoming an object of honourable interest to the examiners."

"One frequently hears it said, 'After being struck on the head with an axe it is a positive pleasure to be beaten about the body with a wooden club,'" said Fa Fei, "and the meaning of the formerly elusive proverb is now explained. Would it not be prudent to avail yourself at length of the admittedly outrageous Tsin Lung's services, so that this period of unworthy trial may be brought to a distinguished close?"

"It is said, 'Do not eat the fruit of the stricken branch,'" replied Hien, "and this person will never owe his success to one who is so detestable in his life and morals that with every facility for a scholarly and contemplative existence he freely announces his barbarous intention of becoming a pirate. Truly the Dragon of Justice does but sleep for a little time, and when he awakens all that will be left of the mercenary Tsin Lung and those who associate with him will scarcely be enough to fill an orange skin."

"Doubtless it will be so," agreed Fa Fei, regretting, however, that Hien had not been content to prophesy a more limited act of vengeance, until, at least, her father had come to a definite decision regarding her own future. "Alas, though, the Book of Dynasties expressly says, 'The one–legged never stumble,' and Tsin Lung is so morally ill–balanced that the proverb may even apply to him."

"Do not fear," said Hien. "It is elsewhere written, 'Love and leprosy few escape,' and the spirit of Tsin Lung's destiny is perhaps even at this moment lurking unsuspected behind some secret place."

"If," exclaimed a familiar voice, "the secret place alluded to should chance to be a hollow cedar–tree of inadequate girth, the unfortunate spirit in question will have my concentrated sympathy."

"Just and magnanimous father!" exclaimed Fa Fei, thinking it more prudent not to recognize that he had learned of their meeting–place and concealing himself there had awaited their coming, "when your absence was discovered a heaven–sent inspiration led me to this spot. Have I indeed been permitted here to find you?"

"Assuredly you have," replied Thang–li, who was equally desirous of concealing the real circumstances, although the difficulty of the position into which he had hastily and incautiously thrust his body on their approach compelled him to reveal himself. "The same inspiration led me to lose myself in this secluded spot, as being the one which you would inevitably search."

"Yet by what incredible perversity does it arise, venerable Thang–li, that a leisurely and philosophical stroll should result in a person of your dignified proportions occupying so unattractive a position?" said Hien, who appeared to be too ingenuous to suspect Thang–li's craft, in spite of a warning glance from Fa Fei's expressive eyes.

"The remark is a natural one, O estimable youth," replied Thang–li, doubtless smiling benevolently, although nothing of his person could be actually seen by Hien or Fa Fei, "but the recital is not devoid of humiliation. While peacefully studying the position of the heavens this person happened to glance into the upper branches of a tree and among them he beheld a bird's nest of unusual size and richness—one that would promise to yield a dish of the rarest flavour. Lured on by the anticipation of so sumptuous a course, he rashly trusted his body to an unworthy branch, and the next moment, notwithstanding his unceasing protests to the protecting Powers, he was impetuously deposited within this hollow trunk."

"Not unreasonably is it said, 'A bird in the soup is better than an eagle's nest in the desert,'" exclaimed Hien. "The pursuit of a fair and lofty object is set about with hidden pitfalls to others beyond you, O noble Chief Examiner! By what nimble–witted act of adroitness is it now your enlightened purpose to extricate yourself?"

At this admittedly polite but in no way inspiring question a silence of a very acute intensity seemed to fall on that part of the forest. The mild and inscrutable expression of Hien's face did not vary, but into Fa Fei's eyes there came an unexpected but not altogether disapproving radiance, while, without actually altering, the appearance of the tree encircling Thang–li's form undoubtedly conveyed the impression that the benevolent smile which might hitherto have been reasonably assumed to exist within had been abruptly withdrawn.

"Your meaning is perhaps well–intentioned, gracious Hien," said Thang–li at length, "but as an offer of disinterested assistance your words lack the gong–like clash of spontaneous enthusiasm. Nevertheless, if you will inconvenience yourself to the extent of climbing this not really difficult tree for a short distance you will be able to grasp some outlying portion of this one's body without any excessive fatigue."

"Mandarin," replied Hien, "to touch even the extremity of your incomparable pig–tail would be an honour repaying all earthly fatigue—"

"Do not hesitate to seize it, then," said Thang–li, as Hien paused. "Yet, if this person may without ostentation continue the analogy, to grasp him firmly by the shoulders must confer a higher distinction and would be even more agreeable to his own feelings."

"The proposal is a flattering one," continued Hien, "but my hands are bound down by the decree of the High Powers, for among the most inviolable of the edicts is it not written: 'Do the lame offer to carry the footsore; the blind to protect the one–eyed? Distrust the threadbare person who from an upper back room invites you to join him in an infallible process of enrichment; turn aside from the one devoid of pig–tail who says, "Behold, a few drops daily at the hour of the morning sacrifice and your virtuous head shall be again like a well–sown rice–field at the time of harvest"; and towards the passing stranger who offers you that mark of confidence which your friends withhold close and yet again open a different eye. So shall you grow obese in wisdom'?"

"Alas!" exclaimed Thang–li, "the inconveniences of living in an Empire where a person has to regulate the affairs of his everyday life by the sacred but antiquated proverbial wisdom of his remote ancestors are by no means trivial. Cannot this possibly mythical obstacle be flattened–out by the amiable acceptance of a jar of sea snails or some other seasonable delicacy, honourable Hien?"

"Nothing but a really well–grounded encouragement as regards Fa Fei can persuade this person to regard himself as anything but a solitary outcast," replied Hien, "and one paralysed in every useful impulse. Rather than abandon the opportunity of coming to such an arrangement he would almost be prepared to give up all idea of ever passing the examination for the second degree."

"By no means," exclaimed Thang–li hastily. "The sacrifice would be too excessive. Do not relinquish your sleuth–hound–like persistence, and success will inevitably reward your ultimate end."

"Can it really be," said Hien incredulously, "that my contemptible efforts are a matter of sympathetic interest to one so high up in every way as the renowned Chief Examiner?"

"They are indeed," replied Thang–li, with that ingratiating candour that marked his whole existence. "Doubtless so prosaic a detail as the system of remuneration has never occupied your refined thoughts, but when it is understood that those in the position of this person are rewarded according to the success of the candidates you will begin to grasp the attitude."

"In that case," remarked Hien, with conscious humiliation, "nothing but a really sublime tolerance can have restrained you from upbraiding this obscure competitor as a thoroughly corrupt egg."

"On the contrary," replied Thang–li reassuringly, "I have long regarded you as the auriferous fowl itself. It is necessary to explain, perhaps, that the payment by result alluded to is not based on the number of successful candidates, but—much more reasonably as all those have to be provided with lucrative appointments by the authorities—on the economy effected to the State by those whom I can conscientiously reject. Owing to the malignant Tsin Lung's sinister dexterity these form an ever–decreasing band, so that you may now be fittingly deemed the chief prop of a virtuous but poverty–afflicted line. When you reflect that for the past eleven years you have thus really had the honour of providing the engaging Fa Fei with all the necessities of her very ornamental existence you will see that you already possess practically all the advantages of matrimony. Nevertheless, if you will now bring our agreeable conversation to an end by releasing this inauspicious person he will consider the matter with the most indulgent sympathies."

"Withhold!" exclaimed a harsh voice before Hien could reply, and from behind a tree where he had heard Thang—li's impolite reference to himself Tsin Lung stood forth. "How does it chance, O two—complexioned Chief Examiner, that after weighing this one's definite proposals—even to the extent of demanding a certain proportion in advance—you are now engaged in holding out the same alluring hope to another? Assuredly, if your existence is so critically imperilled this person and none other will release you and claim the reward."

"Turn your face backwards, imperious Tsin Lung," cried Hien. "These incapable hands alone shall have the overwhelming distinction of drawing forth the illustrious Thang—li."

"Do not get entangled among my advancing footsteps, immature one," contemptuously replied Tsin Lung, shaking the massive armour in which he was encased from head to foot. "It is inept for pigmies to stand before one who has every intention of becoming a rapacious pirate shortly."

"The sedan—chair is certainly in need of new shafts," retorted Hien, and drawing his sword with an expression of ferocity he caused it to whistle around his head so loudly that a flock of migratory doves began to arrive, under the impression that others of their tribe were calling them to assemble.

"Alas!" exclaimed Thang—li, in an accent of despair, "doubtless the wise Nung—yu was surrounded by disciples all eager that no other should succour him when he remarked: 'A humble friend in the same village is better than sixteen influential brothers in the Royal Palace.' In all this illimitable Empire is there not room for one whose aspirations are bounded by the submerged walls of a predatory junk and another whose occupation is limited to the upper passes of the Chunling mountains? Consider the poignant nature of this person's vain regrets if by a couple of evilly directed blows you succeeded at this inopportune moment in exterminating one another!"

"Do not fear, exalted Thang—li," cried Hien, who, being necessarily somewhat occupied in preparing himself against Tsin Lung's attack, failed to interpret these words as anything but a direct encouragement to his own cause. "Before the polluting hands of one who disdains the Classics shall be laid upon your sacred extremities this tenacious person will fix upon his antagonist with a serpent—like embrace and, if necessary, suffer the spirits of both to Pass Upward in one breath." And to impress Tsin Lung with his resolution he threw away his scabbard and picked it up again several times.

"Grow large in hope, worthy Chief Examiner," cried Tsin Lung, who from a like cause was involved in a similar misapprehension. "Rather shall your imperishable bones adorn the interior of a hollow cedar—tree throughout all futurity than you shall suffer the indignity of being extricated by an earth—nurtured sleeve—snatcher." And to intimidate Hien by the display he continued to clash his open hand against his leg armour until the pain became intolerable.

"Honourable warriors!" implored Thang—li in so agonized a voice—and also because they were weary of the exercise—that Hien and Tsin Lung paused, "curb your bloodthirsty ambitions for a breathing—space and listen to what will probably be a Last Expression. Believe the passionate sincerity of this one's throat when he proclaims that there would be nothing repugnant to his very keenest susceptibilities if an escaping parricide, who was also guilty of rebellion, temple—robbing, book—burning, murder and indiscriminate violence, and the pollution of tombs, took him familiarly by the hand at this moment. What, therefore, would be his gratified feelings if two such nobly—born subjects joined forces and drew him up dexterously by the body—cloth? Accept his definite assurance that without delay a specific pronouncement would be made respecting the bestowal of the one around whose jade—like personality this encounter has arisen."

"The proposal casts a reasonable shadow, gracious Hien," remarked Tsin Lung, turning towards the other with courteous deference. "Shall we bring a scene of irrational carnage to an end and agree to regard the incomparable Thang—li's benevolent tongue as an outstretched olive branch?"

"It is admittedly said, 'Every road leads in two directions,' and the alternative you suggest, O virtue—loving Tsin Lung, is both reputable and just," replied Hien pleasantly. In this amiable spirit they extricated Thang–li and bore him to the ground. At an appointed hour he received them with becoming ceremony and after a many–coursed repast rose to fulfil the specific terms of his pledge.

"The Line of Thang," he remarked with inoffensive pride, "has for seven generations been identified with a high standard of literary achievement. Undeniably it is a very creditable thing to control the movements of an ofttime erratic vessel and to emerge triumphantly from a combat with every junk you encounter, and it is no less worthy of esteem to gather round about one, on the sterile slopes of the Chunlings, a devoted band of followers. Despite these virtues, however, neither occupation is marked by any appreciable literary flavour, and my word is, therefore, that both persons shall present themselves for the next examination, and when in due course the result is declared the more successful shall be hailed as the chosen suitor. Lo, I have spoken into a sealed bottle, and my voice cannot vary."

Then replied Tsin Lung: "Truly, it is as it is said, astute Thang–li, though the encircling wall of a hollow cedar–tree, for example, might impart to the voice in question a less uncompromising ring of finality than it possesses when raised in a silk–lined chamber and surrounded by a band of armed retainers. Nevertheless the pronouncement is one which appeals to this person's sense of justice, and the only improvement he can suggest is that the superfluous Hien should hasten that ceremony at which he will be an honoured guest by now signifying his intention of retiring from so certain a defeat. For by what expedient," he continued, with arrogant persistence, "can you avert that end, O ill–destined Hien? Have you not burned joss–sticks to the deities, both good and bad, for eleven years unceasingly? Can you, as this person admittedly can, inscribe the Classics with such inimitable delicacy that an entire volume of the Book of Decorum, copied in his most painstaking style, may be safely carried about within a hollow tooth, a lengthy ode, traced on a shred of silk, wrapped undetectably around a single eyelash?"

"It is true that the one before you cannot bend his brush to such deceptive ends," replied Hien modestly. "A detail, however, has escaped your reckoning. Hitherto Hien has been opposed by a thousand, and against so many it is true that the spirits of his ancestors have been able to afford him very little help. On this occasion he need regard one adversary alone. Giving those Forces which he invokes clearly to understand that they need not concern themselves with any other, he will plainly intimate that after so many sacrifices on his part something of a really tangible affliction is required to overwhelm Tsin Lung. Whether this shall take the form of mental stagnation, bodily paralysis, demoniacal possession, derangement of the internal faculties, or being changed into one of the lower animals, it might be presumptuous on this person's part to stipulate, but by invoking every accessible power and confining himself to this sole petition a very definite tragedy may be expected. Beware, O contumacious Lung, 'However high the tree the shortest axe can reach its trunk.'"

*

As the time for the examination drew near the streets of Ho Chow began to wear a fuller and more animated appearance both by day and night. Tsin Lung's outer hall was never clear of anxious suppliants all entreating him to supply them with minute and reliable copies of the passages which they found most difficult in the selected works, but although his low and avaricious nature was incapable of rejecting this means of gain he devoted his closest energies and his most inspired moments to his own personal copies, a set of books so ethereal that they floated in the air without support and so cunningly devised in the blending of their colour as to be, in fact, quite invisible to any but his microscopic eyes. Hien, on the other hand, devoted himself solely to interesting the Powers against his rival's success by every variety of incentive, omen, sacrifice, imprecation, firework, inscribed curse, promise, threat or combination of inducements. Through the crowded streets and by-ways of Ho Chow moved the imperturbable Thang-li, smiling benevolently on those whom he encountered and encouraging each competitor, and especially Hien and Tsin Lung, with a cheerful proverb suited to the moment.

An outside cause had further contributed to make this period one of the most animated in the annals of Ho Chow, for not only was the city, together with the rest of the imperishable Empire, celebrating a great and popular victory, but, as a direct consequence of that event, the sublime Emperor himself was holding his court at no great distance away. An armed and turbulent rabble of illiterate barbarians had suddenly appeared in the north and, not giving a really sufficient indication of their purpose, had traitorously assaulted the capital. Had he followed the prompting of his own excessive magnanimity, the charitable Monarch would have refused to take any notice whatever of so puny and contemptible a foe, but so unmistakable became the wishes of the Ever-victorious Army that, yielding to their importunity, he placed himself at their head and resolutely led them backward. Had the opposing army been more intelligent, this crafty move would certainly have enticed them on into the plains, where they would have fallen an easy victim to the Imperial troops and all perished miserably. Owing to their low standard of reasoning, however, the mule–like invaders utterly failed to grasp the advantage which, as far as the appearance tended, they might reasonably be supposed to reap by an immediate pursuit. They remained incapably within the capital slavishly increasing its defences, while the Ever–victorious lurked resourcefully in the neighbourhood of Ho Chow, satisfied that with so dull–witted an adversary they could, if the necessity arose, go still further.

Upon a certain day of the period thus indicated there arrived at the gate of the royal pavilion one having the appearance of an aged seer, who craved to be led into the Imperial Presence.

"Lo, Mightiest," said a slave, bearing in this message, "there stands at the outer gate one resembling an ancient philosopher, desiring to gladden his failing eyesight before he Passes Up with a brief vision of your illuminated countenance."

"The petition is natural but inopportune," replied the agreeable Monarch. "Let the worthy soothsayer be informed that after an exceptionally fatiguing day we are now snatching a few short hours of necessary repose, from which it would be unseemly to recall us."

"He received your gracious words with distended ears and then observed that it was for your All–wisdom to decide whether an inspired message which he had read among the stars was not of more consequence than even a refreshing sleep," reported the slave, returning.

"In that case," replied the Sublimest, "tell the persevering wizard that we have changed our minds and are religiously engaged in worshipping our ancestors, so that it would be really sacrilegious to interrupt us."

"He kowtowed profoundly at the mere mention of your charitable occupation and proceeded to depart, remarking that it would indeed be corrupt to disturb so meritorious an exercise with a scheme simply for your earthly enrichment," again reported the message–bearer.

"Restrain him!" hastily exclaimed the broadminded Sovereign. "Give the venerable necromancer clearly to understand that we have worshipped them enough for one day. Doubtless the accommodating soothsayer has discovered some rare jewel which he is loyally bringing to embellish our crown."

"There are rarer jewels than those which can be pasted in a crown, Supreme Head," said the stranger, entering unperceived behind the attending slave. He bore the external signs of an infirm magician, while his face was hidden in a cloth to mark the imposition of a solemn vow. "With what apter simile," he continued, "can this person describe an imperishable set of verses which he heard this morning falling from the lips of a wandering musician like a seven-roped cable of pearls pouring into a silver bucket? The striking and original title was 'Concerning Spring,' and although the snow lay deep at the time several bystanders agreed that an azalea bush within hearing came into blossom at the eighty-seventh verse."

"We have heard of the poem to which you refer with so just a sense of balance," said the impartial Monarch encouragingly. (Though not to create a two-sided impression it may be freely stated that he himself was the author of the inspired composition.) "Which part, in your mature judgment, reflected the highest genius and maintained the most perfectly-matched analogy?"

"It is aptly said: 'When it is dark the sun no longer shines, but who shall forget the colours of the rainbow?'" replied the astrologer evasively. "How is it possible to suspend topaz in one cup of the balance and weigh it against amethyst in the other; or who in a single language can compare the tranquillizing grace of a maiden with the invigorating pleasure of witnessing a well-contested rat-fight?"

"Your insight is clear and unbiased," said the gracious Sovereign. "But however entrancing it is to wander unchecked through a garden of bright images, are we not enticing your mind from another subject of almost equal importance?"

"There is yet another detail, it is true," admitted the sage, "but regarding its comparative importance a thoroughly loyal subject may be permitted to amend the remark of a certain wise Emperor of a former dynasty: 'Any person in the City can discover a score of gold mines if necessary, but One only could possibly have written "Concerning Spring."'"

"The arts may indeed be regarded as lost," acquiesced the magnanimous Head, "with the exception of a solitary meteor here and there. Yet in the trivial matter of mere earthly enrichment—"

"Truly," agreed the other. "There is, then, a whisper in the province that the floor of the Imperial treasury is almost visible."

"The rumour, as usual, exaggerates the facts grossly," replied the Greatest. "The floor of the Imperial treasury is quite visible."

"Yet on the first day of the next moon the not inconsiderable revenue contributed by those who present themselves for the examination will flow in."

"And by an effete and unworthy custom almost immediately flow out again to reward the efforts of the successful," replied the Wearer of the Yellow in an accent of refined bitterness. "On other occasions it is possible to assist the overworked treasurer with a large and glutinous hand, but from time immemorial the claims of the competitors have been inviolable."

"Yet if by a heaven—sent chance none, or very few, reached the necessary standard of excellence—?"

"Such a chance, whether proceeding from the Upper Air or the Other Parts would be equally welcome to a very hard—lined Ruler," replied the one who thus described himself.

"Then listen, O K'ong—hi, of the imperishable dynasty of Chung," said the stranger. "Thus was it laid upon me in the form of a spontaneous dream. For seven centuries the Book of the Observances has been the unvarying Classic of the examinations because during that period it has never been surpassed. Yet as the Empire has admittedly existed from all time, and as it would be impious not to agree that the immortal System is equally antique, it is reasonable to suppose that the Book of the Observances displaced an earlier and inferior work, and is destined in the cycle of time to be itself laid aside for a still greater."

"The inference is self–evident," acknowledged the Emperor uneasily, "but the logical development is one which this diffident Monarch hesitates to commit to spoken words."

"It is not a matter for words but for a stroke of the Vermilion Pencil," replied the other in a tone of inspired authority. "Across the faint and puny effusions of the past this person sees written in very large and obliterating strokes the words 'Concerning Spring.' Where else can be found so novel a conception combined with so unique a way of carrying it out? What other poem contains so many thoughts that one instinctively remembers as having heard before, so many involved allusions that baffle the imagination of the keenest, and so much sound in so many words? With the possible exception of Meng–hu's masterpiece, 'The Empty Coffin,' what other work so skilfully conveys the impression of being taken down farther than one can ever again come up and then suddenly upraised beyond the possible descent? Where else can be found so complete a defiance of all that has hitherto been deemed essential, and, to insert a final wedge, what other poem is half so long?"

"Your criticism is severe but just," replied the Sovereign, "except that part having reference to Meng–hu. Nevertheless, the atmosphere of the proposal, though reasonable, looms a degree stormily into a troubled future. Can it be permissible even for—"

"Omnipotence!" exclaimed the seer.

"The title is well recalled," confessed the Emperor. "Yet although unquestionably omnipotent there must surely be some limits to our powers in dealing with so old established a system as that of the examinations."

"Who can doubt a universal admission that the composer of 'Concerning Spring' is capable of doing anything?" was the profound reply. "Let the mandate be sent out—but, to an obvious end, let it be withheld until the eve of the competitions."

"The moment of hesitancy has faded; go forth in the certainty, esteemed," said the Emperor reassuringly. "You have carried your message with a discreet hand. Yet before you go, if there is any particular mark of Imperial favour that we can show—something of a special but necessarily honorary nature—do not set an iron screen between your ambition and the light of our favourable countenance."

"There is indeed such a signal reward," assented the aged person, with an air of prepossessing diffidence. "A priceless copy of the immortal work—"

"By all means," exclaimed the liberal-minded Sovereign, with an expression of great relief. "Take three or four in case any of your fascinating relations have large literary appetites. Or, still more conveniently arranged, here is an unopened package from the stall of those who send forth the printed leaves—'thirteen in the semblance of twelve,' as the quaint and harmonious phrase of their craft has it. Walk slowly, revered, and a thousand rainbows guide your retiring footsteps."

Concerning the episode of this discreetly-veiled personage the historians who have handed down the story of the imperishable affection of Hien and Fa Fei have maintained an illogical silence. Yet it is related that about the same time, as Hien was walking by the side of a bamboo forest of stunted growth, he was astonished by the maiden suddenly appearing before him from the direction of the royal camp. She was incomparably radiant and had the appearance of being exceptionally well satisfied with herself. Commanding him that he should stand motionless with closed eyes, in order to ascertain what the presiding deities would allot him, she bound a somewhat weighty object to the end of his pig-tail, at the same time asking him in how short a period he could commit about nineteen thousand lines of atrociously ill-arranged verse to the tablets of his mind.

"Then do not suffer the rice to grow above your ankles," she continued, when Hien had modestly replied that six days with good omens should be sufficient, "but retiring to your innermost chamber bar the door and digest this scroll as though it contained the last expression of an eccentric and vastly rich relation," and with a laugh more musical than the vibrating of a lute of the purest Yun-nan jade in the Grotto of Ten Thousand Echoes she vanished.

It has been sympathetically remarked that no matter how painstakingly a person may strive to lead Destiny along a carefully-prepared path and towards a fit and thoroughly virtuous end there is never lacking some inopportune creature to thrust his superfluous influence into an opposing balance. This naturally suggests the intolerable Tsin Lung, whose ghoulish tastes led him to seek the depths of that same glade on the following day. Walking with downcast eyes, after his degraded custom, he presently became aware of an object lying some distance from his way. To those who have already fathomed the real character of this repulsive person it will occasion no surprise to know that, urged on by the insatiable curiosity that was deeply grafted on to his avaricious nature, he turned aside to probe into a matter with which he had no possible concern, and at length succeeded in drawing a package from the thick bush in which it had been hastily concealed. Finding that it contained twelve lengthy poems entitled "Concerning Spring", he greedily thrust one in his sleeve, and upon his return, with no other object than the prompting of an ill–regulated mind, he spent all the time that remained before the contest in learning it from end to end.

There have been many remarkable scenes enacted in the great Examination Halls and in the narrow cells around, but it can at once be definitely stated that nothing either before or since has approached the unanimous burst of frenzy that shook the dynasty of Chung when in the third year of his reign the well–meaning but too–easily–led–aside Emperor K'ong inopportunely sought to replace the sublime Classic then in use with a work that has since been recognized to be not only shallow but inept. At Ho Chow nine hundred and ninety–eight voices blended into one soul–benumbing cry of rage, having all the force and precision of a carefully drilled chorus, when the papers were opened, and had not the candidates been securely barred within their solitary pens a popular rising must certainly have taken place. There they remained for three days and nights, until the clamour had subsided into a low but continuous hum, and they were too weak to carry out a combined effort.

Throughout this turmoil Hien and Tsin Lung each plied an unfaltering brush. It may here be advantageously stated that the former person was not really slow or obtuse and his previous failures were occasioned solely by the inequality he strove under in relying upon his memory alone when every other competitor without exception had provided himself with a concealed scrip. Tsin Lung also had a very retentive mind. The inevitable consequence was, therefore, that when the papers were collected Hien and Tsin Lung had accomplished an identical number of correct lines and no other person had made even an attempt.

In explaining Thang–li's subsequent behaviour it has been claimed by many that the strain of being compelled, in the exercise of his duty, to remain for three days and three nights in the middle of the Hall surrounded by that ferocious horde, all clamouring to reach him, and the contemplation of the immense sum which he would gain by so unparalleled a batch of rejections, contorted his faculties of discrimination and sapped the resources of his usually active mind. Whatever cause is accepted, it is agreed that as soon as he returned to his house he summoned Hien and Tsin Lung together and leaving them for a moment presently returned, leading Fa Fei by the hand. It is further agreed by all that these three persons noticed upon his face a somewhat preoccupied expression, and on the one side much has been made of the admitted fact that as he spoke he wandered round the room catching flies, an occupation eminently suited to his age and leisurely tastes but, it may be confessed, not altogether well chosen at so ceremonious a moment.

"It has been said," he began at length, withdrawing his eyes reluctantly from an unusually large insect upon the ceiling and addressing himself to the maiden, "that there are few situations in life that cannot be honourably settled, and without loss of time, either by suicide, a bag of gold, or by thrusting a despised antagonist over the edge of a precipice upon a dark night. This inoffensive person, however, has striven to arrive at the conclusion of a slight domestic arrangement both by passively waiting for the event to unroll itself and, at a later period, by the offer of a definite omen. Both of the male persons concerned have applied themselves so tenaciously to the ordeal that the result, to this simple one's antique mind, savours overmuch of the questionable arts. The genial and light−witted Emperor appears to have put his foot into the embarrassment ineffectually; and Destiny herself has every indication of being disinclined to settle so doubtful a point. As a last resort it now remains for you yourself to decide which of these strenuous and evenly−balanced suitors I may acclaim with ten thousand felicitations."

"In that case, venerated and commanding sire," replied Fa Fei simply, yet concealing her real regard behind the retiring mask of a modest indifference, "it shall be Hien, because his complexion goes the more prettily with my favourite heliotrope silk."

When the results of the examination were announced it was at once assumed by those with whom he had trafficked that Tsin Lung had been guilty of the most degraded treachery. Understanding the dangers of his position, that person decided upon an immediate flight. Disguised as a wild−beast tamer, and leading several apparently ferocious creatures by a cord, he succeeded in making his way undetected through the crowds of competitors watching his house, and hastily collecting his wealth together he

184

set out towards the coast. But the evil spirits which had hitherto protected him now withdrew their aid. In the wildest passes of the Chunlings Hien's band was celebrating his unexpected success by a costly display of fireworks, varied with music and dancing. . . . So heavily did they tax him that when he reached his destination he was only able to purchase a small and dilapidated junk and to enlist the services of three thoroughly incompetent mercenaries. The vessels which he endeavoured to pursue stealthily in the hope of restoring his fortunes frequently sailed towards him under the impression that he was sinking and trying to attract their benevolent assistance. When his real intention was at length understood both he and his crew were invariably beaten about the head with clubs, so that although he persevered until the three hired assassins rebelled, he never succeeded in committing a single act of piracy. Afterwards he gained a precarious livelihood by entering into conversation with strangers, and still later he stood upon a board and dived for small coins which the charitable threw into the water. In this pursuit he was one day overtaken by a voracious sea–monster and perished miserably.

The large–meaning but never fully–accomplishing Emperor K'ong reigned for yet another year, when he was deposed by the powerful League of the Three Brothers. To the end of his life he steadfastly persisted that the rebellion was insidiously fanned, if not actually carried out, by a secret confederacy of all the verse–makers of the Empire, who were distrustful of his superior powers. He spent the years of his exile in composing a poetical epitaph to be carved upon his tomb, but his successor, the practical–minded Liu–yen, declined to sanction the expense of procuring so fabulous a supply of marble.

*

When Kai Lung had repeated the story of the well–intentioned youth Hien and of the Chief Examiner Thang–li and had ceased to speak, a pause of questionable import filled the room, broken only by the undignified sleep–noises of the gross Ming–shu. Glances of implied perplexity were freely passed among the guests, but it remained for Shan Tien to voice their doubt.

"Yet wherein is the essence of the test maintained," he asked, "seeing that the one whom you call Hien obtained all that which he desired and he who chiefly opposed his aims was himself involved in ridicule and delivered to a sudden end?"

185

"Beneficence," replied Kai Lung, with courteous ease, despite the pinions that restrained him, "herein it is one thing to demand and another to comply, for among the Platitudes is the admission made: 'No needle has two sharp points.' The conditions which the subtlety of Ming-shu imposed ceased to bind, for their corollary was inexact. In no romance composed by poet or sage are the unassuming hopes of virtuous love brought to a barren end or the one who holds them delivered to an ignominious doom. That which was called for does not therefore exist, but the story of Hien may be taken as indicating the actual course of events should the case arise in an ordinary state of life."

This reply was not deemed inept by most of those who heard, and they even pressed upon the one who spoke slight gifts of snuff and wine. The Mandarin Shan Tien, however, held himself apart.

"It is doubtful if your lips will be able thus to frame so confident a boast when to-morrow fades," was his dark forecast.

"Doubtless their tenor will be changed, revered, in accordance with your far-seeing word," replied Kai Lung submissively as he was led away.

CHAPTER XI. Of Which it is Written: "In Shallow Water Dragons become the Laughing-stock of Shrimps"

AT an early gong-stroke of the following day Kai Lung was finally brought up for judgment in accordance with the venomous scheme of the reptilian Ming-shu. In order to obscure their guilty plans all justice-loving persons were excluded from the court, so that when the story-teller was led in by a single guard he saw before him only the two whose enmity he faced, and one who stood at a distance prepared to serve their purpose.

"Committer of every infamy and inceptor of nameless crimes," began Ming-shu, moistening his brush, "in the past, by the variety of discreditable subterfuges, you have parried the stroke of a just retribution. On this occasion, however, your admitted powers of evasion will avail you nothing. By a special form of administration, designed to meet such cases, your guilt will be taken as proved. The technicalities of passing sentence and seeing it carried out will follow automatically."

"In spite of the urgency of the case," remarked the Mandarin, with an assumption of the evenly–balanced expression that at one time threatened to obtain for him the title of "The Just", "there is one detail which must not be ignored—especially as our ruling will doubtless become a lantern to the feet of later ones. You appear, malefactor, to have committed crimes—and of all these you have been proved guilty by the ingenious arrangement invoked by the learned recorder of my spoken word—which render you liable to hanging, slicing, pressing, boiling, roasting, grilling, freezing, vatting, racking, twisting, drawing, compressing, inflating, rending, spiking, gouging, limb–tying, piecemeal–pruning and a variety of less tersely describable discomforts with which the time of this court need not be taken up. The important consideration is, in what order are we to proceed and when, if ever, are we to stop?"

"Under your benumbing eye, Excellence," suggested Ming–shu resourcefully, "the precedent of taking first that for which the written sign is the longest might be established. Failing that, the names of all the various punishments might be inscribed on separate shreds of parchment and these deposited within your state umbrella. The first withdrawn by an unbiased—"

"High Excellence," Kai Lung ventured to interrupt, "a further plan suggests itself which—"

"If," exclaimed Ming–shu in irrational haste, "if the criminal proposes to narrate a story of one who in like circumstances—"

"Peace!" interposed Shan Tien tactfully. "The felon will only be allowed the usual ten short measures of time for his suggestion, nor must he, under that guise, endeavour to insert an imagined tale."

"Your ruling shall keep straight my bending feet, munificence," replied Kai Lung. "Hear now my simplifying way. In place of cited wrongs—which, after all, are comparatively trivial matters, as being merely offences against another or in defiance of a local usage—substitute one really overwhelming crime for which the penalty is sharp and explicit."

"To that end you would suggest—?" Uncertainty sat upon the brow of both Shan Tien and Ming–shu.

"To straighten out the entangled thread this person would plead guilty to the act—in a lesser capacity and against his untrammelled will—of rejoicing musically on a day set apart for universal woe: a crime aimed directly at the sacred person of the Sublime Head and all those of his Line."

At this significant admission the Mandarin's expression faded; he stroked the lower part of his face several times and unostentatiously indicated to the two attendants that they should retire to a more distant obscurity. Then he spoke.

"When did this—this alleged indiscretion occur, Kai Lung?" he asked in a considerate voice.

"It is useless to raise a cloud of evasion before the sun of your penetrating intellect," replied the story–teller. "The eleventh day of the existing moon was its inauspicious date."

"That being yesterday? Ming–shu, you upon whom the duty of regulating my admittedly vagarious mind devolves, what happened officially on the eleventh day of the Month of Gathering–in?" demanded the Mandarin in an ominous tone.

"On such and such a day, benevolence, three–score and fifteen years ago, the imperishable founder of the existing dynasty ascended on a fiery dragon to be a guest on high," confessed the conscience–stricken scribe, after consulting his printed tablets. "Owing to the stress of a sudden journey significance of the date had previously escaped my weed–grown memory, tolerance."

"Alas!" exclaimed Shan Tien bitterly, "among the innumerable drawbacks of an exacting position the enforced reliance upon an unusually inept and more than ordinarily self–opinionated inscriber of the spoken word is perhaps the most illimitable. Owing to your profuse incompetence that which began as an agreeable prelude to a busy day has turned into a really serious matter."

"Yet, lenience," pleaded the hapless Ming–shu, lowering his voice for the Mandarin's private ear, "so far the danger resides in this one throat alone. That disposed of—"

"Perchance," replied Shan Tien; then turning to Kai Lung: "Doubtless, O story–teller, you were so overcome by the burden of your guilt that until this moment you have hidden the knowledge of it deep within your heart?"

"Magnificence, the commanding quality of your enduring voice would draw the inner matter from a marrow–bone," frankly replied Kai Lung. "Fearful lest this crime might go unconfessed and my weak and trembling ghost therefrom be held to bear its weight unto the end of time, I set out the full happening in a written scroll and sent it at daybreak by a sure and secret hand to a scrupulous official to deal with as he sees fit."

"Your worthy confidant would assuredly be a person of incorruptible integrity?"

"The repute of the upright Censor K'o–yih had reached even these stunted ears."

"Inevitably: the Censor K'o–yih!" Shan Tien's hasty glance took in the angle of the sun and for a moment rested on the door leading to the part where his swiftest horses lay. "By this time the message will have reached him?"

"Omnipotence," replied Kai Lung, spreading out his hands to indicate the full extent of his submission, "not even a piece of the finest Ping–hi silk could be inserted between the deepest secret of this person's heart and your all–extracting gaze. Should you, in your meritorious sense of justice, impose upon me a punishment that would seem to be adequate, it would be superfluous to trouble the obliging Censor in the matter. To this end the one who bears the message lurks in a hidden corner of Tai until a certain hour. If I am in a position to intercept him there he will return the message to my hand; if not, he will straightway bear it to the integritous K'o–yih."

"May the President of Hades reward you—I am no longer in a position to do so!" murmured Shan Tien with concentrated feeling. "Draw near, Kai Lung," he continued sympathetically, "and indicate—with as little delay as possible—what in your opinion would constitute a sufficient punishment."

Thus invited and with his cords unbound, Kai Lung advanced and took his station near the table, Ming—shu noticeably making room for him.

"To be driven from your lofty presence and never again permitted to listen to the wisdom of your inspired lips would undoubtedly be the first essential of my penance, High Excellence."

"It is gran—inflicted," agreed Shan Tien, with swift decision.

"The necessary edict may conveniently be drafted in the form of a safe—conduct for this person and all others of his band to a point beyond the confines of your jurisdiction—when the usually agile—witted Ming—shu can sufficiently shake off the benumbing torpor now assailing him so as to use his brush."

"It is already begun, O virtuous harbinger of joy," protested the dazed Ming—shu, overturning all the four precious implements in his passion to comply. "A mere breath of time—"

"Let it be signed, sealed and thumb—pressed at every available point of ambiguity," enjoined Shan Tien.

"Having thus oppressed the vainglory of my self—willed mind, the presumption of this unworthy body must be subdued likewise. The burden of five hundred taels of silver should suffice. If not—"

"In the form of paper obligations, estimable Kai Lung, the same amount would go more conveniently within your scrip," suggested the Mandarin hopefully.

"Not convenience, O Mandarin, but bodily exhaustion is the essence of my task," reproved the story—teller.

"Yet consider the anguish of my internal pang, if thus encumbered, you sank spent by the wayside, and being thereby unable to withhold the message, you were called upon to endure a further ill."

"That, indeed, is worthy of our thought," confessed Kai Lung. "To this end I will further mortify myself by adventuring upon the uncertain apex of a trustworthy steed (a mode of progress new to my experience) until I enter Tai."

"The swiftest and most reputable awaits your guiding hand," replied Shan Tien.

"Let it be enticed forth into a quiet and discreet spot. In the interval, while the obliging Ming–shu plies an unfaltering brush, the task of weighing out my humiliating burden shall be ours."

In an incredibly short space of time, being continually urged on by the flattering anxiety of Shan Tien (whose precipitancy at one point became so acute that he mistook fourscore taels for five), all things were prepared. With the inscribed parchment well within his sleeve and the bags of silver ranged about his body, Kai Lung approached the platform that had been raised to enable him to subdue the expectant animal.

"Once in the desired position, weighted down as you are, there is little danger of your becoming displaced," remarked the Mandarin auspiciously.

"Your words are, as usual, many–sided in their wise application, benignity," replied Kai Lung. "One thing only yet remains. It is apart from the expression of this one's will, but as an act of justice to yourself and in order to complete the analogy—" And he indicated the direction of Ming–shu.

"Nevertheless you are agreeably understood," declared Shan Tien, moving apart. "Farewell."

As those who controlled the front part of the horse at this moment relaxed their tenacity, Kai Lung did not deem it prudent to reply, nor was he specifically observant of the things about. But a little later, while in the act of permitting the creature whose power he ruled to turn round for a last look at its former home, he saw that the unworthy no longer flourished. Ming–shu, with his own discarded cang around his vindictive neck, was being led off in the direction of the prison–house.

191

CHAPTER XII. The Out-passing into a State of Assured Felicity of the Much-Enduring Two With Whom These Printed Leaves Have Chiefly Been Concerned

ALTHOUGH it was towards sunset, the heat of the day still hung above the dusty earth-road, and two who tarried within the shadow of an ancient arch were loath to resume their way. They had walked far, for the uncertain steed, having revealed a too contentious nature, had been disposed of in distant Tai to an honest stranger who freely explained the imperfection of its ignoble outline.

"Let us remain another space of time," pleaded Hwa-mei reposefully, "and as without your all-embracing art the course of events would undoubtedly have terminated very differently from what it has, will you not, out of an emotion of gratitude, relate a story for my ear alone, weaving into it the substance of this ancient arch whose shade proves our rest?"

"Your wish is the crown of my attainment, unearthly one," replied Kai Lung, preparing to obey. "This concerns the story of Ten-teh, whose name adorns the keystone of the fabric."

The Story of the Loyalty of Ten-teh, the Fisherman "Devotion to the Emperor—" The Five Great Principles

The reign of the enlightened Emperor Tung Kwei had closed amid scenes of treachery and lust, and in his perfidiously-spilled blood was extinguished the last pale hope of those faithful to his line. His only son was a nameless fugitive—by ceaseless report already Passed Beyond—his party scattered and crushed out like the sparks from his blackened Capital, while nothing that men thought dare pass their lips. The usurper Fuh-chi sat upon the dragon throne and spake with the voice of brass cymbals and echoing drums, his right hand shedding blood and his left hand spreading fire. To raise an eye before him was to ape with death, and a whisper in the outer ways foreran swift torture. With harrows he uprooted the land until no household could gather round its ancestral tablets, and with marble rollers he flattened it until none dare lift his head. For the body of each one who had opposed his ambition there was offered an equal weight of fine silver, and upon the head of the child-prince was set the reward of ten times his weight in pure gold. Yet in noisome swamps and forests, hidden in caves, lying on desolate islands, and concealing themselves in every kind of solitary place were those who daily prostrated themselves to the memory of Tung Kwei and by a sign acknowledged the authority of his infant son Kwo Kam. In the Crystal City there was a great roar of violence and drunken song, and men and women lapped from deep lakes filled up with wine; but the ricesacks of the poor had long been turned out and shaken for a little dust; their eyes were closing and in their hearts they were as powder between the mill-stones. On the north and the west the barbarians had begun to press forward in resistless waves, and from The Island to The Beak pirates laid waste the coast.

i. UNDER THE DRAGON'S WING

Among the lagoons of the Upper Seng river a cormorant fisher, Ten-teh by name, daily followed his occupation. In seasons of good harvest, when they of the villages had grain in abundance and money with which to procure a more varied diet, Ten-teh was able to regard the ever-changeful success of his venture without anxiety, and even to add perchance somewhat to his store; but when affliction lay upon the land the carefully gathered hoard melted away and he did not cease to upbraid himself for adopting so uncertain a means of livelihood. At these times the earth-tillers, having neither money to spend nor crops to harvest, caught such fish as they could for themselves. Others in their extremity did not scruple to drown themselves and their dependents in Ten-teh's waters, so that while none contributed to his prosperity the latter ones even greatly added to the embarrassment of his craft. When, therefore, his own harvest failed him in addition, or tempests drove him back to a dwelling which was destitute of food either for himself, his household, or his cormorants, his self-reproach did not appear to be ill-reasoned. Yet in spite of all Ten-teh was of a genial disposition, benevolent, respectful and incapable of guile. He sacrificed adequately at all festivals, and his only regret was that he had no son of his own and very scanty chances of ever becoming rich enough to procure one by adoption.

The sun was setting one day when Ten-teh reluctantly took up his propelling staff and began to urge his raft towards the shore. It was a season of parched crops and destitution in the villages, when disease could fondle the bones of even the most rotund and leprosy was the insidious condiment in every dish; yet never had the Imperial dues been higher, and each succeeding official had larger hands and a more inexorable face than the one before him. Ten-teh's hoarded resources had already followed the snows of the previous winter, his shelf was like the heart of a despot to whom the oppressed cry for pity, and the contents of the creel at his feet were too insignificant to tempt the curiosity even of his hungry cormorants. But the mists of the evening were by this time lapping the surface of the waters and he had no alternative but to abandon his fishing for the day.

"Truly they who go forth to fish, even in shallow waters, experience strange things when none are by to credit them," suddenly exclaimed his assistant—a mentally deficient youth of the villages whom Ten-teh charitably employed because all others rejected him. "Behold, master, a spectre bird approaches."

"Peace, witless," replied Ten-teh, not turning from his occupation, for it was no uncommon incident for the deficient youth to mistake widely-differing objects for one another or to claim a demoniacal insight into the most trivial happenings. "Visions do not materialize for such as thou and I."

"Nevertheless," continued the weakling, "if you will but slacken your agile proficiency with the pole, chieftain, our supper to-night may yet consist of something more substantial than the fish which it is our intention to catch to-morrow.

When the defective youth had continued for some time in this meaningless strain Ten-teh turned to rebuke him, when to his astonishment he perceived that a strange cormorant was endeavouring to reach them, its progress being impeded by an object which it carried in its mouth. Satisfying himself that his own birds were still on the raft, Ten-teh looked round in expectation for the boat of another fisherman, although none but he had ever within his memory sought those waters, but as far as he could see the wide-stretching lagoon was deserted by all but themselves. He accordingly waited, drawing in his pole, and inciting the bird on by cries of encouragement.

"A nobly-born cormorant without doubt," exclaimed the youth approvingly. "He is lacking the throat-strap, yet he holds his prey dexterously and makes no movement to consume it. But the fish itself is outlined strangely."

As the bird drew near Ten-teh also saw that it was devoid of the usual strap which in the exercise of his craft was necessary as a barrier against the gluttonous instincts of

194

the race. It was unnaturally large, and even at a distance Ten-teh could see that its plumage was smoothed to a polished lustre, its eye alert, and the movement of its flight untamed. But, as the youth had said, the fish it carried loomed mysteriously.

"The Wise One and the Crafty Image—behold they prostrate themselves!" cried the youth in a tone of awe-inspired surprise, and without a pause he stepped off the raft and submerged himself beneath the waters.

It was even as he asserted; Ten-teh turned his eyes and lo, his two cormorants, instead of rising in anger, as their contentious nature prompted, had sunk to the ground and were doing obeisance. Much perturbed as to his own most prudent action, for the bird was nearing the craft, Ten-teh judged it safest to accept this token and falling down he thrice knocked his forehead submissively. When he looked up again the majestic bird had vanished as utterly as the flame that is quenched, and lying at his feet was a naked man-child.

"O master," said the voice of the assistant, as he cautiously protruded his head above the surface of the raft, "has the vision faded, or do creatures of the air before whom even their own kind kowtow still haunt the spot?"

"The manifestation has withdrawn," replied Ten-teh reassuringly, "but like the touch of the omnipotent Buddha it has left behind it that which proves its reality," and he pointed to the man-child.

"Beware, alas!" exclaimed the youth, preparing to immerse himself a second time if the least cause arose; "and on no account permit yourself to be drawn into the snare. Inevitably the affair tends to evil from the beginning and presently that which now appears as a man-child will assume the form of a devouring vampire and consume us all. Such occurrences are by no means uncommon when the great sky-lantern is at its full distension."

"To maintain otherwise would be impious," admitted his master, "but at the same time there is nothing to indicate that the beneficial deities are not the ones responsible for this apparition." With these humane words the kindly-disposed Ten-teh wrapped his outer robe about the man-child and turned to lay him in the empty creel, when to his profound astonishment he saw that it was now filled with fish of the rarest and most unapproachable kinds.

"Footsteps of the dragon!" exclaimed the youth, scrambling back on to the raft hastily; "undoubtedly your acuter angle of looking at the visitation was the inspired one. Let us abandon the man–child in an unfrequented spot and then proceed to divide the result of the adventure equally among us."

"An agreed portion shall be allotted," replied Ten–teh, "but to abandon so miraculously–endowed a being would cover even an outcast with shame."

"'Shame fades in the morning; debts remain from day to day,'" replied the youth, the allusion of the proverb being to the difficulty of sustaining life in times so exacting, when men pledged their household goods, their wives, even their ancestral records for a little flour or a jar of oil. "To the starving the taste of a grain of corn is more satisfying than the thought of a roasted ox, but as many years must pass as this creel now holds fish before the little one can disengage a catch or handle the pole."

"It is as the Many–Eyed One sees," replied Ten–teh, with unmoved determination. "This person has long desired a son, and those who walk into an earthquake while imploring heaven for a sign are unworthy of consideration. Take this fish and depart until the morrow. Also, unless you would have the villagers regard you as not only deficient but profane, reveal nothing of this happening to those whom you encounter." With these words Ten–teh dismissed him, not greatly disturbed at the thought of whatever he might do; for in no case would any believe a word he spoke, while the greater likelihood tended towards his forgetting everything before he had reached his home.

As Ten–teh approached his own door his wife came forth to meet him. "Much gladness!" she cried aloud before she saw his burden; "tempered only by a regret that you did not abandon your chase at an earlier hour. Fear not for the present that the wolf–tusk of famine shall gnaw our repose or that the dreaded wings of the white and scaly one shall hover about our house–top. Your wealthy cousin, journeying back to the Capital from the land of the spice forests, has been here in your absence, leaving you gifts of fur, silk, carved ivory, oil, wine, nuts and rice and rich foods of many kinds. He would have stayed to embrace you were it not that his company of bearers awaited him at an arranged spot and he had already been long delayed."

Then said Ten–teh, well knowing that he had no such desirable relative, but drawn to secrecy by the unnatural course of events: "The years pass unperceived and all changes but the heart of man; how appeared my cousin, and has he greatly altered under the enervating sun of a barbarian land?"

"He is now a little man, with a loose skin the colour of a finely–lacquered apricot," replied the woman. "His teeth are large and jagged, his expression open and sincere, and the sound of his breathing is like the continuous beating of waves upon a stony beach. Furthermore, he has ten fingers upon his left hand and a girdle of rubies about his waist."

"The description is unmistakable," said Ten–teh evasively. "Did he chance to leave a parting message of any moment?"

"He twice remarked: 'When the sun sets the moon rises, but to–morrow the drawn will break again,'" replied his wife. "Also, upon leaving he asked for ink, brushes and a fan, and upon it he inscribed certain words." She thereupon handed the fan to Ten–teh, who read, written in characters of surpassing beauty and exactness, the proverb: "Well–guarded lips, patient alertness and a heart conscientiously discharging its accepted duty: these three things have a sure reward."

At that moment Ten–teh's wife saw that he carried something beyond his creel and discovering the man–child she cried out with delight, pouring forth a torrent of inquiries and striving to possess it. "A tale half told is the father of many lies," exclaimed Ten–teh at length, "and of the greater part of what you ask this person knows neither the beginning nor the end. Let what is written on the fan suffice." With this he explained to her the meaning of the characters and made their significance clear. Then without another word he placed the man–child in her arms and led her back into the house.

From that time Hoang, as he was thenceforward called, was received into the household of Ten–teh, and from that time Ten–teh prospered. Without ever approaching a condition of affluence or dignified ease, he was never exposed to the penury and vicissitudes which he had been wont to experience; so that none had need to go hungry or ill–clad. If famine ravaged the villages Ten–teh's store of grain was miraculously maintained; his success on the lagoons was unvaried, fish even leaping on to the structure of the raft. Frequently in dark and undisturbed parts of the house he found sums of money and other valuable articles of which he had no remembrance, while it was no uncommon thing for passing merchants to leave bales of goods at his door in mistake and to meet with some accident which prevented them from ever again visiting that part of the country. In the meanwhile Hoang grew from infancy into childhood, taking part with Ten–teh in all his pursuits, yet even in the most menial occupation never wholly shaking off the air of command and nobility of bearing which lay upon him. In strength and endurance he outpaced all the youths around, while in the manipulation of the raft and the dexterous handling of the cormorants he covered Ten–teh with gratified shame. So excessive was the devotion which he aroused in those who knew him that the deficient youth wept openly if Hoang chanced to cough or sneeze; and it is even asserted that on more than one occasion high officials, struck by the authority of his presence, though he might be in the act of carrying fish along the road, hastily descended from their chairs and prostrated themselves before him.

In the fourteenth year of the reign of the usurper Fuh–chi a little breeze rising in the Province of Sz–chuen began to spread through all the land and men's minds were again agitated by the memory of a hope which had long seemed dead. At that period the tyrannical Fuh–chi finally abandoned the last remaining vestige of restraint and by his crimes and excesses alienated even the protection of the evil spirits and the fidelity of his chosen guard; so that he conspired with himself to bring about his own destruction. One discriminating adviser alone had stood at the foot of the throne, and being no less resolute than far–seeing, he did not hesitate to warn Fuh–chi and to hold the prophetic threat of rebellion before his eyes. Such sincerity met with the reward not difficult to conjecture.

"Who are our enemies?" exclaimed Fuh–chi, turning to a notorious flatterer at his side, "and where are they who are displeased with our too lenient rule?"

"Your enemies, O Brother of the Sun and Prototype of the Red–legged Crane, are dead and unmourned. The living do naught but speak of your clemency and bask in the radiance of your eye–light," protested the flatterer.

"It is well said," replied Fuh–chi. "How is it, then, that any can eat of our rice and receive our bounty and yet repay us with ingratitude and taunts, holding their joints stiffly in our presence? Lo, even lambs have the grace to suck kneeling."

"Omnipotence," replied the just minister, "if this person is deficient in the more supple graces of your illustrious Court it is because the greater part of his life has been spent in waging your wars in uncivilized regions. Nevertheless, the alarm can be as competently sounded upon a brass drum as by a silver trumpet, and his words came forth from a sincere throat."

"Then the opportunity is by no means to be lost," exclaimed Fuh–chi, who was by this time standing some distance from himself in the effects of distilled pear juice; "for we have long desired to see the difference which must undoubtedly exist between a sincere throat and one bent to the continual use of evasive flattery."

Without further consideration he ordered that both persons should be beheaded and that their bodies should be brought for his inspection. From that time there was none to stay his hand or to guide his policy, so that he mixed blood and wine in foolishness and lust until the land was sick and heaved.

The whisper starting from Sz–chuen passed from house to house and from town to town until it had cast a network over every province, yet no man could say whence it came or by whom the word was passed. It might be in the manner of a greeting or the pledging of a cup of tea, by the offer of a coin to a blind beggar at the gate, in the fold of a carelessly–worn garment, or even by the passing of a leper through a town. Oppression still lay heavily upon the people; but it was without aim and carried no restraint; famine and pestilence still went hand in hand, but the message rode on their backs and was hospitably received. Soon, growing bolder, men stood face to face and spoke of settled plans, gave signs, and openly declared themselves. On all sides proclamations began to be affixed; next weapons were distributed, hands were made proficient in their uses, until nothing remained but definite instruction and a swift summons for the appointed day. At intervals omens had appeared in the sky and prophecies had been put into the mouths of sooth–sayers, so that of the success of the undertaking and of its justice none doubted. On the north and the west entire districts had reverted to barbarism, and on the coasts the pirates anchored by the water–gates of walled cities and tossed jests to the watchmen on the towers.

Throughout this period Ten–teh had surrounded Hoang with an added care, never permitting him to wander beyond his sight, and distrusting all men in spite of his confiding nature. One night, when a fierce storm beyond the memory of man was raging, there came at the middle hour a knocking upon the outer wall, loud and insistent; nevertheless Ten–teh did not at once throw open the door in courteous invitation, but drawing aside a shutter he looked forth. Before the house stood one of commanding stature, clad from head to foot in robes composed of plaited grasses, dyed in many colours. Around him ran a stream of water, while the lightning issuing in never–ceasing flashes from his eyes revealed that his features were rugged and his ears pierced with many holes from which the wind whistled until the sound resembled the shrieks of ten thousand tortured ones under the branding–iron. From him the tempest proceeded in every direction, but he stood unmoved among it, without so much as a petal of the flowers he wore disarranged.

In spite of these indications, and of the undoubted fact that the Being could destroy the house with a single glance, Ten–teh still hesitated.

"The night is dark and stormy, and robbers and evil spirits are certainly about in large numbers, striving to enter unperceived by any open door," he protested, but with becoming deference. "With what does your welcome and opportune visit concern itself, honourable stranger?"

"The one before you is not accustomed to be questioned in his doings, or even to be spoken to by ordinary persons," replied the Being. "Nevertheless, Ten–teh, there is that in your history for the past fourteen years which saves you from the usual fatal consequences of so gross an indiscretion. Let it suffice that it is concerned with the flight of the cormorant."

Upon this assurance Ten–teh no longer sought evasion. He hastened to throw open the outer door and the stranger entered, whereupon the tempest ceased, although the thunder and lightning still lingered among the higher mountains. In passing through the doorway the robe of plaited grasses caught for a moment on the staple and pulling aside revealed that the Being wore upon his left foot a golden sandal and upon his right foot one of iron, while embedded in his throat was a great pearl. Convinced by this that he was indeed one of the Immortal Eight, Ten–teh prostrated himself fittingly, and explained that the apparent disrespect of his reception arose from a conscientious interest in the safety of the one committed to his care.

"It is well," replied the Being affably; "and your unvarying fidelity shall not go unrewarded when the proper time arrives. Now bring forward the one whom hitherto you have wisely called Hoang."

In secret during the past years Ten—teh had prepared for such an emergency a yellow silk robe bearing embroidered on it the Imperial Dragon with Five Claws. He had also provided suitable ornaments, fur coverings for the hands and face, and a sword and shield. Waking Hoang, he quickly dressed him, sprinkled a costly perfume about his head and face, and taking him for the last time by the hand he led him into the presence of the stranger.

"Kwo Kam, chosen representative of the sacred line of Tang," began the Being, when he and Hoang had exchanged signs and greetings of equality in an obscure tongue, "the grafted peach—tree on the Crystal Wall is stricken and the fruit is ripe and rotten to the touch. The flies that have fed upon its juice are drunk with it and lie helpless on the ground; the skin is empty and blown out with air, the leaves withered, and about the root is coiled a great worm which has secretly worked to this end. From the Five Points of the kingdom and beyond the Outer Willow Circle the Sheaf—binders have made a full report and it has been judged that the time is come for the tree to be roughly shaken. To this destiny the Old Ones of your race now call you; but beware of setting out unless your face should be unchangingly fixed and your heart pure from all earthly desires and base considerations."

"The decision is too ever—present in my mind to need reflection," replied Hoan resolutely. "To grind to powder that presumptuous tyrant utterly, to restore the integrity of the violated boundaries of the land, and to set up again the venerable Tablets of the true Tang line—these desires have long since worn away the softer portion of this person's heart by constant thought."

"The choice has been made and the words have been duly set down," said the Being. "If you maintain your high purpose to a prosperous end nothing can exceed your honour in the Upper Air; if you fail culpably, or even through incapacity, the lot of Fuh—chi himself will be enviable compared with yours."

Understanding that the time had now come for his departure, Hoang approached Ten—teh as though he would have embraced him, but the Being made a gesture of restraint.

"Yet, O instructor, for the space of fourteen years—" protested Hoang.

"It has been well and discreetly accomplished," replied the Being in a firm but not unsympathetic voice, "and Ten–teh's reward, which shall be neither slight nor grudging, is awaiting him in the Upper Air, where already his immediate ancestors are very honourably regarded in consequence. For many years, O Ten–teh, there has dwelt beneath your roof one who from this moment must be regarded as having passed away without leaving even a breath of memory behind. Before you stands your sovereign, to whom it is seemly that you should prostrate yourself in unquestioning obeisance. Do not look for any recompense or distinction here below in return for that which you have done towards a nameless one; for in the State there are many things which for high reasons cannot be openly proclaimed for the ill–disposed to use as feathers in their darts. Yet take this ring; the ears of the Illimitable Emperor are never closed to the supplicating petition of his children and should such a contingency arise you may freely lay your cause before him with the full assurance of an unswerving justice."

A moment later the storm broke out again with redoubled vigour, and raising his face from the ground Ten–teh perceived that he was again alone.

ii. THE MESSAGE FROM THE OUTER LAND

After the departure of Hoang the affairs of Ten–teh ceased to prosper. The fish which for so many years had leaped to meet his hand now maintained an unparalleled dexterity in avoiding it; continual storms drove him day after day back to the shore, and the fostering beneficence of the deities seemed to be withdrawn, so that he no longer found forgotten stores of wealth nor did merchants ever again mistake his door for that of another to whom they were indebted.

In the year that followed there passed from time to time through the secluded villages lying in the Upper Seng valley persons who spoke of the tumultuous events progressing everywhere. In such a manner those who had remained behind learned that the great rising had been honourably received by the justice–loving in every province, but that many of official rank, inspired by no friendship towards Fuh–chi, but terror–stricken at the alternatives before them, had closed certain strong cities against

202

the Army of the Avenging Pure. It was at this crisis, when the balance of the nation's destiny hung poised, that Kwo Kam, the only son of the Emperor Tung Kwei, and rightful heir of the dynasty of the glorious Tang, miraculously appeared at the head of the Avenging Pure and being acclaimed their leader with a unanimous shout led them on through a series of overwhelming and irresistible victories. At a later period it was told how Kwo Kam had been crowned and installed upon his father's throne, after receiving a mark of celestial approbation in the Temple of Heaven, how Fuh-chi had escaped and fled and how his misleading records had been publicly burned and his detestable name utterly blotted out.

At this period an even greater misfortune than his consistent ill success met Ten-teh. A neighbouring mandarin, on a false pretext, caused him to be brought before him, and speaking very sternly of certain matters in the past, which, he said, out of a well-intentioned regard for the memory of Ten-teh's father he would not cast abroad, he fined him a much larger sum than all he possessed, and then at once caused the raft and the cormorants to be seized in satisfaction of the claim. This he did because his heart was bad, and the sight of Ten-teh bearing a cheerful countenance under continual privation had become offensive to him.

The story of this act of rapine Ten-teh at once carried to the appointed head of the village communities, assuring him that he was ignorant of the cause, but that no crime or wrong-doing had been committed to call for so overwhelming an affliction in return, and entreating him to compel a just restitution and liberty to pursue his inoffensive calling peaceably in the future.

"Listen well, O unassuming Ten-teh, for you are a person of discernment and one with a mature knowledge of the habits of all swimming creatures," said the headman after attending patiently to Ten-teh's words. "If two lean and insignificant carp encountered a voracious pike and one at length fell into his jaws, by what means would the other compel the assailant to release his prey?"

"So courageous an emotion would serve no useful purpose," replied Ten-teh. "Being ill-equipped for such a conflict, it would inevitably result in the second fish also falling a prey to the voracious pike, and recognizing this, the more fortunate of the two would endeavour to escape by lying unperceived among the reeds about."

"The answer is inspired and at the same time sufficiently concise to lie within the hollow bowl of an opium pipe," replied the headman, and turning to his bench he continued in his occupation of beating flax with a wooden mallet.

"Yet," protested Ten—teh, when at length the other paused, "surely the matter could be placed before those in authority in so convincing a light by one possessing your admitted eloquence that Justice would stumble over herself in her haste to liberate the oppressed and to degrade the guilty."

"The phenomenon has occasionally been witnessed, but latterly it would appear that the conscientious deity in question must have lost all power of movement, or perhaps even fatally injured herself, as the result of some such act of rash impulsiveness in the past," replied the headman sympathetically.

"Alas, then," exclaimed Ten—teh, "is there, under the most enlightened form of government in the world, no prescribed method of obtaining redress?"

"Assuredly," replied the headman; "the prescribed method is the part of the system that has received the most attention. As the one of whom you complain is a mandarin of the fifth degree, you may fittingly address yourself to his superiors of the fourth, third, second and first degrees. Then there are the city governors, the district prefects, the provincial rulers, the Imperial Assessors, the Board of Censors, the Guider of the Vermilion Pencil, and, finally, the supreme Emperor himself. To each of these, if you are wealthy enough to reach his actual presence, you may prostrate yourself in turn, and each one, with many courteous expressions of intolerable regret that the matter does not come within his office, will refer you to another. The more prudent course, therefore, would seem to be that of beginning with the Emperor rather than reaching him as the last resort, and as you are now without means of livelihood if you remain here there is no reason why you should not journey to the Capital and make the attempt."

"The Highest!" exclaimed Ten—teh, with a pang of unfathomable emotion. "Is there, then, no middle way? Who is Ten—teh, the obscure and illiterate fisherman, that he should thrust himself into the presence of the Son of Heaven? If the mother of the dutiful Chou Yii could destroy herself and her family at one blow to the end that her son might serve his sovereign with a single heart, how degraded an outcast must he be who would obtrude his own trivial misfortunes at so critical a time."

"'A thorn in one's own little finger is more difficult to endure than a sword piercing the sublime Emperor's arm,'" replied the headman, resuming his occupation. "But if your angle of regarding the various obligations is as you have stated it, then there is obviously nothing more to be said. In any case it is more than doubtful whether the Fountain of Justice would raise an eyelash if you, by every combination of fortunate circumstance, succeeded in reaching his presence."

"The headman has spoken, and his word is ten times more weighty than that of an ill-educated fisherman," replied Ten-teh submissively, and he departed.

From that time Ten-teh sought to sustain life upon roots and wild herbs which he collected laboriously and not always in sufficient quantities from the woods and rank wastes around. Soon even this resource failed him in a great measure, for a famine of unprecedented harshness swept over that part of the province. All supplies of adequate food ceased, and those who survived were driven by the pangs of hunger to consume weeds and the bark of trees, fallen leaves, insects of the lowest orders and the bones of wild animals which had died in the forest. To carry a little rice openly was a rash challenge to those who still valued life, and a loaf of chaff and black mould was guarded as a precious jewel. No wife or daughter could weigh in the balance against a measure of corn, and men sold themselves into captivity to secure the coarse nourishment which the rich allotted to their slaves. Those who remained in the villages followed in Ten-teh's footsteps, so that the meagre harvest that hitherto had failed to supply one household now constituted the whole provision for many. At length these persons, seeing a lingering but inevitable death before them all, came together and spoke of how this might perchance be avoided.

"Let us consider well," said one of their number, "for it may be that succour would not be withheld did we but know the precise manner in which to invoke it."

"Your words are light, O Tan-yung, and your eyes too bright in looking at things which present no encouragement whatever," replied another. "We who remain are old, infirm, or in some way deficient, or we would ere this have sold ourselves into slavery or left this accursed desert in search of a more prolific land. Therefore our existence is of no value to the State, so that they will not take any pains to preserve it. Furthermore, now being beyond the grasp of the most covetous extortion, the district officials have no reason for maintaining an interest in our lives. Assuredly there is no escape except by the White Door of which each one himself holds the key."

"Yet," objected a third, "the aged Ning has often recounted how in the latter years of the reign of the charitable Emperor Kwong, when a similar infliction lay upon the land, a bullock–load of rice was sent daily into the villages of the valley and freely distributed by the headman. Now that same munificent Kwong was a direct ancestor to the third degree of our own Kwo Kam."

"Alas!" remarked a person who had lost many of his features during a raid of brigands, "since the days of the commendable Kwong, while the feet of our lesser ones have been growing smaller the hands of our greater ones have been growing larger. Yet even nowadays, by the protection of the deities, the bullock might reach us."

"The wheel–grease of the cart would alone make the day memorable," murmured another.

"O brothers," interposed one who had not yet spoken, "do not cause our throats to twitch convulsively; nor is it in any way useful to leave the date of solid reflection in pursuit of the stone of light and versatile fancy. Is it thought to be expedient that we should send an emissary to those in authority, pleading our straits?"

"Have not two already journeyed to Kuing–yi in our cause, and to what end?" replied the second one who had raised his voice.

"They did but seek the city mandarin and failed to reach his ear, being empty–handed," urged Tan–yung. "The distance to the Capital is admittedly great, yet it is no more than a persevering and resolute–minded man could certainly achieve. There prostrating himself before the Sublime One and invoking the memory of the imperishable Kwong he could so outline our necessity and despair that the one wagon–load referred to would be increased by nine and the unwieldy oxen give place to relays of swift horses."

"The Emperor!" exclaimed the one who had last spoken, in tones of undisguised contempt towards Tan–yung. "Is the eye of the Unapproachable Sovereign less than that of a city mandarin, that having failed to come near the one we should now strive to reach the other; or are we, peradventure, to fill the sleeves of our messenger with gold and his inner scrip with sapphires!" Nevertheless the greater part of those who stood around zealously supported Tan–yung, crying aloud: "The Emperor! The suggestion is inspired! Undoubtedly the beneficent Kwo Kam will uphold our cause and our troubles may now be considered as almost at an end."

"Yet," interposed a faltering voice, "who among us is to go?"

At the mention of this necessary detail of the plan the cries which were the loudest raised in exultation suddenly leapt back upon themselves as each person looked in turn at all the others and then at himself. The one who had urged the opportune but disconcerting point was lacking in the power of movement in his lower limbs and progressed at a pace little advanced to that of a shell–cow upon two slabs of wood. Tan–yung was subject to a disorder which without any warning cast him to the ground almost daily in a condition of writhing frenzy; the one who had opposed him was paralysed in all but his head and feet, while those who stood about were either blind, lame, camel–backed, leprous, armless, misshapen, or in some way mentally or bodily deficient in an insuperable degree. "Alas!" exclaimed one, as the true understanding of their deformities possessed him, "not only would they of the Court receive it as a most detestable insult if we sent such as ourselves, but the probability of anyone so harassed overcoming the difficulties of river, desert and mountain barrier is so remote that this person is more than willing to stake his entire share of the anticipated bounty against a span–length of succulent lotus root or an embossed coffin handle."

"Let unworthy despair fade!" suddenly exclaimed Tan–yung, who nevertheless had been more downcast than any other a moment before; "for among us has been retained one who has probably been especially destined for this very service. There is yet Ten–teh. Let us seek him out."

With this design they sought for Ten–teh and finding him in his hut they confidently invoked his assistance, pointing out how he would save all their lives and receive great honour. To their dismay Ten–teh received them with solemn curses and drove them from his door with blows, calling them traitors, ungrateful ones, and rebellious subjects whose minds were so far removed from submissive loyalty that rather than perish harmlessly they would inopportunely thrust themselves in upon the attention of the divine Emperor when his mind was full of great matters and his thoughts tenaciously fixed upon the scheme for reclaiming the abandoned outer lands of his forefathers. "Behold," he cried, "when a hand is raised to sweep into oblivion a thousand earthworms they lift no voice in protest, and in this matter ye are less than earthworms. The dogs are content to starve dumbly while their masters feast, and ye are less than dogs. The dutiful son cheerfully submits himself to torture on the chance that his father's sufferings may be lessened, and the Emperor, as the supreme head, is more to be venerated than any father; but your hearts are sheathed in avarice and greed." Thus he drove them away, and their last hope being gone they wandered back to the forest, wailing and filling the air with their despairing moans; for the brief light that had inspired them was extinguished and the thought that by a patient endurance they might spare the Emperor an unnecessary pang was not a sufficient recompense in their eyes.

The time of warmth and green life passed. With winter came floods and snow–storms, great tempests from the north and bitter winds that cut men down as though they had been smitten by the sword. The rivers and lagoons were frozen over; the meagre sustenance of the earth lay hidden beneath an impenetrable crust of snow and ice, until those who had hitherto found it a desperate chance to live from day to day now abandoned the unequal struggle for the more attractive certainty of a swift and painless death. One by one the fires went out in the houses of the dead; the ever–increasing snow broke down the walls. Wild beasts from the mountains walked openly about the deserted streets, thrust themselves through such doors as were closed against them and lurked by night in the most sacred recesses of the ruined temples. The strong and the wealthy had long since fled, and presently out of all the eleven villages of the valley but one man remained alive and Ten–teh lay upon the floor of his inner chamber, dying.

"There was a sign—there was a sign in the past that more was yet to be accomplished," ran the one thought of his mind as he lay there helpless, his last grain consumed and the ashes on his hearthstone black. "Can it be that so solemn an omen has fallen unfulfilled to the ground; or has this person long walked hand in hand with shadows in the Middle Air?"

"Dwellers of Yin; dwellers of Chung–yo; of Wei, Shan–ta, Feng, the Rock of the Bleak Pagoda and all the eleven villages of the valley!" cried a voice from without. "Ho, inhospitable sleeping ones, I have reached the last dwelling of the plain and no one has as yet bidden me enter, no voice invited me to unlace my sandals and partake of tea. Do they fear that this person is a robber in disguise, or is this the courtesy of the Upper Seng valley?"

"They sleep more deeply," said Ten–teh, speaking back to the full extent of his failing power; "perchance your voice was not raised high enough, O estimable wayfarer. Nevertheless, whether you come in peace or armed with violence, enter here, for the one who lies within is past help and beyond injury."

Upon this invitation the stranger entered and stood before Ten–teh. He was of a fierce and martial aspect, carrying a sword at his belt and a bow and arrows slung across his back, but privation had set a deep mark upon his features and his body bore unmistakable traces of a long and arduous march. His garments were ragged, his limbs torn by rocks and thorny undergrowth, while his ears had fallen away before the rigour of the ice–laden blasts. In his right hand he carried a staff upon which he leaned at every step, and glancing to the ground Ten–teh perceived that the lower part of his sandals were worn away so that he trod painfully upon his bruised and naked feet.

"Greeting," said Ten–teh, when they had regarded each other for a moment; "yet, alas, no more substantial than of the lips, for the hospitality of the eleven villages is shrunk to what you see before you," and he waved his arm feebly towards the empty bowl and the blackened hearth. "Whence come you?"

"From the outer land of Im–kau," replied the other. "Over the Kang–ling mountains."

"It is a moon–to–moon journey," said Ten–teh. "Few travellers have ever reached the valley by that inaccessible track."

"More may come before the snow has melted," replied the stranger, with a stress of significance. "Less than seven days ago this person stood upon the northern plains."

Ten–teh raised himself upon his arm. "There existed, many cycles ago, a path—of a single foot's width, it is said—along the edge of the Pass called the Ram's Horn, but it has been lost beyond the memory of man."

"It has been found again," said the stranger, "and Kha—hia and his horde of Kins, joined by the vengeance—breathing Fuh—chi, lie encamped less than a short march beyond the Pass."

"It can matter little," said Ten—teh, trembling but speaking to reassure himself. "The people are at peace among themselves, the Capital adequately defended, and an army sufficiently large to meet any invasion can march out and engage the enemy at a spot most convenient to ourselves."

"A few days hence, when all preparation is made," continued the stranger, "a cloud of armed men will suddenly appear openly, menacing the western boundaries. The Capital and the fortified places will be denuded, and all who are available will march out to meet them. They will be but as an empty shell designed to serve a crafty purpose, for in the meanwhile Kha—hia will creep unsuspected through the Kang—lings by the Ram's Horn and before the army can be recalled he will swiftly fall upon the defenceless Capital and possess it."

"Alas!" exclaimed Ten—teh, "why has the end tarried thus long if it be but for this person's ears to carry to the grave so tormenting a message! Yet how comes it, O stranger, that having been admitted to Kha—hia's innermost council you now betray his trust, or how can reliance be placed upon the word of one so treacherous?"

"Touching the reason," replied the stranger, with no appearance of resentment, "that is a matter which must one day lie between Kha—hia, this person, and one long since Passed Beyond, and to this end have I uncomplainingly striven for the greater part of a lifetime. For the rest, men do not cross the King—langs in midwinter, wearing away their lives upon those stormy heights, to make a jest of empty words. Already sinking into the Under World, even as I am now powerless to raise myself above the ground, I, Nau—Kaou, swear and attest what I have spoken."

"Yet, alas!" exclaimed Ten—teh, striking his breast bitterly in his dejection, "to what end is it that you have journeyed? Know that out of all the eleven villages by famine and pestilence not another man remains. Beyond the valley stretch the uninhabited sand plains, so that between here and the Capital not a solitary dweller could be found to bear the message."

"The Silent One laughs!" replied Nau–Kaou dispassionately; and drawing his cloak more closely about him he would have composed himself into a reverent attitude to Pass Beyond.

"Not so!" cried Ten–teh, rising in his inspired purpose and standing upright despite the fever that possessed him; "the jewel is precious beyond comparison and the casket mean and falling to pieces, but there is none other. This person will bear the warning."

The stranger looked up from the ground in an increasing wonder. "You do but dream, old man," he said in a compassionate voice. "Before me stands one of trembling limbs and infirm appearance. His face is the colour of potter's clay; his eyes sunken and yellow. His bones protrude everywhere like the points of armour, while his garment is scarcely fitted to afford protection against a summer breeze."

"Such dreams do not fade with the light," replied Ten–teh resolutely. "His feet are whole and untired; his mind clear. His heart is as inflexibly fixed as the decrees of destiny, and, above all, his purpose is one which may reasonably demand divine encouragement."

"Yet there are the Han–sing mountains, flung as an insurmountable barrier across the way," said Nau–Kaou.

"The wind passes over them," replied Ten–teh, binding on his sandals.

"The Girdle," continued the other, thereby indicating the formidable obstacle presented by the tempestuous river, swollen by the mountain snows.

"The fish, moved by no great purpose, swim from bank to bank," again replied Ten–teh. "Tell me rather, for the time presses when such issues hang on the lips of dying men, to what extent Kha–hia's legions stretch?"

"In number," replied Nau–Kaou, closing his eyes, "they are as the stars on a very clear night, when the thousands in front do but serve to conceal the innumerable throng behind. Yet even a small and resolute army taking up its stand secretly in this valley and falling upon them unexpectedly when half were crossed could throw them into disorder and rout, and utterly destroy the power of Kha–hia for all time."

"So shall it be," said Ten–Teh from the door. "Pass Upward with a tranquil mind, O stranger from the outer land. The torch which you have borne so far will not fail until his pyre is lit."

"Stay but a moment," cried Nau–Kaou. "This person, full of vigour and resource, needed the spur of a most poignant hate to urge his trailing footsteps. Have you, O decrepit one, any such incentive to your failing powers?"

"A mightier one," came back the voice of Ten–teh, across the snow from afar. "Fear not."

"It is well; they are the great twin brothers," exclaimed Nau–Kaou. "Kha–hia is doomed!" Then twice beating the ground with his open hand he loosened his spirit and passed contentedly into the Upper Air.

iii. THE LAST SERVICE

The wise and accomplished Emperor Kwo Kam (to whom later historians have justly given the title "Profound") sat upon his agate throne in the Hall of Audience. Around him were gathered the most illustrious from every province of the Empire, while emissaries from the courts of other rulers throughout the world passed in procession before him, prostrating themselves in token of the dependence which their sovereigns confessed, and imploring his tolerant acceptance of the priceless gifts they brought. Along the walls stood musicians and singers who filled the air with melodious visions, while fan–bearing slaves dexterously wafted perfumed breezes into every group. So unparalleled was the splendour of the scene that rare embroidered silks were trodden under foot and a great fountain was composed of diamonds dropping into a jade basin full of pearls, but Kwo Kam outshone all else by the dignity of his air and the magnificence of his apparel.

Suddenly, and without any of the heralding strains of drums and cymbals by which persons of distinction had been announced, the arras before the chief door was plucked aside and a figure, blinded by so much jewelled brilliance, stumbled into the chamber, still holding thrust out before him the engraved ring bearing the Imperial emblem which alone had enabled him to pass the keepers of the outer gates alive. He had the appearance of being a very aged man, for his hair was white and scanty, his face deep with shadows and lined like a river bank when the waters have receded, and as he advanced, bent down with infirmity, he mumbled certain words in ceaseless repetition. From his feet and garment there fell a sprinkling of sand as he moved, and blood dropped to the floor from many an unhealed wound, but his eyes were very bright, and though sword-handles were grasped on all sides at the sight of so presumptuous an intrusion, yet none opposed him. Rather, they fell back, leaving an open passage to the foot of the throne; so that when the Emperor lifted his eyes he saw the aged man moving slowly forward to do obeisance.

"Ten-teh, revered father!" exclaimed Kwo Kam, and without pausing a moment he leapt down from off his throne, thrust aside those who stood about him and casting his own outer robe of state about Ten-teh's shoulders embraced him affectionately.

"Supreme ruler," murmured Ten-teh, speaking for the Emperor's ear alone, and in such a tone of voice as of one who has taught himself a lesson which remains after all other consciousness has passed away, "an army swiftly to the north! Let them dispose themselves about the eleven villages and, overlooking the invaders as they assemble, strike when they are sufficiently numerous for the victory to be lasting and decisive. The passage of the Ram's Horn has been found and the malignant Fuh-chi, banded in an unnatural alliance with the barbarian Kins, lies with itching feet beyond the Kang-lings. The invasion threatening on the west is but a snare; let a single camp, feigning to be a multitudinous legion, be thrown against it. Suffer delay from no cause. Weigh no alternative. He who speaks is Ten-teh, at whose assuring word the youth Hoang was wont to cast himself into the deepest waters fearlessly. His eyes are no less clear to-day, but his heart is made small with overwhelming deference or in unshrinking loyalty he would cry: 'Hear and obey! All, all—Flags, Ironcaps, Tigers, Braves—all to the Seng valley, leaving behind them the swallow in their march and moving with the guile and secrecy of the ringed tree-snake.'" With these words Ten-teh's endurance passed its drawn-out limit and again repeating in a clear and decisive voice, "All, all to the north!" he released his joints and would have fallen to the ground had it not been for the Emperor's restraining arms.

When Ten-teh again returned to a knowledge of the lower world he was seated upon the throne to which the Emperor had borne him. His rest had been made easy by the luxurious cloaks of the courtiers and emissaries which had been lavishly heaped about him, while during his trance the truly high-minded Kwo Kam had not disdained to wash his feet in a golden basin of perfumed water, to shave his limbs, and to anoint his head. The greater part of the assembly had been dismissed, but some of the most trusted among the ministers and officials still waited in attendance about the door.

"Great and enlightened one," said Ten-teh, as soon as his stupor was lifted, "has this person delivered his message competently, for his mind was still a seared vision of snow and sand and perchance his tongue has stumbled?"

"Bend your ears to the wall, O my father," replied the Emperor, "and be assured."

A radiance of the fullest satisfaction lifted the settling shadows for a moment from Ten-teh's countenance as from the outer court came at intervals the low and guarded words of command, the orderly clashing of weapons as they fell into their appointed places, and the regular and unceasing tread of armed men marching forth. "To the Seng valley—by no chance to the west?" he demanded, trembling between anxiety and hope, and drinking in the sound of the rhythmic tramp which to his ears possessed a more alluring charm than if it were the melody of blind singing girls.

"Even to the eleven villages," replied the Emperor. "At your unquestioned word, though my kingdom should hang upon the outcome."

"It is sufficient to have lived so long," said Ten-teh. Then perceiving that it was evening, for the jade and crystal lamps were lighted, he cried out: "The time has leapt unnoted. How many are by this hour upon the march?"

"Sixscore companies of a hundred spearmen each," said Kwo Kam. "By dawn four times that number will be on their way. In less than three days a like force will be disposed about the passes of the Han-sing mountains and the river fords, while at the same time the guards from less important towns will have been withdrawn to take their place upon the city walls."

"Such words are more melodious than the sound of many marble lutes," said Ten-teh, sinking back as though in repose. "Now is mine that peace spoken of by the philosopher Chi-chey as the greatest: 'The eye closing upon its accomplished work.'"

"Assuredly do you stand in need of the healing sleep of nature," said the Emperor, not grasping the inner significance of the words. "Now that you are somewhat rested, esteemed sire, suffer this one to show you the various apartments of the palace so that you may select for your own such as most pleasingly attract your notice."

"Yet a little longer," entreated Ten-teh. "A little longer by your side and listening to your voice alone, if it may be permitted, O sublime one."

"It is for my father to command," replied Kwo Kam. "Perchance they of the eleven villages sent some special message of gratifying loyalty which you would relate without delay?"

"They slept, omnipotence, or without doubt it would be so," replied Ten-teh.

"Truly," agreed the Emperor. "It was night when you set forth, my father?"

"The shadows had fallen deeply upon the Upper Seng Valley," said Ten-teh evasively.

"The Keeper of the Imperial Stores has frequently conveyed to us their expressions of unfeigned gratitude for the bounty by which we have sought to keep alive the memory of their hospitality and our own indebtedness," said the Emperor.

"The sympathetic person cannot have overstated their words," replied Ten-teh falteringly. "Never, as their own utterances bear testimony, never was food more welcome, fuel more eagerly sought for, and clothing more necessary than in the years of the most recent past."

"The assurance is as dew upon the drooping lotus," said Kwo Kam, with a lightening countenance. "To maintain the people in an unshaken prosperity, to frown heavily upon extortion and to establish justice throughout the land—these have been the achievements of the years of peace. Yet often, O my father, this one's mind has turned yearningly to the happier absence of strife and the simple abundance which you and they of the valley know."

"The deities ordain and the balance weighs; your reward will be the greater," replied Ten-teh. Already he spoke with difficulty, and his eyes were fast closing, but he held himself rigidly, well knowing that his spirit must still obey his will.

"Do you not crave now to partake of food and wine?" inquired the Emperor, with tender solicitude. "A feast has long been prepared of the choicest dishes in your honour. Consider well the fatigue through which you have passed."

"It has faded," replied Ten–teh, in a voice scarcely above a whisper, "the earthly body has ceased to sway the mind. A little longer, restored one; a very brief span of time."

"Your words are my breath, my father," said the Emperor, deferentially. "Yet there is one matter which we had reserved for affectionate censure. It would have spared the feet of one who is foremost in our concern if you had been content to send the warning by one of the slaves whose acceptance we craved last year, while you followed more leisurely by the chariot and the eight white horses which we deemed suited to your use."

Ten–teh was no longer able to express himself in words, but at this indication of the Emperor's unceasing thought a great happiness shone on his face. "What remains?" must reasonably have been his reflection; "or who shall leave the shade of the fruitful palm–tree to search for raisins?" Therefore having reached so supreme an eminence that there was nothing human above, he relaxed the effort by which he had so long sustained himself, and suffering his spirit to pass unchecked, he at once fell back lifeless among the cushions of the throne.

That all who should come after might learn by his example, the history of Ten–teh was inscribed upon eighteen tablets of jade, carved patiently and with graceful skill by the most expert stone–cutters of the age. A triumphal arch of seven heights was also erected outside the city and called by his name, but the efforts of story–tellers and poets will keep alive the memory of Ten–teh even when these imperishable monuments shall have long fallen from their destined use.

*

When Kai Lung had completed the story of the loyalty of Ten–teh and had pointed out the forgotten splendour of the crumbling arch, the coolness of the evening tempted them to resume their way. Moving without discomfort to themselves before nightfall they reached a small but seemly cottage conveniently placed upon the mountain-side. At the gate stood an aged person whose dignified appearance was greatly added to by his long white moustaches. These possessions he pointed out to Hwa-mei with inoffensive pride as he welcomed the two who stood before him.

"Venerated father," explained Kai Lung dutifully, "this is she who has been destined from the beginning of time to raise up a hundred sons to keep your line extant."

"In that case," remarked the patriarch, "your troubles are only just beginning. As for me, since all that is now arranged, I can see about my own departure—'Whatever height the tree, its leaves return to the earth at last.'"

"It is thus at evening-time—to-morrow the light will again shine forth," whispered Kai Lung. "Alas, radiance, that you who have dwelt about a palace should be brought to so mean a hut!"

"If it is small, your presence will pervade it; in a palace there are many empty rooms," replied Hwa-mei, with a reassuring glance. "I enter to prepare our evening rice."

Ernest Bramah, of whom in his lifetime Who's Who had so little to say, was born in Manchester. At seventeen he chose farming as a profession, but after three years of losing money gave it up to go into journalism. He started as correspondent on a typical provincial paper, then went to London as secretary to Jerome K. Jerome, and worked himself into the editorial side of Jerome's magazine, To-day, where he got the opportunity of meeting the most important literary figures of the day. But he soon left To-day to join a new publishing firm, as editor of a publication called The Minister; finally, after two years of this, he turned to writing as his full-time occupation. He was intensely interested in coins and published a book on the English regal copper coinage. He is, however, best known as the creator of the charming character Kai Lung who appears in Kai Lung Unrolls His Mat, Kai Lung's Golden Hours, The Wallet of Kai Lung, Kai Lung Beneath the Mulberry Tree, The Mirror of Kong Ho, and The Moon of Much Gladness; he also wrote two one- act plays which are often performed at London variety theatres, and many stories and articles in leading periodicals. He died in 1942.

Printed in the United States
50958LVS00003B/18